Sweet [illegible]

Books by Kevin Alan Milne

The Paper Bag Christmas
The Nine Lessons
Sweet Misfortune
The Final Note

Available from Center Street wherever books are sold.

Sweet Misfortune

A Novel

KEVIN ALAN MILNE

*Some people are lucky in love.
You aren't one of them.*

CENTER
STREET

New York Boston Nashville

This book is a work of fiction. Names, characters, places, and incidents are the product of the author's imagination or are used fictitiously. Any resemblance to actual events, locales, or persons, living or dead, is coincidental.

Center Street
Hachette Book Group
237 Park Avenue
New York, NY 10017

www.centerstreet.com

Center Street is a division of Hachette Book Group, Inc.
The Center Street name and logo are trademarks of Hachette Book Group, Inc.

The publisher is not responsible for websites (or their content) that are not owned by the publisher.

Printed in the United States of America
Originally published in hardcover by Center Street.

First Trade Edition: April 2011
10 9 8 7 6 5 4 3 2 1

The Library of Congress has cataloged the hardcover edition as follows:

Milne, Kevin Alan.
Sweet misfortune : a novel / Kevin Alan Milne.
p. cm.
Summary: "A story about finding love and proving that happiness is not just a myth"–Provided by publisher.
ISBN 978-1-59995-297-0
1. Happiness–Fiction. I. Title.

PS3613.15919S84 2010
813'.6–dc22

2009037861

ISBN 978-1-59995-296-3 (pbk.)

For my better half, Rebecca

Part I

The Beginning of the End

Chapter 1

Have patience: rainy days will soon return.

September 21, 2009

SOPHIE JONES KNEW EXACTLY WHAT THE SQUATTY LITTLE bus driver was going to say, long before the Gig Harbor Express to Tacoma lurched to a halt in front of her stop on Harborview Drive. She anticipated the woman's words, the disappointment-laden inflections, and even the accusatory facial expressions. Every nuance of what was about to transpire was, for all intents and purposes, a foregone conclusion. As the bus's door swung open with a hydraulic wheeze, Sophie entertained herself by rehearsing the pending exchange in her head. *Again? Oh snap, girl! What's wrong with you? Leave that thing at home!*

Sophie stepped slowly from the curb and up onto the bus, while simultaneously closing the extra-large black umbrella that rested on her shoulder. She half-smiled at the woman behind the wheel but felt instantly silly for trying to be nice. What was the point, since there would not be so much as a courtesy smirk in return?

Knowing not only *what* was about to happen, but also *when*, she began counting down.

Three…

The bus driver scrunched up her face, lowered her chin and opened her mouth just enough to expose a mouthful of shiny amalgam fillings, and then drilled into Sophie and the unwieldy umbrella with her eyes.

Two…

She let go of the steering wheel with both hands and folded her arms across her torso, letting them hang just below her name tag and across the Puget Sound Public Transportation insignia on her stiff cotton shirt.

One…

A nasal sigh, a disappointed shake of her head, and then…

Zero.

"Again? Oh *snap*, girl! What's wrong with you? Leave that thing at home! It's a beautiful Monday morning."

Sophie chuckled softly as she leaned the umbrella nose-down against a safety bar and paid the fare. She found nothing particularly humorous about the woman or her comments, but she did find it mildly amusing that the driver was so predictable.

"And if it rains?" Sophie replied, completely unaffected.

"You see any clouds today? We ain't had a dang sprinkle in a week, thank Jesus Almighty and knock on wood." She thumped the thick metal steering column with her knuckles.

Sophie shook her head in dismay. Though she didn't like the woman's attitude, she couldn't deny that the driver was right about the weather. The air outside was brisk, but the early-morning sky was an unblemished sheet of powder blue from one edge of the horizon to the other, and the local forecast called only for sun. None of that mattered to Sophie. "Expect the worst," she quipped, trying once again to force a smile.

"I know you do, girl," the driver balked. "And *that's* your problem."

The woman said something else under her breath while Sophie found a seat, but the words were drowned out by the revving engine as the bus started to roll. Sophie would have ignored her, anyway. Even on the best of days, it was way too early in the morning to get riled over the offhanded remarks of bus drivers.

But this was not the best of days.

For Sophie, this day was the single worst day of the year, like an annually recurring nightmare that she couldn't escape. If it weren't for the fact that she had a business to run, she'd have gladly turned down the blinds, turned off her cell phone, gone back to bed, and slumbered the day away in peaceful oblivion.

If only, Sophie thought, as she shuffled along the aisle to her favorite seat at the rear of the bus. Few other Gig Harbor commuters ventured that far back, so she usually had the elevated rear bench all to herself. Sophie preferred silent contemplation during her morning travels, and her perch at the back kept her safe from the idle chit-chat and coffee talk that others seemed to thrive on. While the bus rumbled along she stared out at the lush green landscape whistling by, watched as several eager boats left the harbor for a day in the Sound. She studied the tall cable supports of the Narrows Bridge, which connected the town of Gig Harbor and the Olympic Peninsula to Washington's mainland. On most days, those sights would be enough to distract her from the bitter realities of life.

But this was not most days.

For Sophie, this was a day for regrets, and nothing could quell the renewed sense of heartache and disappointment that this particular date evoked each year. No amount of pine trees, sails, or suspension cables passing through the glare of a dirty bus window could help her forget her past. A *day for self-loathing,* she told herself, as she wedged the enormous umbrella into a space between her seat and the floor heater. *My own personal pity party. I can be as miserable as I want on my—*

"Happy birthday, Sophie!"

Jumping at the loud and unexpected verbal intrusion, Sophie blurted out, "What the—?" She gasped audibly before the familiar female voice registered in her mind. "Holy crow, Evi! Are you trying to give me an aneurism? What are you doing here?" Sophie consciously ignored the blatant stares of the handful of commuters who'd craned their necks to see what was going on.

"I thought I'd surprise you! Looks like it worked." Evi smiled as wide as she could and added a wink for good measure while sprawling out on the vacant seat one row up.

Sophie glared back at her with mock contempt. "Brilliant," she deadpanned. "I have one friend in the whole world, and how does she show me that she cares? By sneaking up on me, making a public scene, and reminding me what day it is."

Evi was still beaming. "Like you need any reminders," she teased. "And for the record, I didn't sneak up on you. I got on the bus two stops before you did, but you were so self-absorbed when you got on that you walked right past me. I was even waving!" She stopped to wink. "But forget it. It's your birthday, so I forgive you."

"Yes, my birthday—the worst day imaginable."

"Oh, shut it," Evi countered cheerfully. "We both know that the worst day was forever ago, which makes today just another start of something good."

Evi was a short brunette with an infectious smile, an easy laugh, and beautiful bronze skin that never faded in the winter. Her hair and smile were from her mother, her skin color came from her Latino father, whom she'd never met, and her laugh was simply how she'd learned to deal with life's complexities. She was also one of the few people in the world whom Sophie trusted implicitly. Much to Sophie's chagrin, her friend's full name, Evalynn Marion Mason, had recently been appended to become Evalynn Marion Mason-*Mack*, the hyphenation having been added six months earlier as a result of marrying Justin Mack, a friend of theirs since freshman year at college. Sophie didn't have anything against Justin—in fact, she was glad for her friends—but their union made her worry that life was quickly passing her by, a feeling that was amplified tenfold when Evalynn announced two months later that she was pregnant.

Outwardly, Evi and Sophie were as different as night and day. Evi was short, and Sophie was tall. Evi's hair was straight, brown, and bobbed, while Sophie had golden locks that flowed gracefully past her shoulders. And whereas Evi was gregarious, Sophie was more reserved. Everyone who knew them assumed that their friendship was built solely on the principle that opposites attract, but Sophie knew that it was much more than that. They were more like sisters than anything else, and they depended on one another in ways that people who grew up under more normal circumstances didn't understand. For as different as they might have appeared to outside observers, the pair had at least two things in common that stitched them together like a patchwork quilt: tragedy, and their African-American foster mom.

Sophie exhaled slowly. "You know I hate my birthday."

"Yep."

"You should have just stayed in bed with your hubby this morning and left me alone to sulk."

"I know."

Sophie yawned, and then grimaced. "Then *why* are you here? And don't say, 'Because misery loves company.' I'm proof that that isn't true."

Evalynn tried mimicking the bus driver's sassy derisiveness to lighten things up. "Girl, what's wrong with you? You know I ain't leaving you 'lone on the day you turn twenty-nine!

Snap! Next year you'll be a dang old maid. You best enjoy your twenties while they're still here, girl!"

"Stop! You're embarrassing yourself."

A single giggle escaped Evi's enormous grin. "No, I'm embarrassing *you*. It's what I do best." She poked her friend gently in the ribs. "Oh, c'mon. Smile, Soph! I don't want to spend the whole day with you if you're going to be a grouch."

Sophie raised her eyebrows questioningly but refused to smile. "The whole day?"

"Well, I certainly didn't get on the bus just to wish you a happy birthday. My boss assured me that she can survive with one less legal assistant today, so I took the entire day off, and I'm coming with you to help make the chocolates and stuff. I don't want you to have to be alone today."

"Wait. You're coming to help *make* the chocolates, or to *eat* the chocolates? Last time you 'helped,' as I recall, it was tough to tell what your true purpose was."

Evalynn smacked her on the shoulder. "You know I love those peanut-butter truffles. Just have me work on something else, and I'll be fine. Anyway, I've got other plans, too, that don't involve filling molds and dipping cherries. I made some special arrangements for this afternoon that I think might help you forget it's your birthday."

"Arrangements? I don't like the sound of that. What sort of *arrangements*, Ev?"

Evalynn winked. "Sorry, it's a surprise. My lips are officially sealed. You'll just have to wait until later."

The next bus stop was the park-and-ride on Kimball Drive. A few people on Sophie's bus got off there to transfer to another route, while nearly a dozen new passengers boarded. Among them was a face that Sophie didn't recognize. The man was wearing a navy blazer and khakis, and he stood at least four inches over six feet, making him tall enough that he had to stoop to keep from hitting his head. His wavy brown hair curled playfully just above the ears, and his bright blue eyes twinkled in the morning light. If she hadn't already given up on men, Sophie might have been inclined to give this particular specimen more than a casual once-over. She chided herself for even thinking such things.

Most of the new passengers took the first vacant seat they could find, but the unfamiliar man scanned the full length of the bus's interior for just the right spot, even after the bus had started to roll. He pretended not to notice Sophie looking at him. With a computer satchel in one hand and a map of bus routes in the other, he carefully made his way down the aisle toward the rear, shifting his weight periodically to adjust for the pitch and sway of the moving bus.

Sophie turned her head ninety degrees and looked directly out the window, pretending to be very interested in the passing scenery.

"May I sit here?" he asked courteously a few seconds later, pointing to the empty half of the elevated rear bench.

Sophie continued staring out the window, as though she hadn't heard him.

He cleared his throat. "Excuse me. May I?"

Evalynn let out a nasally laugh as Sophie turned her head back around to face the man.

"It's a public bus," she said coolly. "But what's wrong with the empty seats up there?" She pointed with her eyes to the vacant seats he'd passed by.

The man smiled graciously and sat down, laying his computer bag across his lap and unfolding the map. "The view from up here is infinitely better." He looked right at Sophie as he spoke.

Sophie straightened slightly in her seat, her mind turning briefly to thoughts of her former fiancé. She paused to mentally compare the two. The guy now sitting beside her was, she conceded, easy to look at. Tall. Good-looking. Confident.

But he was no Garrett.

"Suit yourself," she said. "I've only got one more stop anyway."

The man continued smiling. "Well, in that case, maybe you can help me out. I'm new here. Just moved up from Oregon over the weekend, and I'm trying to figure out the transit system. How many stops are we away from downtown Seattle?"

"A lot," she replied, finally allowing herself to smile, if only out of amusement at the man's predicament. "This bus only does a loop between Gig Harbor and Tacoma. Back where you got on, you should have waited for the next bus."

"I see." He nodded quizzically. "So basically, I'm lost."

"Afraid so."

He didn't let it faze him. "In that case, I'm glad I made my way all the way to the backseat. As long as I'm lost, and likely late for my first day on the job, at least I got to meet you."

Now it was Sophie's turn for quizzical glances. "Wait a minute. Is this, like, your little shtick? Ride the bus with a map and pretend to be the new guy in town so you can pick up unsuspecting women?"

He grinned. "If it is, is it working?"

"Absolutely not!" retorted Sophie, sounding quite appalled.

"I'm joking," he said, chuckling. "Actually, I'm really not the pick-up-strange-women type." He caught himself. "Not that you're strange, but...you get what I mean."

Sophie didn't reply. *What's the use?* she wondered. *He can flirt all he wants, and it won't make a bit of difference. I'm through with men.* Another image of Garrett popped into her head.

The man kept talking. "My new boss told me that riding the bus would be easier than fighting morning traffic, but now I'm not so sure."

Pulling her umbrella from its berth beside the seat, Sophie said, "You're really from Oregon?"

He nodded again. "Astoria, on the coast."

"Well, welcome to Washington," she continued politely. "Now, my stop is coming up, so if you don't mind I'd like to get by." She turned to Evalynn. "Ready?"

Evalynn nodded, and the pair stood up.

The man angled his knees so Sophie could scoot by in front of him. "Listen," he said. "I really could use some help. Can you at least tell me how to get to Seattle?"

Leaning in close so she wouldn't have to speak loudly, Sophie said, "There are lots of women on the bus. I'm sure one of them will help."

He didn't say another word.

As soon as they were on the sidewalk and clear of the bus, Evalynn poked Sophie in the side again. "Are you crazy? That guy was adorable!"

Sophie shook her head. "The last thing I need right now is a relationship. I've told you before, I'm perfectly happy without a guy in my life."

"Could've fooled me," Evalynn mumbled under her breath.

Sophie rolled her eyes. "Oh yeah? And do you think you're so much better off now that you and Justin have tied the knot?"

"Having Justin around is great," she said emphatically, then paused and placed her hand on her stomach. "It's just this 'gift' he's given me that I could do without."

Sophie chuckled lightly, but couldn't help wondering if the comment was meant as a joke. Evalynn had made a few similar remarks in recent months, and Sophie was starting to worry that maybe her friend was privately struggling with the idea of stepping into the role of mother. She decided not to pry. If Evi was really having a hard time with it, she would eventually say something.

The pair continued chatting as they walked the remaining

four blocks to Sophie's store, although Evalynn carried most of the conversation. Sophie kept an open ear as she moved along, her umbrella perched on her shoulder, but her mind was elsewhere—*lost in memories of birthdays gone by*. At the forefront of her thoughts was the most important birthday of all, exactly twenty years earlier, which proved to be a day of new beginnings and tragic ends; a day that changed the course of every single day thereafter.

But in Sophie's mind, it would forever be remembered as the day her life shattered.

Chapter 2

You have a good memory, weighed down by bad memories.

September 21, 1989

JACOB BARNES RUBBED HIS FACE ON THE SLEEVE OF HIS coat, trying in vain to wipe away the dizziness from his eyes. He felt as though he might faint again at any moment. His mind raced to piece together details of the last fifteen minutes, but he was still too foggy to recall exactly how he'd gotten to his current position along the side of the road. After steadying himself against a lamppost, Jacob tugged angrily at his silk tie, which suddenly felt like a noose around his neck. The front of his Italian suit was soaked through, but he figured that was just the result of standing around in a daze in the steady downpour of Seattle's infamous liquid weather.

"Dear God," he said aloud, once his mind was clear enough to focus on the world around him. He squinted hard to sharpen his focus as he surveyed the scene. Jacob was never known for having a strong stomach, so what he saw before him, combined with his own fuzzy recollection of how it transpired, made him want to vomit. He fought hard to control the urge.

"It's all my fault," whispered a terrified little voice from nearby.

Jacob's dilated eyes darted around, searching for the voice's owner. A few paces off, sitting all alone on the curb near a yellow fire hydrant, was a young girl. She, too, wiped her face on her sleeve, but only to hide the evidence that she was crying. But it didn't matter; it was raining hard enough that she could have wiped all night and her face would still be wet. Her nose and lips were bruised and swollen, and a gash on her cheek sent a small trickle of red cascading down past her jaw and onto her neck. The white blouse she wore also bore random flecks of crimson.

The girl wrapped her shivering arms around her legs to protect them from the rain and the unusually cold September wind. "I...I just wanted a p-piece of chocolate," she sobbed. "Just *o-one* piece."

Jacob felt woozy. He shifted his position against the pole, hoping that would be enough to keep him from passing out again. "You think you caused this?" he asked in a voice more gruff than intended. "What has chocolate got to do with anything?"

The girl answered his first question with a nod, then she began rocking slowly back and forth, carefully studying the commotion down the street. Jacob followed her gaze—the steady whirring of sirens and passing cars, lights spinning and blinking, flares glowing with bright red brilliance, police officers darting here and there while trying to guide traffic, firefighters barking out orders, ambulance drivers, broken glass, bent metal, and blood—so much blood. The sights and sounds, and even the smell and taste of the horrific scene, filled his senses to overflowing. The girl turned again to look at him, but still said nothing.

Just then a policewoman and a young-faced EMT came running over. It occurred to Jacob that he and the girl were far enough away from the accident that they might have been mistaken for onlookers by the first wave of emergency personnel who'd arrived earlier.

"Sir," the EMT said to Jacob, looking very worried, "let me help you sit down." He quickly placed his tackle box of first-aid equipment on the ground, then wrapped a giant arm around Jacob's midsection and lowered him to the curb. "Can you do me a favor? Raise your left hand above your head and keep it elevated while I get you some bandages. Can you do that for me?"

Jacob was more confused by the EMT's odd request than he was by the young girl blaming the accident on chocolate. "Why? I'm fine. Can't you see that? Help that kid—she looks a little banged up."

"Sir, have you—"

"It's Jacob."

"Fine. Jacob, you're in shock. I think you've probably lost a lot of blood, and I want to make sure you don't lose any—"

"Blood? From where? Why am I bleeding?"

"It's okay. If you follow my directions, you'll be fine. Just hold your arm up like this." The EMT lifted Jacob's left arm for him. Jacob used his other arm to prop it up when the EMT let go.

Another jolt of queasiness coursed through Jacob's body. "Is the blood from my head? My face?" His voice picked up speed as he started to panic. "How the blazes is holding my arm above my head going to help that? Won't it just cause more blood to run down to my head and increase the blood loss? Are you sure you know what you're doing? Are you even old enough to be an—"

"Jacob!" shouted the EMT, his voice like ice. "It's not your face. Look at your hand!"

Jacob tilted his head absently. Squinting through the pouring rain and the streetlamp's hazy luminescence, he focused for the first time on the hand he was holding above his head. The sight sent another rush of nausea throughout his abdomen. All four fingers on his left hand were gone, severed completely where they met the palm. Only his thumb remained. He tried instinctively to wiggle his fingers. Oddly, his brain told him that all of them were moving, but only his thumb waved back. "I... I think I need to lie down," he groaned.

While the EMT attended to Jacob's hand and a few other less severe injuries, Jacob diverted his attention to the little girl and the policewoman. From his position on his back he could see and hear everything they said. The officer's name was Ellen, or at least that was how she identified herself to the child. She started by dabbing gently at the girl's face with a cotton swab while making small talk. Then she sat down next to her on the wet curb. The girl kept stealing glances at Jacob's mangled hand.

"Everything's gonna be fine, sweetie. Just fine." Ellen paused to look at the carnage, as if wondering if anything could ever really be *just fine* in the wake of something like this. "Now, can you tell me your name?" she asked cautiously.

The child looked up at her with a vacant stare, as though she were trying to process the words. Then she nodded and whispered quietly, "Sophia Maria Jones."

"Wow, that's a beautiful name. I'm glad to meet you, Sophia Maria."

The girl swallowed. "I go by Sophie."

"Then Sophie it is. How old are you, Sophie?" The officer must have been trained to ask the simple questions first, in order to prime the pump for the more difficult questions that, eventually, always have to be asked.

The girl wiped her nose again on the sleeve of her blouse. "Eight. No—nine."

"Wow," replied the officer soothingly, "that's a great age. I remember when I was nine. When was your birthday?"

A new, giant tear formed at the inside corner of Sophie's eye and spilled out onto her cheek. "*T-t-today*," she said, choking on the word.

"Oh, I see," Ellen said softly. "Were you out celebrating your birthday tonight?"

She nodded.

"Sophie, were you in one of these cars?"

Another nod.

A lump formed in Jacob's throat as he continued listening. He hardly noticed the EMT who was working swiftly above him, wrapping his injured limb with a gauze bandage.

"Can you tell me which one?" Ellen coaxed, looking up once more to survey the wreckage. A blue Datsun rested on its side fifty paces away, just in front of a late-model station wagon that had damage to its rear and front. Neither would ever be driven again, but the passengers at least had walked away. The other four cars involved in the accident—a Volvo, a small pickup, a Mercedes sedan, and a large UPS delivery truck—were spread out east to west along the four-lane road. The pickup had been struck on the passenger side and flipped over completely, probably hitting the Datsun in the process. The Volvo had suffered the most damage, apparently having been hit head-on by the much larger delivery truck. Jacob's Mercedes was right-side-up near the opposite curb. Jacob didn't remember it, but it looked like it had rolled a time or two before coming to a stop. He watched as emergency workers used a hydraulic machine to pry off the Volvo's crushed door so they could retrieve the lifeless body of a victim trapped inside. On the ground, near the rear of the same car, crews carefully draped a blue sheet over another unfortunate person they had pulled from within. Twenty yards farther down the road, an ambulatory team worked feverishly on the bent and broken body of the UPS truck driver.

"Can you tell me which car you were in, sweetie?" Ellen asked again.

Sophie reticently nodded a third time. She looked sadly at Ellen, begging with her eyes not to have to say. But she seemed to sense that the officer needed to know. Slowly, bravely, Sophie lifted one hand and pointed to the Volvo. "There. That's my mommy," she whispered, just as two firefighters gingerly coerced the limp body of a slender woman in her early thirties from the hole in the passenger side, where the crumpled front door had been only moments before.

Jacob couldn't contain the lurching in his stomach any longer. He turned his head in the opposite direction and vomited all over the ground, not caring that the bile was running right back toward him. He closed his eyes and silently wished he could undo the past hour of his life.

OFFICER ELLEN MONROE wanted to cry, but she knew that wouldn't help anything or anyone. Instead, she swooped up Sophie in her arms and tucked the girl's head against her shoulder, then carried her quickly to the far side of a row of ambulances where the view of the accident was blocked.

"Looks like you got your hands full," said another officer, as the pair approached. "Anything I can help with?"

Ellen grimaced. "We're okay," she said softly, trying to hide her growing concern for the child in her arms. "But can you put in a call to *double-S* for me? I got a hunch we're going to need 'em."

"Double-S?"

Ellen didn't want to have to say the words *Social Services* in front of the girl. She hinted with her head at Sophie, as she shot the man a look that said, *Use your brain, idiot*!

"Ah," he said, finally catching on. "Of course. Double-S. I'll get them on the horn right away."

Ellen set Sophie down gently on the back end of an ambulance and found a blanket to wrap around her. "You're gonna get through this, kiddo. You know that, right?"

Sophie only smirked.

"Well you are. There are lots of people who are here to help." Sophie's smirk drifted to a frown. Ellen changed the subject, hoping to keep the girl from clamming up entirely before the psychological cavalry arrived. "Earlier, when I first showed up, I thought I heard that man say something to you about chocolate. Do you like chocolate? 'Cuz I happen to have a Kiss right here in my vest. You want it?" She reached into her pocket and pulled out a silver-wrapped Hershey's Kiss. Sophie's eyes acknowledged the treat with open interest. "Here you go. It's all yours."

Sophie unwrapped the foil and popped it into her mouth, then relaxed noticeably.

Works every time, thought Ellen. "So tell me, Sophie, what was this cute little nine-year-old doing tonight to celebrate her birthday? You have such a lovely outfit on. Did you go out with your mom for dinner?"

"Uh-huh."

"Cool. Where did you go? Someplace fun, I bet." Though she wasn't a mother herself, Ellen had a special way with kids. Even if she'd never met them before, she could speak to them like they'd been pals forever. It was a skill she found particularly useful in such heart-wrenching circumstances.

"I dunno the name. A Japanese place. We only go there for special times." Sophie looked down at her hand and then clenched her fingers tightly.

"You got something in there you want to show me?" Ellen motioned to Sophie's tight fist.

"I don't want you to see it."

"Okay," she replied casually. "That's cool. So, did you have fun at the restaurant?"

"Yes." She paused. "They cook it on the table. The chef made a burning volcano out of onions. That was my favorite part."

"Wow, Sophie. That sounds like a great time. So after dinner, then what?"

"Dad said we had to go, because of school tomorrow."

Dang! That must've been her dad under the sheet. "Just you, your mom, and your dad?"

"And Grams. She lives with us, ever since Grandpa died."

Her grandmother, too! "I see. So you all headed home together?"

"Yes." Sophie clenched her hand tighter.

"And then... did you stop anywhere else?" *C'mon, Sophie, what happened? Help me understand what you've been through tonight so I can help you.*

Sophie looked up and down the street, her eyes finally settling on a point a few hundred yards away. "I wanted to. But Dad... he was in a hurry to get home, I guess. I told him the wish of my heart was to get a piece of chocolate at that candy store up there." She pointed. "They have the best chocolate in town. At least Mom says they do."

"I'll be sure to try it sometime. What happened then?"

"Dad said no."

"No chocolate?"

"Yes. Not tonight, because we already had dessert at the restaurant. But I told him it was the wish of my heart."

Ellen raised her eyebrows at the use of that phrase again. "What did he say to that?"

Sophie looked down at her clenched fist, then at the policewoman, and then back up the street to the chocolate store. "He... he must've forgotten."

"How do you mean?"

"Well, the wish of my heart was to get some chocolate. But he must have forgotten, so I showed him—" Sophie raised her white-knuckled hand. "I showed him that we *would* stop."

"You showed him your hand?"

Sophie shook her head. "I showed him what's in my hand. He told me at the restaurant that it would come true, so I wanted him to remember. And then..."

Ellen rubbed the young girl's shoulder softly. "It's okay, sweetie. What happened next?"

"He turned around to see it. Then a horn honked. He didn't have time to turn back around." The last words were barely audible. Sophie's head sagged between her shoulders. "It's all my fault," she said, crying once more.

Just then the other officer returned. "They're on their way," he said quietly, trying not to intrude.

"Thanks, Pete. Hey, Sophie's grandmother was in the car, too. Can you—?"

Pete cut her off midsentence with a look that said, *Don't ask. You won't like the answer.*

Ellen rubbed Sophie's shoulder and arm a little harder. "It's all gonna be okay, Sophie Jones. I promise you that. One way or another, it's going to be okay. And it's *not* your fault."

Sophie wrapped herself tighter in the blanket and looked down once more at her clenched fist.

"You care to show me now what you're hiding there in your hand?"

Nodding, Sophie slowly peeled open her fingers. Cradled inside her shivering hand was a crumpled slip of paper from a fortune cookie. Ellen leaned in closer so she could read the message, and then she understood.

Happiness is a gift that shines within you.
The wish of your heart will soon come true.

"It's not true, is it?" Sophie asked. "None of it. Fortune cookies aren't real, are they? My dad lied."

Ellen didn't know what to say that wouldn't further ruin

the girl, if that were even possible. "Well, they do come true," she fibbed. "Eventually."

Sophie's eyes opened a bit wider, but her expression was one of doubt. "Really?"

"Sure." Ellen shrugged. "Your dad wouldn't lie to you, now would he? And I wouldn't, either. It *will* come true."

Sophie took a moment to weigh Ellen's words. "Okay. If you really think it will, then the new wish of my heart is to have my family back. I saw them in the car, and... and I'm old enough to know they're gone. But I want them back! *That's* my wish."

Ellen felt like her heart was being ripped out of her chest. For the first time ever on the job, she allowed the emotions that swelled inside her to spill over in the form of tears. "Oh, sweetie, I'm so sorry," she cried. "I know that's your wish. That's my wish too. But—but—"

"But I can't have that wish, can I?"

Ellen breathed out a long, painful sigh, then brushed away the tears that were running down her own face and tucked a wisp of hair behind the girl's ear. "I'm afraid not, sweetheart."

Sophie wadded up the tiny paper and threw it on the ground in front of her. It landed without a sound in a small current of water running along the edge of the street. She watched as it floated slowly away, carrying with it all of her hopes and dreams. Part of her wanted to chase after it, to pick it up and dry it off, and pretend like everything would be okay. But it wouldn't be okay, and she refused to kid herself. Her parents were gone, her grandparents were gone, and there was nobody left in the world to love her. Her mind flashed back to scenes of the wreckage—the UPS truck driver, the cars flipped every which way, the man with the missing fingers, and especially her own parents' lifeless bodies. "It's *my* fault," she whispered numbly to herself again. "All my fault."

Chapter 3

Something you lost will soon turn up,
but some lost things are better left unfound.

September 21, 2009

SOPHIE'S STORE WAS LOCATED IN A SMALL RETAIL SPACE on Commerce Avenue, marked by a sleek, brushed-nickel sign that protruded horizontally from the building just above the front entrance. The laser-embossed lettering read, Chocolat' de Soph, followed by a much smaller cursive subscript: Confections of the Heart.

The interior of the store was decidedly upscale. Several large postmodern paintings hung on the walls at varying heights and angles, their colorful patterns providing sufficient visual interest against the gloss-black paneling and stainless-steel trim to keep the clean, contemporary décor from getting stale. Four Austrian-crystal dishes sat atop an etched-glass display case; they would be used later to hold free samples of the day's fresh fudge. Matching granite tables, each supported by a thick, hammered-steel base, stood in opposite corners near the store's tinted bay windows. The tables and their barstools provided both space and ambiance for patrons who wished to sit and enjoy a warm drink while nibbling on Sophie's rich chocolate creations.

The morning hours passed as they always did, with Sophie quietly rushing from one task to another. There were nuts to chop, molds to fill, butters to melt, powders to blend, creams to stir, liquids to measure, sweeteners to add, and a thousand other tasks to complete before the doors opened at 10:00 AM. Compounding all of that, Sophie had to make sure that Evalynn stayed clear of the peanut-butter balls in the refrigerator until they were firm enough to dip.

Evalynn, for her part, offered little noticeable help. Most of her effort was spent fingering the chocolate creams to determine which one she liked best. Sophie didn't mind. Even though she would have rather been alone with her thoughts, she appreciated her friend's gesture; Evi's presence alone had helped lighten her weighty emotional load.

At nine forty, with nearly everything ready, Sophie grabbed a pen and a handful of narrow slips of paper from the small office that adjoined the kitchen area at the rear of the building and sat down to complete her morning preparations. Writing out those unique fortunes had become her favorite part of the job, and it was probably the main reason her niche business had managed to stay afloat in a slowing economy.

"Any specific theme today?" asked Evalynn.

"Nope." Sophie tapped the pen on her lips while pondering what to write.

"You aiming for mild disappointment, or full-blown heartache?"

Sophie glanced up, annoyed. "Sshh. Neither. The goal is reality, nothing more."

Evi stifled a laugh. "Your reality or mine?"

"Stop."

"Can I help you write them?"

"Nope."

"Well then, can I at least have a peanut-butter truffle?" she asked hopefully.

With a hint of a growl, Sophie hissed, "Be quiet! I can't think. Just turn your mouth off for a few minutes. Please."

"I'll take that as a yes," whispered Evalynn, as she started for the other room, where a tray of fresh truffles was on display.

"Fine," said Sophie, frustrated. "Knock yourself out. But just give me a few minutes' peace so I can finish."

Fifteen minutes later, satisfied that she had enough slips of paper filled out to meet the day's demand, she gathered them together and joined Evalynn in the front of the store.

"How'd you make out?" asked Evi.

Sophie handed her the small stack of tiny slips. "See for yourself. And when you're done, would you mind sliding them into the fortune cookies? I have a couple more things to clean up in the back before we open."

Morning sales can be notoriously slow, even for the best chocolatiers, so it didn't surprise Sophie that nobody was beating the door down when she turned on the neon Open sign that hung in the window. Chocolat' de Soph opened promptly at ten, but the first customers didn't arrive until ten thirty, and they were more interested in free samples than anything else.

Shortly after eleven o'clock the lunch rush started, and sales began to pick up. As always, the big customer draw was Sophie's Misfortune Cookies, each of which included one of her unique, handwritten prognostications of gloom, doom, or pending hardships. By design, Misfortune Cookies weren't the best-tasting treat in the store. After bending and baking the cookies to the traditional fortune cookie shape, they were dipped in a vat of unsweetened chocolate stock imported directly from a cocoa plantation in Brazil. The resulting taste was shock-and-awe on unsuspecting mouths. When she dreamed up the odd cookies eleven months earlier, Sophie figured they'd be a short-term gimmick at best, a novelty that would fizzle. But to her great surprise, the bitter morsels had grown into a high-volume, high-margin staple, gaining enough local infamy to keep them flying off the shelf. She'd even started getting mail orders from other parts of the country.

Just prior to two o'clock in the afternoon, while Sophie was ringing up a husband and wife who seemed perfectly giddy to find out from their Misfortune Cookies that their car would soon break down and that others talked about them behind their backs, Evi tapped on her watch and mouthed, *It's almost time!*

Sophie's brow furrowed tightly as she remembered the arrangements her friend had spoken of earlier. She handed the couple their change and waited for them to exit before turning back to her friend. "Okay, Ev. Spill it. What's the big surprise?"

Evalynn glanced again at her watch. "I told you, my lips are sealed."

"Is something being delivered to the store?" There was no reply. "Is it a tangible something-or-other?" Still nothing. "Oh c'mon, give me a clue, Evi. You know I hate surprises."

"Fine. Yes, something is coming to the store. Something tangible. But that's all you're getting out of me." She zipped her fingers across her lips, then twisted an imaginary key at the edge of her mouth and dropped it down the front of her blouse.

"When? It better not be until later in the day."

Evalynn glanced beyond Sophie's shoulder toward the door, then back at her watch, and then she began tiptoeing toward the kitchen. "Oh," she said slowly, drawing out the word while stealing another quick peek at the window near the entrance, "I'm guessing, right about..." Evi ducked out of sight as she called over her shoulder, "Now!"

At the same moment, the bell that hung from the front door jingled lightly. Sophie kept her back to the door, unwilling to face whatever surprise had just entered her store. Her stomach churned with dread as her mind raced to deduce what kind of a surprise would arrive with such obvious punctuality at precisely two o'clock. *A singing telegram? No, that would be too cheesy, even for Evi. A delivery of... what? Definitely not chocolates. Maybe flowers? Yes! She said she'd made arrangements. That could be an arrangement of flowers, right? A nice bouquet, perhaps? I hate surprises! Please be flowers. Please...*

Sophie turned reluctantly. Before she made it all the way around she closed her eyes in a final attempt to delay the inevitable. After a few shallow breaths, interspersed here and there with unkind murmuring about Evalynn for doing this to her, Sophie forced one eyelid up, just a crack. Then she gasped, and both eyes shot wide open.

"What the—" Her face flushed instantly. She tried to gather her composure before uttering, "Oh. Crap." It wasn't exactly what she intended to say, but she delivered the words with as much grace and poise as could be expected, then followed up eloquently with, "I think I'm going to be sick."

Chapter 4

An apple a day keeps the doctor away.
You should invest in an apple orchard.

SICK? MAYBE YOU SHOULD SEE A DOCTOR." HE HELD A dozen long-stemmed roses peppered with fresh lilies, and he had a perfect mouth, even when he spoke. He was half a foot taller than Sophie, strong jawed, and well proportioned. Everything about him—the thick, dark hair, the dimples, the soothing timbre of his voice—was just as she remembered.

Sophie felt a strange urge to smooth her hair and straighten her blouse, but she resisted. *Bad habits die hard*, she thought. "I see one. That's my problem." She paused. Her eyes wandered circumspectly around the room, hoping to find something more worthy of her stare than him. "Umm. Why are you here?"

He took a couple of steps forward so he could close the door behind him. His sympathetic smile remained fixed in place. "Can we back up a sec? How about we start with a simple greeting, like 'Hello' or 'Good to see you'?"

She folded her arms and bit her lower lip nervously. "Do we have to?"

He took a long breath. "No, but I'd like to."

She sized him up once more, and then relented. "Fine."

"Yeah?"

"Sure." She waited. "Oh, you want *me* to start?"

"It's your candy store," he said with a wink.

Sophie recalled how she used to love those winks. Now she wasn't so sure. "Fine. Umm. Hello... Garrett. You're—here. Uninvited, I might add. Welcome."

"Hi, Sophie," he replied softly. "Happy birthday." He held up the flowers and started stepping closer, slowly, like a cautious mouse moving in to inspect a trap. "You look great. How've you been?"

Sophie didn't respond immediately. Looking down briefly at the display case, she caught a glimpse of her own reflection in the glass, and what she saw jolted her. No longer was she a confident, independent woman or a capable business owner. She was a teenage girl, a starry-eyed kid dreaming of the day that she would fall in love. She looked once more and saw the same girl, a few years older, in college, feeling very much alone, like she might never find someone who would care for her unconditionally. Again the reflection changed. Now she was moving from one bad relationship to another, each suitor blending curiously with the next, but all of them ending in heartache. Then, as if by a miracle, in the blink of an eye she was showing off an engagement ring to Evi, holding Garrett's hand, making wedding plans, and sending out invitations. Sophie squinted hard once more, but the image faded away. She knew it would.

"I've been better. Now back to my original question. What are you doing here?"

Garrett kept inching forward until the only thing standing between him and Sophie was the glass display case. He looked at her and his demeanor softened even further. The curve of his dimpled smile flattened into a solemn, serious line. "I've missed you, Soph."

It took only a split second for Sophie's mind to list all of the possible reactions to such an incredible statement: cry pathetically, turn and walk away, cheer, run into his arms, scream hysterically, vomit, panic, faint, call the police, throw the nearest half-empty bowl of Oreo fudge in his face, all of the above, or...

Sophie laughed. A single, simple, "that's just about the stupidest thing I've ever heard" kind of a laugh. She then glanced out the window to make sure no customers were about to enter the store.

Only then, when she was absolutely positive that the coast was clear, she yelled as loud as she could. "Evalynn Marion Mason-Mack! Get in here right now!"

A faint reply echoed from somewhere in the back. "Umm... just a minute."

"Now!" she repeated. "And get your filthy fingers out of the peanut-butter dough!"

There was a momentary pause, followed by a barely audible cry of dismay. "What the heck? Are there hidden cameras in the refrigerator?" A few seconds later Evi poked her head sheepishly around the wall that hid the kitchen from the rest of the store. She curtsied playfully. "You screamed, my lady?"

Sophie reached out and yanked her into full view by the sleeve of her shirt. "Explain," she commanded, motioning to Garrett, who was smiling again.

"Hey, careful with the pregnant lady," joked Evalynn.

"Explain, *now.*"

"Oh, c'mon, Sophie. I just thought... you know, that maybe you could use a little extra spark for your birthday."

"A spark?" she howled. "This is an explosion! Or an implosion. Either way, what were you thinking?"

"Well, I...," stammered Evalynn, "I see your point, I guess. But...really I just thought...Oh, c'mon, don't you see the twisted humor here? What spark burns brighter than an old flame, right?"

Sophie wanted to scream again, but she held her tongue. "So *this* was your big surprise? Twenty years since the worst day of my life, and to celebrate it you invite over the guy who's responsible for the *second* worst day of my life? Brilliant."

Evalynn shrugged. "Well, when you put it like that, I suppose—"

"Wait a minute, ladies," piped Garrett, wearing his serious expression again. Sophie imagined that was the look he used when he had to give patients bad news. "Can I say something?" Neither woman responded, so he continued. "Sophie, I contacted Evi a few days ago when I made up my mind that I was coming to see you. She didn't seek me out or invite me. In fact, she told me flat out to leave you alone. But when she couldn't change my mind, she chose to come today as well, just in case you needed her."

Sophie turned to Evalynn. "Is that true?"

Evi nodded.

"And I know very well," Garrett continued, "that I hurt you. I won't make excuses, but you should know that what I did hurt me, too. Your second worst day happens to be my very worst day, and that's why I came today. There were things I wasn't ready to tell you back then, but I feel like you need to know the truth. And I think if you'll give me a chance, you'll find that your birthday is the perfect day to hear what I need to say." Garrett held out the flowers and looked deep into Sophie's eyes.

She reluctantly took the bouquet, glaring at him as she did so. Then she glared equally hard at Evalynn, and then once more at Garrett. "Are you out of your mind? Usually I ask that the nuts get delivered to the back door, and yet here you are. Garrett, I really don't think we have anything to talk about. It was almost a year ago, for crying out loud. You left. You had your reasons. End of story."

Garrett's face sank. "You won't indulge me for one little date to sit and talk, so I can tell you what—?"

"I thought you said you just came to talk! Now you want a date, too?"

"Sophie," Garrett said, "listen. What I have to say to you is important. You probably won't like it, but it's important that you hear it anyway. Can you give me just one evening to say what I need to say, so both of us can have some sort of closure?" He paused, begging with his eyes. "*Please?*"

She shook her head sternly. "No. Not going to happen."

"But I—"

She lifted a finger. "No."

"Just one date," he pressed. "I know I should have handled things better than I did, but is it too much to ask for an hour of your time to say what should have been said before?"

Sophie ignored him. "If you don't mind, I have a business to run here. Evi, I think I can handle everything up front, so you're welcome to go work on the dishes."

Evalynn nodded apologetically and went to the back.

Garrett looked like he'd been punched. He stared longingly at the beautiful woman who'd stolen his heart a year earlier. But he'd taken her heart as well, held it in his hands like a treasure, and then, when she least expected it, dropped it like a rock and stomped on it. "Well as long as I'm here," he said, letting out a long breath, "can I at least buy some of your chocolates?"

Sophie considered his question briefly, looking for any hidden ploy. "Fine. I won't turn away a paying customer," she responded flatly.

He scanned the full length of the glass display case. "Anything new since the last time I was in?"

A mischievous grin played at the corner of Sophie's mouth, but she tried to hide it. "Actually, yes. These right here are the top sellers," she said proudly, pulling a basket of chocolate-dipped fortune cookies from behind the counter. "Believe it or not, you were part of the inspiration behind them."

"Really?" he asked, sounding both doubtful and flattered at the same time. "They look delicious. How much?"

"Three dollars."

"Okay, one of those. Plus half a dozen truffles for the road. A random assortment is fine."

Sophie gathered the chocolates and boxed them up, but left the Misfortune Cookie out on a napkin. She knew it was cruel, but she hoped he would eat it before leaving the store so she could watch his reaction. He didn't disappoint. Garrett pulled out his wallet and handed her some cash, then grabbed the cookie and took a bite. Sophie watched expectantly, her wry grin growing wider as his pearly white teeth closed around it.

Garrett's initial reaction was one of calm deliberation. He allowed several contemplative seconds for his taste buds to make sense of the strange new experience. Then his eyes grew as big as tires and his lips puckered wildly.

"Sophie that's...," he sputtered. "It tastes like baking chocolate."

Sophie scrunched her face into a deliberate pout. "Oh, you hate them. I'm crushed."

He wiped a piece of the bitter brown from his lip and spit several times into the napkin. "You really sell these to people? I mean, they pay money for them?"

Now, for the first time since he'd entered the store, she flashed a genuine smile. "Isn't it great? I call them Misfortune Cookies. Only real diehards eat the whole thing. Most people just buy them to read the fortune."

Garrett broke off another chunk of cookie so he could easily get at the small slip of paper tucked inside. His eyes scanned the message. Then he read it aloud, his voice questioning every word. "*Your job seems secure now, but have patience. Nothing lasts forever!* What is that supposed to mean?"

Sophie shrugged. "Beats me, Doctor Black. I just write them."

"It's the most depressing fortune cookie I've ever read."

"Well, buy some more," she replied with a twinkle in her eyes. "I'm sure you'll find one that can top it."

His mouth hung open. "You're telling me that people come in here just to get fortunes like this? Why would they do that?"

Beaming, Sophie handed Garrett his change. "Yes to the first question, and the jury's still out on the second. Evi thinks people like them because they're unique, one of a kind. But my hypothesis is that people just want an occasional dose of reality now and then. Life stinks, you know. It's as bitter as that chocolate, so why pretend like it's not, right?"

Garrett stared at her blankly, not knowing quite what to say. "Wow," he finally managed, exhaling. "I guess Evalynn was right. You really aren't happy, are you?"

Sophie's smile disappeared. She looked back over her shoulder to see if her friend was in sight. "She said that?"

He nodded.

She shrugged. "Well, maybe she's right. I mean, it's not like I'm sad, and I'm far from depressed. But I don't know that I'm particularly happy."

"Hmmm. How long have you felt that way?"

"Oh, don't go trying to make a diagnosis, Doctor. You're a podiatrist, remember, not a shrink. Besides, what is happiness anyway? I'd say there's more than an outside chance that people who claim to be happy couldn't even answer that simple question. And those that think they know what happiness is are probably just making something up to feel better about themselves."

Frowning, Garrett shoved his hands deep into his pockets. "You don't honestly believe that, do you?"

She tucked a loose strand of wavy blond hair behind her ear. "Why not? Look at the world. The things that people attribute to happiness are just fleeting. Take our relationship, for example.

You, I, we...*fleeted*. It's like your fortune said— *nothing lasts*."

"I think you're wrong."

Sophie stared at him, really looked hard at the man on the opposite side of the counter. She hadn't studied his face like that for a long time. Privately, she couldn't deny that she still enjoyed looking at him. It gave her butterflies the way he was able to look at her like she was the only other person on the face of the planet. "Then tell me, Garrett. What is happiness?"

He tugged at his earlobe while considering her question. "To me? Hmm. Right now I'd have to say that happiness is being completely honest with the people you care about."

The comment caught Sophie off guard. She smoothed her apron. "Meaning what, exactly?"

"Meaning that for the past eleven months I've been living with a secret, and it's killing me. I can't be happy until you know the truth about me."

Sophie retreated in surprise. "Oh crap," she gasped. "There's a *truth* about you? What is it? No, wait! Let me guess." Her mind was reeling. In the wake of her unceremonious dumping, Sophie had spent countless hours wondering what she'd done to drive Garrett away. But she'd also considered the possibility that maybe there were things he didn't want her to learn about him, and the only way to avoid that was to leave. Now all those thoughts came flooding back. "You were cheating, weren't you!" She wanted to cry.

"No, I could never—"

"What then? You're not actually a doctor? There's a large alimony check you never told me about? An STD?" She gasped again and put her hand over her mouth. "Oh. Don't tell me that *I* was the other woman. You're married, aren't you!"

"Sophie!" he shouted, trying to get her to listen. "No! Nothing like that! I can't believe you'd even think those things about me!"

"Then what?"

Speaking more softly than before, he said, "I told you, I can't tell you here. I need to sit down with you where we can really talk. It's complicated, and it deserves your full attention. One date, that's all I ask. You choose the place."

Just then the bell on the door jingled lightly, and a young mother with two small children entered. Garrett backed away from the counter and sat down on one of the empty stools near the window, making room for the kids to get a complete view of the treats in the display case. He hoped they didn't pick the Misfortune Cookies.

While the mother helped the kids pick their goodies, Sophie considered what Garrett had said about her. *He's cruel*, she thought. *Yanks happiness away from me, and then shows up out of the blue and accuses me of not being happy.* But as she stood there thinking, Sophie knew that Garrett had not been the first person to take happiness and love away from her without warning. *That's the story of my life. How can I blame him for adding another chapter?*

Dropping her hands to her side, Sophie glanced down again at the display case. At first she saw the children's faces from the other side, licking their lips as they evaluated each chocolate one by one. Looking harder, her own reflection took shape once more in her mind. Like a forgotten friend, there she was, a smiling little girl, laughing and playing on her father's lap, then giggling as her mother tickled her toes. Sophie's eyes watered, causing the image in her mind to shift. Now she was a few years older. Not old enough to fully comprehend the slim odds that she was even alive, but old enough to remember every detail of the accident. She was cold. Cold and miserably wet, and nothing in the world seemed real. Everything felt wrong, because she knew that it was all her fault. Sophie blinked hard and the image vanished. The only thing looking back at her was the familiar face of an almost-thirty-year-old woman. *Happiness is fleeting*, she reminded herself again.

"Garrett," she said, after the family was gone. "Listen. Whether or not I'm happy is really no concern of yours. You left, remember? You don't get a say in my life. And as far as this awful *thing* goes, that you want to share with me? Honestly, I think I'd rather not know." She paused, watching him carefully. "I really think we should just leave the past alone. All right?"

Garrett sat quietly, staring at the floor. After several long moments he stood up and spoke. "Sophie, just for the sake of argument, what if you're wrong? What if happiness *does* exist? The kind that lasts. What if we had it right there in our hands and I blew it? What if...?" He hesitated, and took a slow step toward her. "What if there's still a chance that we could have that?"

"There's not," she insisted. "And that's a lot of *what ifs*."

"Then how about a *what would*?"

"Huh?"

"What would it take to get you to agree to one date? What I have to tell you isn't just about me, Soph. It's also about *you*."

Sophie tapped her fingers lightly on the countertop, watching the man who had once treated her like she was the sun, the moon, and the stars, all rolled into one. *Right up until the day he walked away*, she reminded herself.

"Tell you what," she said. The finger tapping stopped so she could twirl more golden hair. "I'll make a deal with you."

Garrett's eyes perked up. "What sort of deal?"

The kind of deal you have no chance of winning, she thought. "Well, ever since Evalynn got married, she keeps telling me that I need to find a man so we can better commiserate. Last week she even tried to get me to place a personal ad in the newspaper."

Garrett chuckled. "Like, 'Single white female seeking—'?"

"'Seeking anything but a foot doctor.' Yes, something like that. Anyway, I told her I've always thought those ads are just people looking for a fling—they're not really searching for lasting happiness. But true happiness shouldn't require a relationship, right?" She waited for him to answer. "*Right?*"

"Oh. Yeah, of course. I mean…it can help. But it's not an absolute must."

She grinned. "Good. Then since you brought up happiness, and you're so sure that it exists, how about you try to find it for me?"

Garrett's brow narrowed. "How?"

Sophie's grin expanded. "The newspaper! There are ads for everything else in there. Why not one for happiness?"

"I don't get it. You want me to run a personal ad for you?"

"No. I want a *want ad*. Something simple, like, 'Wanted. Happiness.' You run that in the *Seattle Times*, and if you can get, say, one hundred people to respond with something intelligent, then I'll consent to a date. *One date*."

"Can I put the ad online?"

She shook her head. "That would run the risk of reaching too many people. Printed paper only, please."

Garrett studied her. He knew the likelihood of anyone responding to an ad like that was slim at best, and a hundred replies would be near impossible. "You really don't want to hear what I have to say, do you?"

"Eleven months ago, yes. Now? Not so much. But hey, at least I'm giving you a fighting chance, right?"

He frowned, looking slightly dejected. "Sure. So are there any other stipulations to this deal that I should be aware of?"

Sophie tapped her fingers again on the glass while she thought. "Ummm…yes. This has to be completely anonymous. You can't recruit any of your friends, patients, or anyone else to send in responses. And everything has to go to the PO box I have for business stuff. I don't want any nutjobs showing up at my house or here at the store hoping to make me happy."

He kept his gaze fixed on her. "And what will constitute an 'intelligent response'?"

Sophie laughed. "Whatever I decide when I read them. Obviously, I only want rational, thoughtful statements of happiness. Nothing sexual. Nothing creepy or weird. And most importantly, nothing that fleets."

Garrett made a little snorting sound through his nose. "I can only post this in the *Seattle Times*, I have to get one hundred responses, and none of those things count?"

"Those are the rules if you want a date."

"Is there a time limit?"

"Nope. The offer stands until the day I die, which is probably about how long it'll take to find one hundred happy people through the want ads." Sophie was pleased with her idea, and her ruthless smile showed it.

Garrett, on the other hand, was obviously frustrated. It had taken him eleven months to build up the nerve to share his secret with Sophie, and now that he'd made the effort, she was shutting him down. He turned and walked to the door, his shoulders sagging. He paused only a moment, as if considering stopping right there and telling her everything he wanted to say. But he must have thought it was too complicated for that, because then he kept going. Before opening the door, he turned and looked back over his shoulder. "Good-bye, Sophie."

Part of Sophie wished that she hadn't been so hard on him. After all, it wasn't like she didn't think about him all the time, silently wishing that she were still his. But she knew that that was an impossibility, and she refused to let her heart get crushed again. "Good-bye, Garrett."

His eyes scanned Sophie from head to toe, taking in every detail. "I'll be sure to stop by periodically to see how the responses are coming. But if we never reach one hundred," he added softly, "please know that I always loved you, Soph. Even if I was a coward and a jerk, my feelings for you never changed."

Sophie didn't allow herself to cry until after he was gone. "Me too," she whispered, once the door had closed.

Chapter 5

You'll never really be happy. How sad.

ALTHOUGH SOPHIE ENCOURAGED EVALYNN TO GO HOME to her husband on three different occasions after Garrett left Chocolat' de Soph, her friend didn't budge.

"It's not like you're paying me to be here," she balked. "I chose to spend the day with you, so unless you physically remove me from the premises, you're stuck with me until we get off the bus in Gig Harbor."

"I'm not riding the bus home," Sophie muttered.

"Whatever," Evalynn said, thinking she was teasing.

"I'm serious, Ev. If you're riding the bus, you're on your own."

"Why's that? Afraid another cute guy might try hitting on you?"

Sophie showed her disappointment with a frown—after so many years, Evalynn should have known without being told. "Because there's something else I need to do tonight."

It finally registered. "Oh, yikes! I'm sorry, Soph. Of all the insensitive things. You're going to the cemetery, aren't you?" Evalynn paused, watching Sophie's expression tighten. "Do you want me to come with you this year? I mean...can I?"

Sophie relaxed her face enough to smile. "You've done enough already. Really. But this is something I need to do alone. And you need to go be with Justin."

Evalynn smiled back, then gave Sophie a hug that said, *It's going to be all right.* But inside Evi was thinking, *When is it going to be all right? It's time to get over the past and move on.* It wasn't for lack of understanding that Evalynn felt that way. Like Sophie, tragedy was something she knew a thing or two about, having lost her mother to a prison sentence when she was eight. It was their mutual lack of family that ultimately brought the pair together as children and forged an inseparable bond between them. But for reasons Evalynn didn't fully understand, Sophie's scars ran deeper than her own, and losing Garrett had only heightened her feelings of loss and hopelessness.

Evalynn released her grip on her foster sister. "Are you absolutely sure? You don't always have to go alone, you know. And Justin would be perfectly content if I didn't come home right away and interrupt Monday night football."

"I'm sure."

BY THE TIME the evening help showed up at the store at five o'clock, in the form of a redheaded college kid named Randy, Sophie was completely spent. Physically, the day hadn't been any more demanding than every other day, but emotionally she was wearing thin. Usually she would stay for a short while after Randy arrived to get a jump on preparations for the following day, but the September sun was already starting to dip, so time was becoming a critical factor.

Hailing the first empty cab she could find, Sophie made her

way north to Seattle. She couldn't bring herself to visit the cemetery more than once per year, but that was often enough that she knew the route by heart. She gave the cabbie directions, even though he swore up and down that he knew exactly where he was going without her help.

Traffic along I-5 was, predictably, a nightmare. By the time the cab pulled up in front of Evergreen Washelli Cemetery on Aurora Avenue, the sun had dropped much lower on the western horizon. Sophie paid the fare and got out quickly, hoping to avoid spending any amount of time among the headstones after dark.

Inside the cemetery's fenced perimeter, she followed the main road as it curved around to the east. The road split near the base of a famous World War One statue called *The Doughboy*, which depicted an American soldier returning from battle with mud on his boots and a smile on his face. From the statue she took the path to the left, heading north over and around several small, rolling hills lined with tall cedar trees. "There, by the hedge," she said several minutes later, as her eyes fixed on a point at the top of the next hill. Nobody was around to hear, but speaking out loud helped calm her nerves.

Picking up the pace, Sophie stepped off the main road for the final hundred yards, zigging and zagging around shrubs, small trees, and scores of graves until she reached the tall row of birch trees at the top of the rise. With twenty-five yards to go, she reached a point where the hedge no longer blocked the view of her parents' burial spot. She stopped dead in her tracks. A man was there, squatting down in the grass, looking at the handful of graves at the precise location to which she was heading. The man's hands were tucked deep in the front pocket of his sweatshirt, his back turned to her.

Sophie wondered what the odds were that the only other person in the entire cemetery happened to be visiting a grave right next to her parents. *Not very good*. She didn't panic, but the thought of being alone near dusk in a cemetery with a strange man who happened to be hovering over the tombstone of her dead family gave her a chill. Turning slowly, she tried to slip away undetected.

She made it only three paces.

"Hello! Don't go! I'm leaving now." It was definitely a man's voice, but there was a strange, singsong quality to it. Something decidedly... unique.

Sophie spun back around.

The man was short with broad shoulders, and he wore dark sunglasses in the piercing last rays of daylight. He walked toward her, smiling, and she noticed a peculiar skip in his step. "Really," he continued in the same voice. "I'm done here."

Sophie watched the man as he approached. He was younger than she, maybe nineteen or twenty years old. Under different circumstances she might have felt terror, but something about his demeanor told her not to worry. As he got closer, she noticed that his head was a bit larger than normal, and that his face was slightly more rounded. She wanted to see his eyes, but they were hidden beneath mirrored lenses. Sophie swallowed the lump in her throat. "Did you find what you were looking for?" she asked tentatively, when he was just a couple of steps away.

He grinned but didn't stop, or even slow down. "I was just passing through," he said with a little laugh. "Had something to do for my dad." The man smiled even wider, shoved his hands deeper into his sweatshirt, and continued walking right on by.

Sophie watched the stranger with curiosity for several more seconds. She was contemplating the unusual pitch of his voice—a tempered lisp that rang out like a melody—when another movement near the base of the small hill caught her attention. It was an arm, waving.

"Sophie! Wait up!"

She didn't need to hear anything more than her name to know who the voice belonged to. Remaining completely still, Sophie watched as Evi, who was also wearing shades, hurried past the curious young man and continued at a quick pace up the hill to where she stood.

"I thought I told you I wanted to be alone."

"Did you?" Evalynn asked.

"Don't play dumb."

"Fine... here's the thing. Justin thought I'd be out late, so he invited some friends over to watch a football game. I'd have been a fifth wheel, so I hopped in the car and drove up." She paused just long enough to watch Sophie's expression tighten into a frown. "I figured this way you won't have to pay for a cab ride home when you're done." She smiled mischievously. "You can pay me instead."

The muffled laugh that escaped Sophie's mouth helped lighten her mood. "Not on your life. But I'll be happy to buy us both something to eat on the way. I'm starving, and I really feel like drowning my sorrows in a greasy plate of onion rings and a large chocolate shake."

Evalynn smiled. "Sounds perfect. Now, can we go see your parents?"

Sophie led Evalynn to a simple headstone on the far side of the hedge, directly beneath the outstretched boughs of an aged cedar, which marked the final resting spot of Thomas and Cecilia Jones. The engraving read,

Husband and Father
Wife and Mother
Loved their daughter and each other fully and forever.

"That's sweet," whispered Evalynn after reading the inscription. Then she looked around at the surrounding grave markers. "Is your grandmother nearby, too?"

"No. She'd wanted to be buried with her husband—my grandpa—at a cemetery somewhere else in the state. Camas, I think. I've never been there."

Evalynn nodded. "Tell you what, I'll just hang back a bit so you can do your thing without me hovering." She stepped away.

"No need," Sophie said, waving her forward. "Believe it or not, this will be a quick stop."

Evalynn watched with curiosity as Sophie reached into her handbag and pulled out a small chocolate box from its depths. Opening the box, Sophie picked up one small truffle from within and placed it carefully on the gravestone in the space between her parents' names. Then she reached once more into her purse, this time finding a small slip of paper and a straight pin. She knelt down in front of the headstone, then gingerly poked the pin through the paper and stuck them both into the center of the truffle.

Before standing, Sophie did one final thing that perplexed Evalynn. A flat, smooth rock, perhaps two inches in diameter and half an inch thick, lay near the corner of the gravestone. It was clearly not there by accident. Much of the rock was translucent agate, including several sections that were nearly see-through. The rest of it was opaque, but with brilliant flecks of silver and burgundy peppered throughout. Sophie stared at it momentarily, marveling at its beauty. Then, without any fanfare, she picked it up, dropped it in her purse, and jumped up off of her knees. "Let's go," she said.

"What?" Evalynn asked, surprised. "That's it?"

"I told you. Quick stop. I'm all done."

Sophie took several steps back the way they'd come.

Evalynn didn't move. "But Soph, it's the twentieth anniversary. Don't you want to, you know... say something to them? Or at least spend a little more time?"

"Why?"

"*Because*," Evalynn shot back, her voice rising above a

whisper for the first time in several minutes. "They're your parents!"

"It's okay, Ev. I did what I came here to do. I've made my annual peace."

Evalynn looked down at the grave marker. "The chocolate? Do you leave one every year?"

Sophie nodded.

Glancing once more at the gravestone, Evalynn asked, "What's with the paper you stuck on it? Is that an annual thing, too?"

Sophie shook her head. "That's a new addition this year. After..." She stopped, biting her lip nervously. The words were clear in her mind, but speaking them out loud—even to Evalynn—was hard. "After the whole thing with Garrett, I think my perspective on life changed a bit. The note is just my way of sharing what I feel, without having to verbalize it."

Evalynn smiled sympathetically. "That's good! You need to express it one way or another. Do you mind if I...?" She hinted with her eyes at the paper.

Sophie shrugged. "This is a public place. Knock yourself out."

Evalynn turned and knelt down. Reading the words on the paper proved to be a difficult task in the waning light, especially with sunglasses on. It would have been easier to pick up the ensemble and hold it to her face, but she didn't want to disrupt what Sophie had taken such care to assemble. Getting on all fours and leaning her head close to the ground, she lifted the sunglasses to her forehead, squinted hard, and then slowly read the tiny words aloud. "*You will take a chance in the near future, and win.*" From her position on the ground, Evalynn snapped around and looked up at Sophie, who was now smiling contentedly. "Sophia Maria Jones! You come all the way here to visit your parents, just to leave them a message from your stupid cookies?"

Sophie chuckled dismissively. "Hey, that's not one of mine. I certainly wouldn't write something so rosy. I stopped by Panda Express yesterday after work. There were actually two fortunes in the cookie, and I had a hard time choosing between them. The other one said, '*Opportunity knocks. Will you answer?*' Nice, right?"

Evalynn stood and brushed off her hands and knees. "Oh, for crying out loud. I don't care where it came from. What I care about is *you*. I thought you said this was your way of expressing how you feel. How does this even remotely express your feelings about your parents?"

"I said it expressed how I feel, but I didn't say it's how I feel about them."

"What is that supposed to mean?"

Sophie looked around and squinted at the setting sun. "Think of it this way. Right now, today, it's beautiful outside, sunny and warm. But what about tomorrow? I expect that by then the rain will have set in, the wind will be blowing, and that fortune will be gone. *Ruined*. And the truffle? A hungry squirrel or raccoon will likely scarf it down by dawn. So the fortune and the piece of chocolate are just little reminders—to my parents, to me, to *anyone*—that eventually, hopes and dreams just disappear." She looked down and silently read the inscription below her parents' names one more time. "It's the story of my life. Everything fleets."

Evalynn watched her without speaking.

For a moment Sophie refused to look at her best friend, choosing instead to stare at the ground and rub her arms slowly with her hands. Finally she looked up and saw the concern on Evalynn's face. And the confusion. And maybe even a little disappointment. She let a deep breath escape in a long, heavy sigh. "This is why I wanted to come alone. I don't expect you to understand, Ev. I'm sure now you think I'm nuts, if you didn't already."

Evalynn still didn't say anything.

"Look," Sophie continued, "I know it's probably not how you choose to cope, but it works for me. Okay?"

Part of Evalynn wanted to walk over and shake some sense into Sophie, while another part of her would have liked to track down Garrett Black and make him pay for what he'd done to her heart. But Evalynn knew she could do neither. She simply gave a nod and a wan smile. "Okay, Sophie."

Together they made their way back down the hill to the road, neither of them speaking as they walked. With their backs to the Joneses' headstone, they failed to notice the lone figure behind the large hedge near the cedar tree. They didn't hear the twig that snapped beneath his foot as he stepped from his cover and stood above Thomas and Cecilia Jones.

After several moments, he bent down and placed a small, round stone on the lower corner of the tombstone. With the opposite hand, he gently lifted the truffle, pulled out the pin and its tiny paper fortune, and popped the morsel in his mouth. Then he quietly disappeared into the deepening shadows and trees.

Chapter 6

Is it love or pity? Try not to dwell on it.

FIVE DAYS AND ELEVEN HOURS LATER, THE CELL PHONE on Sophie's nightstand started vibrating, yanking her from another restless night long before she was ready to wake up. She squinted at the screen to check the time—6:26 AM—then stared at the picture of the caller, debating whether or not to answer.

"This is my one day off," Sophie groaned, as she reluctantly picked up. "You're horrible for calling at this hour."

"Couldn't be helped," replied Evalynn cheerfully. "And it's not like you need beauty sleep." She shifted to the Zsa Zsa Gabor impersonation that she'd perfected in high school. "You're gor-ge-ous, darling, simply gor-ge-ous."

Sophie hesitated. "Thanks, but you're still horrible. Besides, it's too early in the morning for flattery." She paused to rub her eyes. "What do you want, Mrs. Mason-Mack?"

"First, I want you to *never* call me that again. *Mrs.* makes me sound old. And second, Justin and I are heading out early today, but before we leave I wanted to let you know that you should go pick up a copy of the Sunday *Times*. I think you'll want to check out page G4."

"What's on page G4?" she asked groggily, still trying to shake off the cobwebs of sleep.

"Well, do you want me to spoil the surprise, or do you prefer to wait and read it on your own?"

"Ev. It's o'dark hundred. Tell me whatever it is you've found, so I can go back to sleep."

Evalynn snickered into the phone. "Honestly, Soph, you're so going to laugh. Okay, maybe not laugh, but . . . just swear to me you'll go get a copy of the paper for yourself. For posterity's sake."

"Posterity? That's laughable."

"You swear?" Evalynn asked, still bubbling with excitement.

"Evi Mack, get on with it, already, or I'm hanging up."

"Okay fine. Here goes. Two words. Ready?"

"Evalynn!"

"All right! I just love the buildup. Here it is. '*Wanted. Happiness.*'" She drew the two words out slowly and clearly, articulating every syllable.

There was a long moment of silence. Then Sophie groaned. "He actually placed the ad?"

"Yep."

"I totally expected him to ditch the idea. There's no way he'll ever get a hundred responses."

"I guess he thinks otherwise."

Another groan. "How did you find it?"

"Dumb luck. I was looking to see if there were any garage sales near my in-laws. Justin is dragging me along to visit his family today in Everett, and I know his mom likes hunting for deals, so I thought I'd take her out, see if I can't get her to like me."

Sophie heard Justin in the background tell Evalynn, unconvincingly, that his mom "usually" liked her.

"She hates my guts," whispered Evalynn into the phone, and then returned to her normal, loud voice. "Anyway, I was scanning down through the ads, and this one just jumped off the page. The heading is in very large print. And bold."

"Please tell me he didn't use my name."

"Nope. No name, no phone number. Just your PO box in Tacoma. Oh, and a little blurb at the end that says women need not respond, 'cuz you're a smokin' hot lady lookin' for Mr. Right."

"Shut it."

"Wait, I misread. It actually says, 'Grumpy single woman with no sense of humor whatsoever. Will settle for misery and despair.'"

A giant yawn escaped Sophie's mouth. "Stop. I already told you, it's too early for flattery."

"Fine, I've got to run anyway. Justin is literally pulling on my sleeve to go. Says if we don't leave now we'll run into Seahawks traffic in the city."

"Great. Well thanks for waking me up with such wonderful news, Ev," Sophie deadpanned. "You're a real pal."

"Oh, I see how it is. Flattery is out, but it's obviously not too early for sarcasm."

"It's what I do best."

"Ciao, Soph!"

Sophie put the phone back and pulled the covers up over her head, but after tossing and turning, and stuffing her head beneath the pillow, and still finding it impossible to go back to sleep, she rolled out of bed and made her way to the bathroom. Once she got in the hot bath she didn't want to get out, so she remained in long enough that her skin was pruned. Then she threw on a sweatshirt and her most comfortable pair of jeans, slung an umbrella over her shoulder, and went for a walk in the morning sun.

There was a small market just around the corner from her house, but it didn't open until nine o'clock on Sundays, so Sophie crossed to the shore side of the road, walking south along the harbor to the next intersection. Half a mile from there, near the top of a steep hill, was a shopping plaza with a drugstore that sold newspapers from vending machines out front. One dollar and fifty cents later, she was thumbing through the *Seattle Times*.

Shortly thereafter she found section G, turned to page four, and scanned it for bold letters.

Sophie grunted when she saw the ad halfway down the second column, just below a notice that someone was giving away kittens. She tried hard to force a frown, but found resistance in the form of a smile that kept playing at the corner of her mouth as she read, and then reread, the want ad.

Wanted: Happiness

Please help me find what I've lost. Send suggestions to PO Box 3297, TACOMA, WA 98402 (Lasting happiness only, please. Nothing that fleets.)

"Garrett Black," she said aloud, shaking her head while her lips still fluxed between grimace and grin. "Don't get your hopes up. Everything fleets."

Part II

The Beginning

Chapter 7

You will soon fall in love.
Caution: when people fall, something usually breaks.

October 2007

"YOU DIDN'T," GARRETT GROANED INTO THE PHONE. "Please tell me you're joking."

Olivia DeMattio was on the other end of the line at her home in Seattle, and she sounded as giddy as a schoolgirl. DeMattio was her married name—second marriage, the first having ended almost before it began. Although Olivia liked the sound of her married surname, she'd always disliked her first name—perhaps because no one ever used it. Her husband of sixteen years, Ken DeMattio, Jr., an accountant working for Microsoft, sometimes called her Liv. Either that or Sugar, Cookie, Sugar Cookie, or his personal favorite, Cookie Sheet. Friends at the police station usually called her Livie, unless they were on patrol, in which case she answered to "Dispatch." Her own mother, who had named her Olivia in the first place, had only ever addressed her as Olive, which was like torture to Olivia growing up. "My daughter, Olive," her mother would tell friends, "is quite a little pickle. Like her very own vegetable platter."

Garrett never called Olivia by any of those names. To him she was simply Mom.

"Oh, c'mon, Garrett. Don't pretend like you're not interested."

Garrett waited before responding. "It just feels an awful lot like a blind date, and you know how I hate those."

"Why is it a blind date? Because she doesn't know who you are? *Pfff*. Even if it were a blind date—*which it's not*—but if it were, a blind date is better than no date, right?" Olivia paused. "And who knows, the two of you might end up finding something you didn't know was missing. I mean, we already know you have a lot in common."

"Incredible. You just jumped from a blind date to... what? A missing something-or-other with a woman I've never even met?"

Olivia was momentarily mute. "So you're going to turn down this opportunity?"

Garrett pulled the phone away from his ear long enough to tell his head nurse that he'd be right there. "Fine," he said reluctantly into the receiver, after the nurse was out of earshot. "I'll go. But don't count on anything coming of it. I'm only going out of curiosity. One date, nothing more."

"Whatever you say, Garrett."

"Good. As long as that's understood. Now, does Sophie know anything about me?"

"Just what I've told Ellen at work, which isn't much."

"Is there anything else you can tell me about her?"

Olivia paused to think. "Nothing comes to mind that you don't already know. But I saw pictures today."

"And?"

Olivia snorted. "And you'll just have to wait and see." She hesitated. "But Garrett?"

"Yes."

"Just remember to take a look at what she's got on the inside."

He knew what that meant. As a kid, whenever the subject of girls came up, Garrett's mother never missed an opportunity to tell him that "the real gems of the female race are often disguised behind imperfect exteriors." Olivia herself had never been what one would describe as a beauty queen, and Garrett was pretty sure she considered herself to be one of those hidden gems.

"Don't worry," he promised. "I'll be nice, no matter what she looks like."

Garrett knew what was coming after the next bit of silence.

"You're a good boy, Garrett."

"Not a boy anymore, Mom."

"You know what I mean."

"Hey, I've got to run. Can you just e-mail me the details for this date?"

"No. It's seven o'clock this Friday. You can remember that without an e-mail. But she doesn't want you to pick her up, so I need you to tell me where you'd like to meet, so I can pass it on to Ellen."

"Oh. Ummm... well, there's a fantastic little KFC not too far from—"

"Garrett."

"Fine. How about the Space Needle? I've only ever gone up there for the view, but I hear the restaurant is great."

"I think that'll be nice. You make the reservations, and I'll let Ellen know you'll meet Sophie in the gift shop at seven."

He checked his watch, noting that his next patient had already been waiting for five minutes. "How will I recognize her?"

Olivia let out a little laugh. "Just look for a hidden gem who's all alone, and that'll probably be her."

Garrett sighed heavily into the phone. "One date only," he reminded her.

"Talk to you later, Garrett."

The phone clicked off.

FRIDAY CAME MUCH faster than Garrett Black wanted it to. He toyed once or twice with the idea of calling his mom and telling her he was sick in bed, but he feared that she'd send one of her detective friends to check out his story, and then there'd be hell to pay.

At a quarter after six he reluctantly left his office in Tacoma, and by five minutes to seven he'd found an empty parking space a few blocks south of the Space Needle along Fourth Avenue. After feeding a crisp ten-dollar bill to the parking meter, he walked the remaining quarter-mile to Seattle's most recognizable landmark—the Space Needle, a towering, 605-foot structure that was built as the centerpiece of the 1962 World Fair, and which was adorned at the top by what clearly resembled a UFO.

Checking his watch once more before entering the gift shop at ground level, Garrett saw that he was already two minutes late. Inside, he scanned the dozens of people who were wandering around eyeing souvenirs, but the handful of women who fit the somewhat homely image he'd contrived in his head of a diamond in the rough were either already with a man or had children hanging on them. One of the women, with a young boy, smiled at him when she caught him looking, and he smiled back, then chuckled softly to himself. He'd dated women with children before and had nothing against it, but the thought of going on a first date with the children in tow? Not an ideal situation.

Continuing his search for Sophie Jones, Garrett made two full loops around the doughnut-shaped store, but still didn't find anyone who fit the bill. "I hate blind dates," he muttered.

As he passed the south elevators for the third time to start another loop, someone tapped him on the shoulder. Turning to his right, Garrett found himself face-to-face with one of the most striking women he'd ever laid eyes on, though it wasn't the first time he'd ever seen her. He'd already noticed her on each of the previous loops, but had purposefully diverted his gaze out of fear that he'd be caught ogling. She was nicely dressed in slacks and a V-neck sweater. The woman's blond hair fell a little past her shoulder in thick, wavy locks, her lips and dimpled cheeks formed a very cute smile, and her bright blue eyes sparkled and smiled all on their own.

"You look lost," she said.

"Oh," he replied, stammering. "No. I'm just... I'm looking for someone. Supposed to meet a girl... lady... a woman, actually." *Idiot.*

Her smile grew. "Well, can I help you out?"

Yes, he thought. "No. I'm fine. I'm sure she'll turn up sooner or later. Hopefully sooner, because we have dinner reservations in one minute."

"What does she look like?" she asked, grinning.

"Good question. But I don't have a good answer. This is sort of a blind date, as pathetic as that may sound."

She nodded. "That does sound pathetic."

"Even more pathetic is the fact that my mom was the one who set me up."

"Ouch."

"I know."

The slender blonde pointed to a stout woman with matted brown hair who'd just come through the main entrance. "She seems nice. Maybe that's her."

Garrett shrugged. "Maybe."

"Well why don't you go introduce yourself?"

He shrugged again, then walked over and asked the woman if her name was Sophie Jones. She tossed her hair to the side, stepped closer to him, touched him on the arm, and told him she could be Sophie Jones if he wanted her to. Taking that as a no, he returned to the blonde, who was trying hard not to laugh.

"Not her?" she asked.

"Afraid not."

The woman bit her lower lip and twirled a tuft of hair around her finger. "I have a great idea," she said after a few seconds. "Why don't you go to the front desk and have her paged? That'll save you both the effort of finding each other."

He looked at his watch, then nodded. "That'll help save time, too. Thanks."

The main desk was just a little ways back, near the elevator. The woman followed Garrett up to the counter.

"Can I have someone paged?" he asked the young lady standing behind the desk.

"Of course. Are they lost?" she asked. "Not your children, I hope." She looked back and forth between Garrett and the woman standing next to him.

"Oh... no... we're not," Garrett said, stammering again, while glancing at the blonde. "I'm looking for someone. She's just helping me out."

"Okay," the receptionist said. "What's the name?"

"Sophie Jones."

"Thank you. One moment please." The young woman adjusted her Space Needle–embroidered vest and leaned in toward a small microphone behind the counter, then pressed a button on the base of the short microphone stand. "Sophie Jones to the front desk. Sophie Jones to the front desk, please. Your party is waiting."

People all throughout the store stopped to listen to the announcement. Then they continued about their business.

The blond woman next to Garrett snickered. But her

snickering quickly grew to a giggle, which in turn advanced to mild cackling, which rapidly escalated to outright laughter. She held her side with one hand and wiped at a small tear with the other.

The receptionist and Garrett both stared at her, dumbfounded.

"I...am...so...sorry!" she managed to say between fits of laughter. She extended her hand. "*I'm*...Sophie Jones."

Garrett's jaw dropped as they shook hands. "But you...I mean you're...*you're* Sophie?" She wasn't anything close to the diamond in the rough that he'd envisioned. She was *better.*

She nodded, still giggling. "I figured it was you—or you were him—when I first tapped you on the shoulder. But you never said who you were looking for, so I just played along." She wiped again at her eyes. "I really am sorry. But thank you for that. I needed a good laugh."

"Glad I could oblige," Garrett said, still stunned that *this* woman was his date. He thought back to his mother's advice that he should look hard at what she had on the inside, and it suddenly seemed all the more prudent. It would have been very easy with someone as attractive as Sophie to be taken in on looks alone.

Since they were already running late, Sophie and Garrett caught the very next elevator to the Space Needle's restaurant, five hundred feet up and just below the topmost observation deck. A waiter named Andre was ready to seat them as soon as the elevator doors opened.

"Careful," Andre said, as the pair stepped into the dining area. "The floor moves." He led them halfway around the O-shaped restaurant to a black granite table beside the Needle's outer window. As they walked, Andre explained how, unlike the rest of the Space Needle, the restaurant spun continually in a circle, making a complete rotation at least once per hour so that patrons could enjoy a 360-degree view of the surrounding landscape. After a few other facts and figures about the history and purpose of the structure, Andre handed each of them a menu. He recommended that they try the Alaskan Salmon and Pacific Northwest Dungeness Crab Cakes, and then he left to fetch drinks.

Once they'd placed their orders—neither of them chose the salmon and crab cakes—Sophie retrieved a pen from her purse and scribbled some words around the edge of a pink packet of Sweet'n Low that she'd grabbed from a small basket in the center of the table. When she was done, she placed it on the windowsill next to the table.

"What's that for?" Garrett asked.

"Souvenir," she remarked. "It's kind of a tradition here. I wrote our names and today's date on it, plus where we're from. Everyone in the restaurant will see it in the window as they pass by, and a few of them will add their names to it just for fun. Some might even write us a message. So thirty or forty minutes from now, when we've come full circle, I'll have a little memento of our visit." She paused. "Would you like one?"

"Sure. Just not pink. A white sugar packet would be great."

Sophie made a few scribbles on a spare sugar packet and placed it in the window. At the rate they were spinning, the Sweet'n Low was already ten feet away. "There you go. Years from now, you'll have something sweet to remember me by." She tucked a strand of hair behind her ear, then unfolded her napkin and placed it on her lap.

"After announcing your name over the intercom, I don't think I'll be forgetting you anytime soon."

She bit her lip and smiled. "I really am sorry," she said. "Tell you what. Why don't we start over with some basic introductions? We sort of missed the get-to-know-you formalities downstairs because we were in a hurry."

"Which formalities, exactly?"

"You know. 'Hi, my name is Sophie. It's a pleasure to meet you.' That sort of thing."

"Okay."

"Yeah? Good."

Garrett waited, but she just stared at him, smiling. "Oh, you want me to start?" he asked.

"Well...it would be the gentlemanly thing to do." She winked.

Grinning sheepishly, he replied, "I was thinking ladies first. But okay." He cleared his throat. "Hi, my name is Garrett. Umm...Garrett Black. And it's a pleasure to meet you."

"Well done. Okay, my turn. Hello, I'm Sophie Jones. You may have heard of me before. They announced my name over the loudspeakers earlier, so if it sounds familiar, that's probably why."

Garrett shook his head and laughed. "Very funny. Tell me, Sophie Jones, how is it that you and I ended up on this date tonight? Was it more the doing of my mother or yours?"

Sophie's brow furrowed and her smile dimmed slightly. She took a drink of water before answering. "I think they were equal partners in crime. If they didn't work for the police department, I'd say we should have them arrested. But..."

"But?"

"Nothing. It's just that...Well, she's not really my mother. Ellen is my foster mom."

Idiot! "Oh? How long have you known her?"

"Since I was nine."

Garret pondered briefly what to say next. Moving on to a completely different subject might come off as insensitive, he thought, but digging into her past right from the get-go carried the same risk. "I know this probably doesn't fall under the umbrella of get-to-know-you questions that you had in mind, but...do you mind if I ask how you came to live in a foster home?"

Sophie took another drink of water. "The first-date response to that question is, 'My parents died.'"

"I'm sorry. That must've been incredibly hard for you. I lost my dad when I was twelve. My parents divorced when I was a baby, so I wasn't real close to him, but still it was tough."

Sophie relaxed, suddenly feeling like she had an ally. She allowed her easy smile to return. "Let's not dwell on the past. There must be better things than that to discuss, right?"

"Right," he said with a nod.

Not long after that Andre showed up with the first course of the meal, tomato bisque with a tray of assorted breads and cheeses. As they ate, Garrett learned all the typical first-date information about the stunning woman who sat across from him. Things like where she went to high school, what she studied in college, and what she did for a living.

"A chocolatier?" he said, when she told him about her candy store. "I can barely say the word, and I can honestly say that I've never personally known a chocolatier before."

"I wish I could say that I've never known a doctor before," she teased. "But a foot doctor? Honestly, how many problems can there be with feet that we should need specialists to work on them?"

He chuckled at her sarcasm. "You'd be surprised. Just wait until your arches collapse, and see if you don't go running to the nearest podiatrist."

The waiter approached. "More water?" he asked, but then began filling Sophie's glass before she could reply. "And you, sir?"

He nodded.

While Andre cleared a few dishes, Garrett took a moment to glance at his watch. By his calculations, their date was probably halfway over, and he found himself already disappointed that his evening with Sophie Jones would eventually come to an end.

"Can I borrow your pen?" he asked Sophie.

She gave him a questioning look but handed it across the table. He took one more sugar packet and quickly wrote a few words across the top.

"I'll be right back," he said, then stood and walked partway around the restaurant, and placed the sugar in the windowsill beside an empty table.

"What was that all about?" she said, when he returned.

"One more souvenir," he responded. "I want to make sure it gets back to us before we leave, so I gave it a head start."

She gave him another funny look, but mostly she was just looking at the way his dimples danced when he smiled. "I see."

Several minutes later, while they were eating their entrees, Sophie's Sweet'n Low came into view again, and a few minutes after that it was within her reach beside their table.

"Four names," she said proudly, after picking it up. "Two from Spokane, one from Portland, and one all the way from Connecticut." She flipped it over. "Oh, and a message on the back! 'Saccharine causes cancer!' "

They both laughed out loud.

"I'm not sure that's been proven," Garrett quipped, "but it's funny anyway."

It wasn't much longer before Garrett's first sugar packet arrived. He let Sophie do the honors, since she'd put it up there for him to begin with. "Darn," she said, pretending to be upset. "You got more signatures than me. Two from Spokane again; probably the same ones as mine. Then one from Seattle, and three from California."

"But no messages?"

Sophie flipped it over and burst out laughing.

"What? Don't tell me someone thinks sugar is a carcinogen, too."

The lighting in the restaurant wasn't ideal, but Garrett could have sworn that Sophie was blushing. "No," she said, suppressing more laughter. She paused to read it once more to herself, and then closed her fist around it. "You really want to hear it?"

"Of course. I like a good laugh."

"Very well. It says, 'Hey Blondie, ditch the dork. We have an extra seat at our table.' Signed, Rodney and friends."

"It doesn't really say that, does it?" Garrett asked, his brow suddenly furrowed.

Sophie started laughing out loud again as she handed it across the table. Then she looked past Garrett and waved politely.

Garrett felt blood rushing to his face as soon as he read the brief message. Spinning around to see who Sophie was waving at, his face turned even redder when he saw that the culprits—three men in their fifties—were practically falling off their chairs and laughing hysterically. One of them, probably Rodney, had laughed himself to tears. They all waved and pointed at Garrett, and continued laughing.

"I'm sorry," Sophie said, still trying to quell a chuckle. "For what it's worth, I disagree with their assessment. You really don't strike me as being dorky."

Garrett knew that his cheeks were still flushed, but he tried not to think about it. "Hey, don't go jumping to conclusions," he joked. "Think about it. What says *dork* more than getting set up on a blind date by your mother?"

Sophie tilted her head at an angle and fiddled with a long strand of hair. She kept her eyes locked on his. "Good point. The only thing that comes to mind is getting set up on a blind date by your foster mother." She smiled warmly, then turned her attention once more to her plate of food.

Garrett's second sugar packet arrived at the table just as they were finishing dessert. They could both see from where they sat that it was filled with handwritten words, and Garrett knew only a few of them were his own.

"Are you going to pick it up?" Sophie asked. "Or can I make it three for three?"

"Go ahead. But just to warn you, this one's a little bit different than the others."

She didn't say anything but gave him a quizzical look that spoke volumes.

Here goes nothing, Garrett thought.

Sophie picked it up and cupped it in her hands, studying both sides for what felt like an eternity, though in reality it was probably under ten seconds. Finally she spoke. "I take it you're planning a date with someone?"

He grinned. "As a matter of fact, I am."

She raised her eyebrows. "Someone special?"

He thought for a moment about Olivia's counsel. "A real gem, near as I can tell."

"Wow. Sounds great. Have you asked her out yet?"

"No, I haven't gotten that far."

Sophie was smiling, which Garrett found encouraging. "So this little sugar-packet survey is intended to help you plan your next date with this 'special gem'? Is that right?"

"That was the general idea, yes. Are there any good ones?"

She laughed. "Shall I read what it says?"

He smiled back and nodded. "Yes, please."

Sophie tucked more hair behind her ear, and then read the question Garrett had written at the top of the sugar packet. "'Ideas for a second date?'" She looked up at him. "Just to let you know, a couple of the responses—I'm guessing from Rodney and company—are fairly crude. Can I skip over those? I'm sure your special someone wouldn't agree to them anyway."

"By all means, filter out the junk."

"Great," she said, and then started over. "'Ideas for a second date?'" She paused once more, clearing her throat. "And I quote, 'Three Bs: Bowl, Bar, Beer.'"

"That could be Rodney, too," quipped Garrett.

She snickered. "No doubt. Next up, 'Dinner Cruise on Puget Sound.' Sounds nice. 'Laser Tag.' Hmmm. I'm guessing a teenage boy wrote that one. This next one is very small print, but I think it says, 'Dinner and a movie.' Completely overdone, if you ask me. The next one cracks me up. 'Meet the parents!' Right." She flipped the sugar over. "'Hike Mt. Rainier.' Yikes, not this time of year. 'Hot tubbing.' Not on the second date. And finally, 'Spend an entire evening gazing at the stars.' I'm sure a woman wrote that one." Sophie looked up from the sugar in her hand and smiled.

"Why is that one from a woman?"

"Because it's the only suggestion that is even remotely romantic."

"Ah. So romance is important?"

"Romance is *everything*. I'm willing to bet your ladyfriend wants a man who's tender and thoughtful and does all the little things that are important. A truly romantic man must be willing to do whatever it takes to win the lady's heart."

"Oh? And then what? Ride off into the sunset?"

She lowered her chin and smiled. "Something like that."

"Romance sounds daunting," he commented, still wearing his giant, dimpled smile. "So if I had to pick something from this list for my next date, you'd definitely go with stargazing?"

She winked. "Definitely."

Andre showed up then with Garrett's credit card and a receipt, and thanked them for coming. The way he stood there waiting, Sophie and Garrett gathered that it was time for them to leave. Andre led them to the main elevator, and forty-three seconds later they were back down on Planet Earth.

"Sophie," Garrett said, before they reached the main exit of the souvenir shop, "I want to apologize for not planning more for tonight than dinner. It just seemed like a safe bet for a blind date."

"It was great," she said, sounding like she meant it. "Are you going to let me know how that second date turns out with your special someone?"

"I'd be happy to. How can I get a hold of you?"

Her eyes twinkled as she pulled out another pink packet of Sweet'n Low that already had her name, address, and phone number on it. "For you." Garrett wasn't sure when she'd had time to write that information down without him noticing, but it was clearly premeditated. "So when do you think you'll be going on that date?"

Garrett could feel his heart thumping against the inside of his chest. "Tomorrow night," he stated nervously. "If she's available."

Sophie smiled coyly. "If she's the gem you say she is, I'm sure she'll make herself available." She hesitated. "I'll bet she's free at seven thirty."

Reaching once more into her purse, Sophie found the sugar packet with suggestions for a second date and handed it to him. She placed it in his palm in such a way that their hands cupped together briefly. His heart pounded faster.

"Thanks," he said, too nervous to come up with anything more intelligent to say.

"Good night, Garrett," said Sophie pleasantly, biting her lip and smiling at the same time.

As she turned and started to walk away, Garrett scanned the words on the sugar packet she'd just handed to him. He flipped it over, quickly reading both sides twice. Then his heart really started to thump in his chest. "Sophie!" he shouted, but the door had already closed behind her. He ran to the exit and stepped out into the night. "Sophie!" he called again.

She turned around and smiled, like she knew what he was going to say.

"It doesn't say, 'Gaze at the stars.'"

Grinning mischievously, Sophie walked back to where he stood. "Really?" She took the sugar from his hand, wrote on it with her pen, and then placed it back in his palm. "Well, now it does. Good night, Garrett Black." She winked.

"Good night, Sophie Jones."

Chapter 8

Trust your intuition. It's bound to be right sooner or later.

IT WASN'T HARD FOR GARRETT TO FIND SOPHIE'S HOUSE the next day in Gig Harbor. The town was small, and she lived on the main arterial street that coursed along the harbor's shore. The home itself was a small, two-story bungalow built in the 1940s, but the slate-blue siding and shingled roof looked less than a decade old, while the crisp white trim around the windows and eaves gave it a certain classic charm. He showed up right at seven thirty wearing a light sport coat and slacks.

Sophie met him at her front door in a thick winter parka, a wool scarf, and mittens. They both took a moment to evaluate the other's choice of clothing.

"You look warm," Garrett said, smiling. "Er—you look great. *And warm.*"

"It's chilly out, and I thought we might be spending some time outside. Is that not the case?"

He chuckled and pulled a small packet of sugar from his

pocket. "Actually, I was going through these ideas for a second date," he said brightly, holding up the sugar, "and even though I liked the idea of gazing at the stars, I'm afraid it's too cloudy for that tonight. So I chose the next best thing."

"Which is?"

"The three Bs! Bowl, bar, and beer."

Her face dropped. "You're joking, right?"

"Yes," he replied, beaming. "I'm actually not much of a bar and beer guy, and even less of a bowler. But it really is too cloudy outside for stargazing, so I've made some other arrangements."

She flashed a generous smile. "I see. And do I get to know what those arrangements are? I'm not a huge fan of surprises."

Garrett rubbed his chin thoughtfully. "Well, I can tell you there will definitely be dinner. And there will also be an activity. But beyond that, you'll just have to wait and see."

She frowned, but he saw that her eyes were still smiling. "Fine. But at least tell me if I'm dressed too warm."

He scanned her once more from head to toe. "You'd probably be safe shedding a layer or two, but it's completely up to you."

Sophie chose to swap the parka and scarf for her peacoat, but kept the mittens just in case. A few minutes later they were on the interstate heading back across the Narrows Bridge toward Tacoma, and a few minutes after that they were on I-5 heading north toward Seattle. Along the way, Sophie kept digging for hints about where they were going or what they'd be doing, but Garrett repeatedly dodged the questions.

"All right, I give in," he said, after her third attempt. "I didn't want to ruin the surprise, but we're going back to the Seattle Center for corn dogs and laser tag."

She knew he was bluffing.

The next time she probed about it he told her they were doing dinner and a movie.

The time after that he said they were taking a dinner cruise.

"Really?" she asked excitedly.

"No," he said cheerfully. "Not really. Sorry."

After taking an exit just north of downtown, Garrett slowed the car, retrieved a solid black sleeping mask from his glove box, and handed it to her while he continued driving. "Would it freak you out if I asked you to put this on?" he asked. "If you see where we're going it'll spoil the surprise."

She looked at him very skeptically. "Yes, as a matter of fact, it would freak me out. I think I'll pass."

Garrett grinned playfully. "You don't trust me?"

"Trust isn't one of my strong suits. And I barely know you. Besides, I've already been your blind date once, and that was enough, thank you very much."

He kept smiling as he reached into the inside pocket of his jacket and pulled out a cell phone, then flipped through a series of menus to get to a number he'd dialed recently. He pushed Send to place a call. "I wouldn't expect you to put it on without some assurance that it's safe," he said, handing the phone to her. "Here. It's for you."

She looked at him like he was crazy. "Huh?"

"Just say hello," he whispered.

"Uhh...hello?"

"Sophie, is that you?"

"Ellen?" Sophie shot Garrett another questioning look. "What's going on?"

"Oh, don't worry, Sweets. Garrett's mom gave him my number, and he and I spoke earlier. He seems very nice, by the way. Is he as cute as he sounds on the phone?"

Sweets was a nickname that Ellen had given to Sophie as an affectionate reference to her love of candy. She couldn't always afford to buy sweets for the girls when they were younger, but that didn't stop Sophie from asking for them every time she saw some at the store as a child. The name officially stuck when Sophie was a teenager, and her fascination grew from eating candy to making it. By the time she graduated from high school and started college, she already had an index file full of recipes for her own unique confections, which she later used to open Chocolat' de Soph.

Sophie paused and looked at Garrett again, hoping he didn't hear the question. "Maybe."

"Good! I can't wait to meet him. Anyway, he said he'd probably be calling right around now. You can rest assured that I know exactly where you guys are going, and there's nothing to worry about. Okay? Just enjoy yourself."

"And the blindfold? You know about that?"

"Yes, ma'am. Put it on. The unknown can be an adventure."

Sophie paused again. "Thanks, El." She ended the call, then turned her attention back to Garrett. "We're not going anywhere creepy, right?"

"Trust me," he said reassuringly.

Sophie sighed, then reluctantly pulled the mask over her eyes and fastened the Velcro strap in the back.

"Can you see?"

"Not at all."

"Excellent."

They were only a few minutes from their destination, but Garrett drove around in circles for an extra five minutes just to throw her off. When the car was stopped and the engine turned off, Sophie asked if she could take off the mask.

"Not yet," he told her. "There's just a short walk, and then we're there."

Walking around to the passenger side of the car, Garrett helped Sophie out, then he took her arm in his and guided her to a nearby building.

"Where are we?" she kept asking, once they were inside. "It sounds like we're all alone."

Garrett didn't offer any hints as he led her through the building. They walked up a flight of stairs, down a long hallway, and through a set of thick double doors.

Finally, he told her to sit down carefully. He helped lower her to the ground, where a large blanket was laid out. She felt with her hands to the edge of the blanket, noting with some concern that it was on a concrete floor. What was even more disconcerting was the complete lack of sound. There were definitely no other people around, and she started feeling like maybe the blindfold and secrecy wasn't such a good idea after all, no matter what Ellen believed they were up to.

Garrett could see the worry in the lines around her mouth. "You ready to take off the mask?" he asked, as he sat down next to her.

"Very."

"Okay, then. We're here. Take it off."

Sophie carefully reached up and broke the Velcro seal on the elastic band that surrounded her head. She squinted to adjust to the new light as the mask came loose.

Only... it was still very dark.

She looked all around the strange, bare room. There appeared to be only one continuous wall that surrounded them like a dome, curving to the center of the room as it got taller. In front of her on the ground were two empty plates beside a couple of small take-out boxes.

"Go ahead, Vance," Garrett said, craning his neck back toward the door. A few seconds later the lights dimmed even further.

Sophie studied Garrett's face as the room darkened. He was staring back at her with boyish glee. As their surroundings faded to near pitch-black, a new, subtle flickering began to emanate from the domed walls. Sophie turned her head in every direction and watched with amazement as thousands of tiny lights unexpectedly burst to life. And then she understood.

"Stars!" she exclaimed. "Oh my gosh! I haven't been to a planetarium since a field trip in fifth grade! How did you arrange this?"

"I know a guy," he said, smiling. "Vance is a patient of mine, and he runs the Pacific Science Center. I gave him a call last night, and he said we could have the whole place to ourselves."

"It's amazing," she said, taking it all in.

"I'm glad you like it."

Sophie shifted her weight on the concrete. "I thought there used to be chairs in here."

"Yeah, sorry about that. They're remodeling, swapping out the old seats for something more comfortable."

"Well, chairs or not, this is incredible. I can't believe it." She looked all around at the growing constellations. "Thank you so much for this."

Garrett smiled in the darkness.

The remainder of the evening was spent doing exactly what Sophie had requested: gazing at the stars. Garrett hoped she found the setting romantic; he thought she did, but it was too dark to get a good read on her. While they gazed at the expanding universe around them, they also did a great deal of talking, mingled here and there with mouthfuls of pad Thai and coconut rice, using two small flashlights that Garrett had brought along so they could see what they were eating. It wasn't quite the romance of flickering candles, but it was as close to a candlelit dinner as the fire codes would allow.

During the conversation, Garrett learned that Sophie had a special affinity for astronomy. She'd even taken several elective courses on it in college and could easily name and identify the twelve zodiac constellations of the Western world, along with a handful of lesser-known constellations of Asian origin. When Garrett asked what, specifically, she liked most about the stars, her answer intrigued him.

Lying on her back on the hard concrete floor, she kept her eyes focused on the twinkling lights overhead. "Looking at stars is a glimpse of history," she said dreamily. "Some of the things we can see in the sky are *millions* of light-years away. The Andromeda galaxy, for instance, is two and a half million light-years from earth, and that's a relatively close one." She took his hand in hers and pointed to a faint blur that made up one of the points in the Andromeda constellation. "So what we're seeing—well, if we were looking at the real thing outside—is literally millions of years old. We're living in the present, but in a very real way we're staring at the past." She paused, briefly glancing at Garrett from the corner of her eye. "Everything in the universe has a past, but stars don't try to hide it. They just keep shining, for everyone to see."

Garrett studied those sections of Sophie's face that were illuminated by the mock starlight. "Andromeda. That's Greek, right?"

"Very good. She was a princess in the mythological kingdom of Aethiopia. But she also went by a different name. The Chained Lady."

"Oh yeah? What do you suppose she was chained to?"

Sophie's eyes locked onto Garrett's for a brief moment before answering. "The past."

Though Sophie looked away almost immediately, Garrett couldn't help but continue staring at her. Everything about her captivated him. The subtle shift in her voice as she talked about Andromeda made him wonder if she somehow viewed herself as a modern Chained Lady, tied to some hidden past. *Or maybe she's more like a star and less like the Greek princess*, he told himself. *Perhaps understanding her in the present means looking at her past.* But if she was a star—and just by the way Sophie shined when she smiled, Garrett knew that she was—then it stood to reason that they shared something fundamental in common: a *past that would eventually come to light*.

He didn't care. Looking at her profile, Garrett wanted to learn as much as he could about this woman. He wanted to take every opportunity to see her in the present, with a hope of getting a glimpse of that past, all while keeping an eye toward making himself a part of her future.

Chapter 9

Don't get caught up with a hopeless romantic.
The romance will end, and then it's just hopeless.

FOR GARRETT, A BLIND DATE SPINNING AROUND THE Space Needle followed by an evening gazing at faux stars from the comfort of a concrete floor was more than enough time with Sophie Jones to realize that his original plan to meet her only once was very shortsighted. Curiosity had given way to infatuation, and now he wanted to spend as much time with her as possible. He felt slightly silly for allowing himself to be so completely affected by her, but ten minutes after dropping Sophie off at her house at the end of their second date, he decided it was time to ask her out again. He pulled into an empty parking lot and took out his cell phone. Sophie had mentioned earlier in the evening that she was getting good at texting back and forth with Evalynn, so for fun he sent her a quick text message. As he punched in the letters on the tiny keypad, it occurred to him that he hadn't asked anyone out in writing since he left a note on a girl's desk in fifth grade and told her to circle yes or no for a bike ride after school.

While pushing send, he decided that the text-invite was much more to his liking, because he didn't have to sit on the other side of the room and watch her reaction when she got the message.

U free tomorrow? he typed.

Thirty seconds later a reply came that made him laugh. *Free? No. Not cheap either.*

Ha! Can I see u again? Dinner @ 7??

Sorry. I have 2 work. My 1 employee is going out of town.

Mind if I drop by your store then?

Garrett expected a quick response, but it was several minutes before Sophie's reply came, and the curtness of her answer caught him off guard. *Yes... I mind.*

Hoping she was joking, Garrett quickly thumbed another brief text: *So that's a definite no???*

Yes... sorry.

Sitting in his car, Garrett stared at the words, suddenly feeling just like he did back in fifth grade when his would-be date circled no with a big red pen, and then passed it around the room for everyone to see.

A large pit rumbled in his stomach. He'd been so sure that Sophie had enjoyed herself on both of their previous dates, that he couldn't believe that she simply didn't want to see him again. *Then again*, he thought, *I'm no expert on women. Maybe she was just being nice.* After five minutes debating whether or not he should send another text message, Garrett decided just to leave it alone. He threw the car into gear, peeled out onto the road, and drove home.

Lying on her bed an hour later, Sophie stared at the last note she'd sent to Garrett. *Yes... sorry.* She wished she'd conveyed the message a little more delicately. It wasn't that she didn't want to see him again; she simply didn't want to see him so soon. Sophie had had relationships before that started out fast, but they always fizzled just as quickly, and that was something she wanted to avoid with Garrett if at all possible.

For the next thirty minutes Sophie stayed sprawled out on her bed, phone in hand, hoping that Garrett would send another note, but nothing came. After another half hour she began to worry that he might never ask her out again, and so she caved in and crafted a message of her own. *Hey Garrett! Where'd you go??*

Garrett was sitting next to his phone as well, and didn't waste any time responding. *Just sitting here trying to figure out what I did wrong. :-(*

SOOOO sorry! I can be lame, I know. But I want 2 see u 2. PLEASE come by the store tomorrow. U can help me make fudge!!

Why the change of heart?

Just come to the store after work... I'll explain there.

Fine. But only 'cuz I'm a sucker for fudge.

Perfect! G'night!

Garrett dwelled nervously throughout the entire next day on what Sophie was going to say about why she'd circled no on his message, but when he showed up at Chocolat' de Soph that evening, he quickly learned that his worry was unwarranted. As soon as he walked in the door Sophie approached him, smiling, and gave him an affectionate hug, then sat him down on one of the stools near the window.

"Do all customers get a hug?" he asked coyly. "I'll have to come here more often."

"It's why I'm still in business," she shot back with a giggle. Then she sat down on the empty stool next to him and got more serious. "Listen, about last night. It was nerves," she said. "I don't exactly have a great track record with..." She then spotted a clump of dried chocolate on her apron and began scraping at it with her fingernail.

"'With'?" he nudged, then waited patiently for her to continue.

Sophie kept scraping until the spot was gone, and only then did she look up at him, noting that Garrett's eyes were the same shade of brown as the creamy dark chocolate. There were several correct ways she could have finished the sentence she'd started, but she wasn't sure which one she wanted to share with the man she'd just hugged. *A lousy track record with handsome men? With opening up my heart? With reciprocating affection? With commitment? With relationships in general?*

"With trust," she said finally.

He looked at her funny. "You don't trust me?"

She chortled lightly, patting him on the knee beneath the table. "No, you seem completely trustworthy. It's *me* that I don't trust. I have a bad habit of ruining relationships, so when you said you wanted to see me again so soon, I got a little nervous, that's all. I guess I don't trust myself to not mess things up. Does that make sense?"

"I think I follow."

Sophie grabbed a lock of hair and tucked it behind her ear. "It's kind of ironic, if you think about it. Out of fear of driving guys away, I drive them away anyway."

Garrett let out a little snicker. "Stop. Any guy would be nuts to let you drive him away."

Sophie liked the sound of Garrett's voice. It was reassuring and confident, and strangely comforting. She also liked the way his dimples sank into his cheeks when he smiled and spoke at the same time. "That's what the last guy who came to my store to help make fudge said, and do you know where he is now?" She watched his face to see if he had an answer. "Me neither!" she laughed. "But I'm sure it's far away from here."

Garrett kept smiling, finding Sophie's self-deprecating

humor oddly endearing. "Have I told you what my mom always says about relationships?"

"Avoid them at all costs, because they can only bring heartache?"

"Close," he said happily. "She says that every relationship will be a complete failure, right up until the one that isn't, and that's what makes all the failures a success—that you're able to get past them to find the right one."

Sophie folded her arms, grinning playfully. "And do you believe dear old Mom? I mean, this is the same woman who set you up on a date with me, so you have to wonder about her judgment."

"I do. As bitter as the failures can be along the way—and I should know, because I've had a lot of them—I'm still holding out hope that the right person will come along. And that'll turn the bitter into sweet."

"Ahh," she said, gently teasing. "You're not just a romantic, you're a hopeless romantic."

"A *hopeful* romantic," he countered. "There's a difference. And I hope that's not a bad thing."

She returned his gaze, trying to read what he was thinking by the look in his eyes. "No. It's not a bad thing." Then she paused. "Just remember what I said about me and trust, okay? I don't want you thinking that just because this is the third night in a row that we've spent time together that your string of failures is about to end. Consider yourself warned, Garrett Black—the more I see a guy, and the more I like him, the more likely I am to do something to really mess it up." She paused again. "It's inevitable."

Garrett stood up and stepped closer, gently touching her arm. "I'll take that as a challenge." He smiled at her, looking directly in her eyes, and then dropped his hand to his side. "Now, are you going to show me how to make chocolates, or what?"

She tipped her head and stood up, too. "Chocolates it is. Follow me."

Sophie led Garrett to the kitchen and taught him a few basic tricks to making fudge come out just right. Then they moved on to truffles and dipped fruit. For the rest of the evening they worked side by side making all sorts of different confections for the next day. When the bell on the front door rang, Sophie would quickly scramble out front to the cash register and help the customers, but the rest of the time they spent talking, teasing, joking, dipping cherries or filling molds, and otherwise enjoying themselves in the kitchen.

Having Garrett there helped the work move faster than normal. By the time the store closed at nine o'clock, Sophie was pretty much finished with the preparations for the following day. The only thing still simmering, in a quart-size double boiler, was a new concoction Sophie had been tinkering with in her spare time for several weeks. It was a melted brew of complimentary dark chocolates, sweetened condensed milk, a touch of crème de menthe, and an assortment of various creams, butters, and sugars. While Garrett stacked pots on a counter, Sophie carefully dabbed a finger into the chocolaty mix, then licked it clean.

"Come try this," she said, motioning at Garrett to join her next to the stove. "I've been working on a new recipe, and I need an honest opinion." She grabbed a spoon and dipped it in the pot, then lifted it to his mouth, cupping her other hand underneath to catch any drips.

He leaned in and took a slow bite.

"So?"

Licking his lips, Garrett replied, "It's good." And then, without thinking, he leaned in even closer. Sophie didn't resist as he gave her a single, gentle kiss. "No," he said, as he pulled back. "It's more than good. It's probably the best I've ever had."

Sophie cocked her head to the side and laughed. "The new recipe? Or...?"

Garrett beamed. "Both."

Chapter 10

You are vigilant in hiding your true self to others . . . and for good reason.

As much as Sophie didn't want to rush things with Garrett—and despite her constant reminders that the more time they spent together the more likely it was that he would want to cut and run—she and Garrett were, by anyone's standards, hooked on each other. After their first kiss at Chocolat' de Soph, they spent as much time together as they could squeeze between their jobs. On most days after work, Garrett would pick Sophie up at her store and drive her home so she wouldn't have to wait for the bus. Then they'd enjoy the evening talking, walking, eating, laughing, whatever filled the time, so long as they were together.

For the first few months of their relationship, Sophie made a point of telling Garrett as often as she could that even though they were seeing a lot of each other, it didn't mean they were an exclusive item. She insisted that both of them could date other people, *if they wanted*. It was her way of making sure he knew there was an easy out, in the event that he needed one. And although she loved being with him and secretly hoped for things to continue going well between them, in the back of her mind Sophie always expected that sooner or later he'd take the out. Each time she mentioned it, Garrett would patiently remind her that unless she had plans of calling it quits, she was stuck with him.

In January, the fourth month since meeting in the lobby of the Space Needle, Garrett took Sophie for a day trip to Cannon Beach, a quaint town tucked along the northern coast of Oregon, just south of the Washington state line. The weather was too cold to enjoy the ocean water, but searching rocky tide pools for starfish and hermit crabs followed by a fresh bowl of clam chowder at Mo's restaurant seemed like a perfect way to spend a lazy winter Sunday. As he guessed she would, during the three-hour drive to their destination Sophie casually asked him how much longer it was going to be before he found some other pretty woman that he liked more than her.

He sighed out loud, buying extra time to think before responding. If he was honest with himself, Garrett had to admit that the constant questioning of his loyalty to her was beginning to wear thin. In his mind, he wondered if Sophie would ever really trust him—or herself—enough to keep the relationship going. When he spoke, his words lacked the usual reassurance and conviction that they normally possessed. "C'mon, Soph," he said without looking at her. "Do we have to go there again?"

Sophie picked up on the difference in his voice. She'd been in enough relationships to recognize the familiar tone, and she knew exactly what it meant: they'd finally reached the beginning of the end. "I'm just being practical," she said flatly. "All good things must come to an end, right?"

Now Garrett pulled his eyes from the road and looked right

at Sophie in the seat beside him, then reached out and took her hand in his. "No. That's completely wrong. What do you think I've been trying to show you these past few months? Not all good things have to end! Why can't you just accept that I don't want anyone else?"

She looked at him for a long time, then finally turned away and shrugged. "I don't know."

He tried to smile. "Well, one way or another, we have to figure that out. Because I'm not going anywhere."

She squeezed his hand. "I believe that you believe that. I just…it's hard for me to imagine that what we have won't eventually vanish. It's like it's too good to be true."

Garrett snickered. "Is that because your old boyfriends didn't put up with you as long as I have?"

"Be nice!" she said, poking him in the ribs. Sophie knew he was joking, but she took a moment to consider the question. "I don't think it was just the guys I've dated. It's deeper than that."

"What is?"

"The fear. The nagging sense that all good things eventually end. It's not just because of the men I've known."

Garrett took his eyes off of the taillights of the car in front of them long enough to see that the look on her face matched the sadness in her voice. She'd danced around this subject several times since they'd met, but had never really gotten to the heart of the matter. "Your parents?" he ventured.

Sophie nodded almost imperceptibly.

"Care to share?"

She let go of his hand so she could adjust her seat belt. Not because she wanted to shift positions, but because it suddenly felt constrictive. "Not really."

Garrett's soothing, reassuring voice was back. "I'm sure your feelings are very natural. Try me."

Sophie let out a little laugh. "You sound like the psychologist

I saw as a teenager. You know what he told me? He said I was right! That I should get used to the fact that all things go away. We all die, he said, and if nothing else, that brings things to an end, so we should just enjoy the relationships we have while they last, and move on once they're over."

"Well, that's a callous thing to tell a kid."

"Yeah," she affirmed. "I stopped seeing him after that."

"So, you think because you lost your parents, that all relationships are somehow going to end up the same way?"

Looking at Garrett, Sophie allowed a tiny grin to turn up at the corners of her mouth. "Gee, Dr. Black, if people's feet stop giving them problems, you should try your hand as a shrink."

"So that's it?"

She shrugged. "I assume so. I can't imagine what else it would be." Sophie knew there was more to it than that—like the fact that she'd played a major role in how things turned out for her family, and that she didn't want to risk hurting someone she loved like that ever again—but that was way more than she wanted Garrett to know. "Starting with their deaths, relationships in my life have felt very…temporary. And it wasn't only the loss of my parents. After that, I had several foster families, and they all went south. One of my foster parents even died."

"What about Ellen? She hasn't gone anywhere. Or Evalynn."

"*Pfft.* Ellen's a cop. She's constantly in harm's way. I always worried—in fact, I still worry to this day—that she'll get in a shoot-out or something, and that'll be that. And Ev? I already lose her for weeks at a time while she works on issues between her and Justin. And if they ever tie the knot…who knows? I might lose her once and for all."

Garrett reached over again and squeezed her leg. "Well you don't have to worry about any of those things with me, Sophie Jones. I'm not a foster parent, a cop, or a best friend who's dating someone. I'm just the guy who's falling in love with you."

The comment took Sophie by surprise. Not only was it the first time he'd used the L word, it was the way he said it that really pricked her ears. She'd had guys occasionally tell her they loved her, but the way Garrett said it actually sounded sincere. There was no hidden agenda in the words, no sense that he was saying it as a means to something else. She didn't even get the impression that he expected her to reciprocate the gesture, which was good, because she wasn't prepared to admit to loving him, even though everything in her heart said that was exactly what she was feeling. Instead of saying anything, Sophie unclicked her seat belt so she could stretch far enough to kiss him on the cheek.

"Careful," he said jokingly, as he squeezed her leg again. "I lose most of my mental and physical faculties when your lips are near my face, so if you're going to kiss me while we're moving, at least keep your seat belt on for safety."

Sophie poked him again in the ribs, then took his hand in hers, interlocking their fingers. There were lots of thoughts running through her head. A few of them were the same old worries that Garrett might eventually run for the hills, but mostly she was thinking about how much she cared for the man who, she'd just noticed, had hands that fit with hers like a glove.

"Garrett," she said after a few moments of silence, "I'm glad your prying mother works with my snooping foster mom."

He gave her fingers a little tug. "Me too."

Chapter 11

When offered the dream of a lifetime, SAY NO!
Remember, it's just a dream.

FOR SOPHIE, THE JANUARY TRIP TO CANNON BEACH with Garrett, and in particular his unexpected expression of love, was a turning point in her willingness to accept that maybe—*just maybe*—their relationship had a chance of withstanding the cruel test of time. After that, she began opening up to the idea that he really did care for her as much as he claimed, and she even found herself dropping hints that she felt the same way about him.

Valentine's Day was the busiest day of the year at Chocolat' de Soph, which meant that Sophie had to work all day long, even after Randy arrived. It took both of them working nonstop just to keep up with the tidal wave of customers looking for last-minute goodies to share with their loved ones. Garrett came by at six thirty and stuck around to help out in the back, hoping to help move things along so he could spend some time with Sophie, but by the time the store closed and everything was cleaned up, the night was pretty well shot. Besides, Sophie was so exhausted from fifteen hours of work without a break that her eyelids were drooping, so Garrett drove her home, gave her a kiss good night, and sent her straight to bed.

The next evening, however, he surprised Sophie with a post-Valentine's date that more than made up for the lack of romance the previous day. Picking her up right at five thirty, they drove north to a private airstrip near Sea-Tac International Airport, where they boarded a small prop plane that Garrett had chartered. The pilot flew them around the Seattle metropolitan area for twenty minutes, then veered west, landing thirty minutes later on a narrow gravel runway in a remote section of hills north of Mt. Rainier.

When Sophie asked why they were landing, Garrett grinned. "Aren't you hungry?"

The runway, Sophie learned, was maintained by a restaurant. In decades past, the site had been an old logger's lodge. But when environmental litigation put the logging company out of business, a group of entrepreneurs scooped up the property for pennies on the dollar and turned it into a gourmet, hunter-style restaurant, catering almost exclusively to small-aircraft enthusiasts. In the ten years since opening, the establishment had become a regular hot spot for flight clubs all over the Pacific Northwest.

The pilot read a magazine in the restaurant's lobby while Sophie and Garrett dined.

"You've got to be kidding me!" Sophie said, when she saw the prices on the menu. "It's like two weeks' worth of groceries just for one meal."

"Don't look at the prices," he chided. "That's what I'm trying to do." Then he added, "I bet people who can afford to own their own airplane don't bat an eye at the cost of a meal here."

"Yeah. Either that, or they know that the safety record of small airplanes justifies an expensive meal, since it may very well be their last."

Garrett chuckled. "You make me laugh, Soph. I think that's what I love most about you."

The timing may have been a bit awkward, but without even thinking about it Sophie blurted out, "I love you, too."

Both of them sat in stunned silence after the words escaped her lips. Garrett was trying to figure out if he'd heard her correctly, and Sophie was trying to figure out if she'd really just said what she thought she said, or if it was a figment of her imagination.

"Whoa," Garrett managed eventually. "Did you just—? I mean...did you mean that?"

Without looking away, and sounding as surprised about it as he was, she said, "I guess I must have." She paused, biting her lip nervously. "Is that...okay?"

He smiled warmly and reached across the table to hold her hands. "It's perfect."

She smiled back in the same manner. The way Garrett was looking at her, Sophie felt an odd sense of vulnerability, but it was balanced out by an even odder feeling of safety and assurance that he wouldn't hurt her. It was a sensation she'd never experienced before, and she relished it. *This is what it's supposed to feel like*, she told herself.

The rest of the evening was as enjoyable a time as Sophie could ever remember having, though the specifics about what made it so wonderful were sketchy, even to her. The only concrete details she could recall the following day were the rough landing back at Sea-Tac airport and the smooth kiss good night in Gig Harbor. "I know we did a lot of talking, but I don't have a clue what either of us said," she told Evalynn by phone the next evening. "I think emotionally I was so overwhelmed by what I'd told him about how I felt, that that's all I could think about for the rest of the night. Everything beyond that was a happy blur."

Two and a half weeks after Valentine's Day, Garrett attended a weeklong podiatry convention in New Orleans. It was the first significant time he and Sophie had spent apart since meeting almost six months earlier.

Evalynn thought Sophie's behavior while Garrett was away was gag-worthy, and she told her as much on both of the evenings that they had dinner together. "Are we going to have an actual conversation while we eat?" Evalynn complained on the second night out, "or are you just going to text-flirt with Dr. Dreamy all night again?"

Sophie hardly heard her. "Just a minute," she replied. "He just sent the *sweetest* note! Let me write him back real quick and then... we'll..." Sophie's thumbs were in high gear before she could finish her sentence.

"Excuse me," Evalynn mumbled under her breath, as she stood up from the table and wiped her mouth on her napkin. "I have to go to the bathroom and puke."

Sophie didn't even look up.

Garrett returned from Louisiana on Saturday, March 8. Sophie was still working when his flight arrived, so he told her not to bother coming to the airport. Instead, he wanted to see her immediately after work for dinner. He wouldn't say where they were going, but he did let her know that she should dress up.

Sophie carried an extra dress with her to work so she would have something nice to change into before Garrett showed up. As soon as Randy arrived for the evening shift, she went to the kitchen and washed her face in the sink, tussled her hair in the mirror, and then slipped into the privacy of her office to put on the dress. Garrett arrived in a suit ten minutes later.

"Well, don't we look dapper tonight," Sophie said when she saw him, then gave him a quick hug and kiss to say hello.

"Dudes," Randy said jokingly. "I'm trying to work here! Take it outside."

They ignored him, but went outside anyway and climbed into Garrett's car.

After driving north for forty-five minutes in traffic, Garrett produced the infamous black sleep mask that he'd made her wear on their second date. "How would you feel about putting this on again for a few minutes?"

She laughed. "What's with you and blindfolds?"

"It's the element of surprise that I like," he answered with a wry smile, "not the blindfold."

"And if I say no, are you going to call Ellen again and have her twist my arm?"

"If I have to," he said, pretending to be very serious. "Believe me, I'm not afraid of calling the cops, if that's what it takes."

"No," she said, smiling. "I trust you." As she fastened the strap around her head, Sophie pondered what it meant that she could say those particular words to him and really mean it. It wasn't simply that she trusted him enough to wear a blindfold for a special surprise. She trusted that he would keep his promises. She trusted that he cared for her, and that he would put her happiness above his own. She didn't know how, but somehow he'd managed to show her that love and trust are inseparable; the more her love for him grew, the more she trusted that he wouldn't suddenly vanish from her life.

Five minutes after Sophie put on the blindfold, she and Garrett arrived at their destination four blocks east of the waterfront on the north end of Seattle. Parking spaces downtown on a Saturday night were a sparse commodity, so Garrett decided it was worth the extra cash to use the drive-up valet service. He got out of his Mercedes, gave the key to an attendant, and then helped walk Sophie the short distance to the front doors.

Once inside, he told her she could take off the mask.

"Good," she said, relieved. "Because even without seeing, I can *feel* people staring." As she unfastened the Velcro and let the mask fall from her face, Sophie knew immediately where they were. "The Space Needle!" she said, looking to her left and right. But Garrett wasn't there. She turned quickly around to look behind her, but he wasn't there either. Doing a complete circle in place, Sophie scanned the face of every man wearing a suit to see if she'd somehow overlooked him in the throng of people nearby. No such luck.

Perfect, she thought half-jokingly. *Just when I was beginning to think he might stick around, he vanishes into thin air.* Just then, a woman's voice echoed throughout the souvenir shop over the sound system: "Sophie Jones to the front desk. Sophie Jones to the front desk, please. Your party is waiting."

Sophie couldn't help but break into a huge grin as she made her way around the doughnut-shaped store to the reception desk near the elevators. There, next to the young woman who'd paged her, was Garrett, holding a single red rose.

"What are you doing?" Sophie asked, somewhat embarrassed but nonetheless pleased.

"It's our six-month anniversary," he said, as he gave her the rose along with a quick kiss on the cheek. "I thought it might be fun to go back to where it all started."

"You're nuts," she said, still beaming. "But it's very sweet."

Taking her arm in his, Garrett redirected Sophie to the elevators at her left. "We're a few minutes early, but I bet if we head up they can get us seated."

After getting a table five hundred feet above ground level and hearing the usual spiel of Space Needle facts from their waiter, Sophie and Garrett pulled out pens and wrote their names on packets of sugar, then stuck them up on the window's ledge. While they waited for their food, they swapped stories about the previous week, happily telling the other how glad they were to finally be back together. Sophie knew that

Evalynn would have gagged if she'd overheard the conversation. But Garrett was there, Sophie was happy, and what anyone else thought was of little consequence.

By the time Sophie and Garrett were through with their main course, the restaurant had spun back to where the sugar packets rested against the window. Garrett was closest, so he grabbed the first one, looked at it just long enough to see that five people had signed it, then handed it to Sophie. A few moments later he plucked the second sugar packet from the windowsill and checked it for signatures.

"Weird," he said, flipping the small white package over and back in his hand. "Nobody signed this one but me."

"Nobody wrote anything?"

"Well, someone wrote a question on the back, but they didn't give their name or where they're from."

"What's the question?"

"It just says, 'Will you'?" he said slowly, then handed it across the table. "Here, take a look."

Sophie took the packet of sugar and held it in her hands, noting that it was thicker—*and heavier*—than the other one she'd just read. A puzzled look crossed her face. "I think there's something in it."

"Yeah, Soph. It's called sugar," quipped Garrett.

"Shut it," she said nicely, looking up at him. "There's something else."

"Like a bug or something? Sick. How'd you like that in your coffee?"

Sophie squeezed the packet gently between her thumb and index finger. "No. It's too hard for that."

"Well, open it up. Now you've got me curious."

"Ooh. I don't know. What if it's something gross?"

"Whatever it is, I'm sure it's not alive. C'mon, rip it open."

Grimacing, Sophie tore gently on one end of the packaging, then dumped the contents onto a clear spot on her plate. In the middle of the pile of sugar was the most dazzling diamond ring she'd ever seen. The sight of it caused her to gasp "Holy crow!" as she picked it up and dusted it off.

She looked up at Garrett, who was smiling sheepishly. "How about you remind me what that question says on the back?"

Sophie was still so surprised by what she'd discovered in the sugar that she had barely heard him. "What?"

"The question?"

"Oh," she replied, picking up the empty paper wrapper again. " 'Will you?' " she read.

Garrett hesitated a few seconds, watching her study the ring with giddy fascination, waiting for her to catch on. "So? Will you?"

She blew at a tiny sugar crystal that was wedged between the center diamond and the white gold that held it in place. "Will I what?" she responded vacantly, still studying the ring. But a moment later a lightbulb flickered to life in her brain. Her eyes shot up to meet Garrett's. "Oh...my...gosh," she said, suddenly short of breath. "Did you just...?"

Sophie narrowed her view to focus solely on Garrett's dimpled mouth, just to make sure that if she couldn't hear what he was about to say above the whirring sound of her own thoughts, at least she could read his lips.

"If you're asking if I just proposed, then yes. *Will you marry me,* Sophia Maria Jones?"

"Oh...my...gosh," Sophie repeated, more stunned than before. Then she started to ramble. "What? That's huge! How can we? I mean...we've only been dating for six months. Six months! That's a blink of an eye! Do you know me well enough? Do I know you well enough? How could we possibly...?"

Garrett just chuckled, taking it all in stride. "I wondered if you might say that. And I know this may seem a little sudden, but I know I'm in love, and I know you are, too. And since I know my feelings for you aren't going to do anything but grow, I figured, why wait?"

"Well, because... things could change. What if something happens to you? Or to me?"

"I thought you might say that, too. When I was in New Orleans I did a lot of thinking about what that psychologist told you as a kid about enjoying relationships while they last, and I think maybe he was on to something. I mean—the way he explained it to a kid who'd lost both parents was harsh, but I think perhaps what he was getting at was that we shouldn't measure the worth of a relationship by its duration."

She took a long look at him. "So, say we get married, and two months later I get sick and die. Will that have been worth it to you?"

"Yes!" he said emphatically. "Because those would have been the best two months of my life. Oh, I'd hate the fact that you were gone. But I'd much rather have two months of marriage with you than none at all." He hesitated. "I know you're scared. I'm nervous about it too—marriage is a *big* step. But I've never been happier since I met you, and I want you to be more than just the beautiful woman I'm dating. I really want you to be my wife."

Garrett's words helped put Sophie at ease, but she wasn't yet ready to give him an answer to the big question. Instead, she redirected the conversation. "So how'd you get the ring in there?"

He winked at her. "A little glue on the plane ride home. I went through five packets of sugar before I was able to make it look like it hadn't been tampered with. I think the lady in the seat next to me thought I was smuggling stolen jewelry."

She held the ring up and examined it more closely. "I can't believe you left this on the window for forty-five minutes. It could have been stolen."

"It was in my pocket the whole time," he explained. "I

swapped it with the other one while you were reading yours." Garrett reached out and grabbed one of Sophie's hands. "So, what do you say?"

"I'm thinking," she assured him.

"Well don't," he replied, grinning. "Don't think about it. Just go with your gut."

She snickered. "My gut is churning. I think it's saying it wants to vomit. Are you sure I should trust it?"

"No, better not. Let's pick something a little higher in your torso. What does your heart say?"

Now Sophie sat back in her chair and looked out at the lights of the Seattle skyline. When she spoke, her voice was steady, but cautious. "It says...that guys like you come along once in a blue moon." Her gaze remained fixed outside.

"Okay, now at least we've picked a trustworthy organ. Is it saying anything else?"

"That I've never been happier in my entire life."

"I like the sound of that. Anything else?"

Sophie turned and faced Garrett again. "Yes. My heart still wants to make sure that you're not going to break it."

Sitting up in his chair, Garrett took a moment to watch Sophie. She was the most beautiful woman he'd ever known, inside and out. Funny, intelligent, patient, caring, witty—everything he'd ever wanted in a companion. Looking at her, he was sure that nothing could ever change his feelings and that he would do anything to keep from hurting her. "Soph," he said softly, "I honestly love you more that I thought I could love anyone. I didn't even know this type of love existed until I met you. I can't promise you that we won't experience difficult things in our life. And as much as I'd like to, I can't even promise you that I—*or you*—won't be taken from this life before either of us would like. Life's just not that predictable. But without a doubt, I can promise you that I will *never* break your heart." He paused to smile. "Tell that to your heart, and see what it says."

Sophie tilted her head to the side, as though she were weighing something in her mind. "It says yes," she said finally.

"Yes what?"

She held up the empty sugar packet with Garrett's handwritten proposal. "Just 'yes.' "

Garrett wanted to jump out of his seat, but he contained himself. "We're getting married?"

Sophie slid the ring onto its intended finger. *Just like Garrett*, she thought. *A perfect fit.* "We're getting married."

Chapter 12

Yesterday was the high point of your life. Sorry.

OCTOBER 25 WAS THE DATE THAT SOPHIE AND GARRETT set for their wedding. It gave them a full seven months to prepare, which Garrett thought was more than enough time to plan and make all the necessary arrangements. For Sophie, however, it felt like a tight schedule, especially with the demands on her time running Chocolat' de Soph.

By the end of the first week of their engagement, she'd already made a comprehensive list of things that needed to be done. When she went over it with Garrett, he was surprised to find out that there was much more to planning a wedding than simply inviting family and friends to the ceremony. He read through her list several times, shaking his head at the level of minutiae. *Wedding colors, wedding dress, bridesmaids and groomsmen, attire for bridesmaids and groomsmen, flowers, guest list, gift registry, wedding venue, reception venue, minister, decorations, rehearsal dinner, photographer, invitations, hors d'oeuvres, entrees, centerpieces, wedding favors, guest book, music, DJ, seating chart, cake, cake topper, cake knife...*

"We have to pick out a knife to cut the cake?" he asked. "I've got plenty of knives we can use."

"Do they match the pen set that people will use to sign the guest book?"

"Probably not."

She poked him in the side. "Then they aren't the right ones."

Garrett chortled. "For a woman who doubted whether she'd ever get married, you sure seem to know a lot about weddings."

"Even when we have doubts, every girl dreams," she said.

As much as possible, Garrett and Sophie tackled the massive to-do list together, setting aside time each week to scratch off a few more items. The magnitude of the effort made time fly, and before either of them knew it, it was September, just four weeks from the big date.

Sophie's birthday fell on the third Sunday of that month. She was glad it was a Sunday, because it meant that she didn't have to go to work. Although there were several open items on their wedding-prep list, Sophie decided that those things could be put off a few more days so she could relax and enjoy her birthday with Garrett.

"I have a surprise for you today," she told him over brunch.

"But it's your birthday. I'm supposed to be doing the surprising."

"Well, it's not so much a surprise as something I want to share with you. Sort of a birthday tradition. Can we go for a little drive this afternoon?"

He agreed, so a few hours later they got in the car and Sophie directed him to the Evergreen Cemetery, making a point not to tell him where they were going until they actually got there.

"This is your big surprise?"

"Tradition," she said, smiling.

They parked the car and got out at the base of a small hill, and then walked hand in hand the rest of the way to a large hedge near the base of an old cedar tree.

"Here it is," Sophie said, pointing, once they'd reached the gravestone of Thomas and Cecelia Jones.

Garrett carefully read every word engraved on the marker. Sophie noticed that his jaw muscles tightened dramatically. "They died on your birthday," he said solemnly. "I never knew that."

Sophie shrugged. "It's not something I like to talk about."

His eyes locked once more on the tombstone, and he read it aloud, mostly to himself. "September 21, 1989...wow. Soph, that's...Did any of the newspapers back then ever mention that you lost your parents on your birthday?"

She put her arm around his waist. "Not that I know of. But who knows?"

"Well if they didn't, they should have. That makes the whole thing all the more tragic."

"It's definitely made my birthdays more...*significant*, that's for sure." She paused and looked at his face. "You know, not counting the first few times when I was a little girl and someone had to drive me here, this is the first time I've ever come to visit them with someone else. I didn't think I'd like sharing this with anyone, but facing the past doesn't seem quite so daunting when I'm with you. Thank you for that."

He gave her a gentle squeeze, but kept his eyes on the grave marker. "Yeah...sure."

Sophie brushed off his sudden introspectiveness. Everyone she'd ever told about her parents' deaths had reacted oddly when they learned that her birthday was their death day, so why should he be any different? Allowing him a chance to ponder, she dug into her purse and found a small box of chocolates. She picked one of the bunch and bent down to set it on the grave, then she picked up the beautiful round rock that was resting on the lower left corner of the gravestone and dropped it in her bag.

"What's the chocolate for?"

"Just a little reminder," she said softly.

"Of what?"

Sophie stood back up and wrapped her arm around him again, grabbing hold of a belt loop on his waist with one finger. "If you're nice to me, maybe someday I'll tell you."

He looked down at her. "I'm not nice to you?"

"Oh, you are." She laughed. "And if you keep it up, eventually I'll share all of my little secrets with you."

"I see. How about the stone? Are you going to tell me about that?"

She stretched up on her tiptoes and gave him a quick peck on the lips. "Yep. You've earned at least that much." Then she kissed him a little longer.

With her eyes closed, Sophie didn't see that Garrett was still looking at the gravestone.

Chapter 13

He who throws dirt is losing ground.

After leaving the cemetery, Garrett's mood perked back up, for which Sophie was very grateful. They spent the remainder of the afternoon walking around the Pike Street marketplace in Seattle, eventually choosing to get an early dinner from a street vendor whose shish kabobs had both of them salivating from the smell as they passed by.

Once they were full, they leisurely made their way back to the place where they'd parked and began driving back south toward Gig Harbor. But after crossing the Narrows Bridge, Sophie reminded Garrett that she still needed to explain what she did with the rock that she'd taken from her parents' graves. They took the first exit past the bridge, then doubled back along a little road that meandered eastward through a thickly treed residential area. She told him to stop along the side of the road near a pathway that split the property line between two homes.

"What are we doing here?"

"From here, we walk," she said. Sophie grabbed the rounded stone from her purse and exited the car, then started walking.

Two hundred yards farther down the path, they came to the shore of the Narrows, the well-named stretch of water that separated the Washington mainland from the Olympic Peninsula. The highway loomed overhead in the form of the Narrows Bridge.

Sophie had to speak loudly to be heard above the noise of passing cars. "Do you know what's out there?" she asked, pointing to a spot in the water beneath the bridge.

Garrett looked at her funny. "Is this a trick question?"

"Nope."

"Okay. Then you must mean either the bridge or the water."

"Nope," she said again. "*In* the water. Below the surface."

"No clue," he said after scanning the surface once more for a hint.

"When I was in second grade my dad brought me out here a couple of times. He had a fascination with suspension bridges. Anyway, he told me all about the *old* Narrows Bridge, though I don't think much of the history stuck until I studied it on my own a few years later. When it opened to the public in 1940, the old bridge was considered state of the art, an engineering marvel."

"What happened to it?"

"Four months after it opened, it collapsed. The wind blowing across the Narrows caused it to start pitching and rolling. They say cars on it at the time felt like they were on a roller coaster. After too much twisting and bending, the whole thing broke apart and fell into the water."

Garrett scratched his chin. "Amazing. But why is that important to you now?"

Sophie pursed her lips. "It was a tragedy of epic proportions, Garrett. An entire bridge—*the best of its kind*—gone, just like that. But the reason I come here now is because of what happened after it fell. First, the engineering community learned a ton about how not to build suspension bridges. The lessons they learned have had a lasting impact on every new suspension bridge in the world since 1940. Plus, believe it or not, the old bridge, which is now resting a hundred and eighty feet below the surface, has become the world's largest man-made reef, providing a home for countless numbers of sea animals."

Wrapping a thick arm around her shoulders, Garrett said, "I think I understand. Something good came out of something bad. Is that it?"

She nodded.

"Then why do you come here with the rock you took from the grave?"

"For this." Sophie ducked out from beneath Garrett's arm and flung the stone as far as she could across the water. It skipped seven or eight times, sending ripples in every direction, before sinking beneath the surface. "It's probably lame, but when I turned ten and found a rock on my parents' graves—on the first anniversary of the accident—I thought it looked like a good skipping stone. I asked Ellen to bring me here, because this place reminds me of my dad. Anyway, I made a wish back then that like the old bridge, something good could come out of my family's tragedy." She paused, staring out at the tiny ripples that were still moving along the surface where her rock had struck the water. "I come back here every year and make the same wish."

He nodded knowingly. "Still waiting for it to come true, aren't you?"

Sophie grimaced. "Yep." She took Garrett's hand in hers, and together they made their way back to the car, both of them quietly lost in their own thoughts.

Chapter 14

Sharing too much of yourself with loved ones can have dire consequences.

NINETEEN DAYS BEFORE THE WEDDING, GARRETT GOT A call late at night from the disc jockey he'd hired to do the music at the wedding reception. The man was calling to inform him that, due to "a whole lot o' messed-up crap," he wouldn't be able to make the wedding. Moreover, DJ Danny-B was going out of business and would be unable to refund the deposit for his services.

"You're joking, right?" Garrett said into the phone, his voice cracking nervously. "Tell me you're joking—please."

"Ummm..."

"Wait! Before you say anything else, I want you to understand that the only thing I had to do for this wedding all on my own was find someone to do the music, which I did. I put my faith and trust in *you*, DJ Danny, so please...tell me you're joking."

"Sorry, boss man. No jokes tonight."

The wedding preparations had worn both Garrett and Sophie thin; emotionally he was too spent right then to deal with this kind of a snafu. He groaned audibly, and then started yelling. "You're telling me I've got to find a new DJ for a wedding that's less than three weeks away? *Plus* I'm out five hundred bucks? That's highway robbery!"

"I feel ya," said DJ Danny unremorsefully. "But hey, if it's any consolation, the dude having a bar mitzvah the day after your wedding is out nearly a grand. Later, bro."

The phone went dead.

The next day, Sophie and Garrett spent five hours flipping through the yellow pages and searching the Internet for someone to replace Danny-B. It wasn't easy finding a qualified DJ who wasn't already booked, and when they did finally stumble across one who was available, his fees were nearly double the standard going rate.

To Garrett, DJ Diddy Dan's voice sounded an awful lot like Danny-B on the phone. "Supply and demand, bro. Take it or leave it."

He took it but wasn't happy about it. Garrett wondered if this was some sort of a racket by DJ Danny to increase revenues—take the deposit money and run, then jack up the price when they find you under a different name. Sophie calmly reminded him that there are much worse things that can go wrong with a wedding—*like the bride not showing up*, she teased—so he let it go.

After closing the deal with the DJ and taking care of a few other odds and ends, they drove up to 13 Coins, a restaurant in Seattle known for its live jazz and blues music. It was the place Sophie had chosen for the rehearsal dinner, on account of its Room Thirteen, a large hall that offered private dining in a space perfectly suited for the number of guests that were invited, and with ambience to boot. The manager of 13 Coins wanted them to come in once more to confirm the entrée selections and taste the planned dessert offerings.

By the time they were finished sampling imported custards and fresh tarts, the nearly-weds were ready for something slightly more filling. Garrett punched a series of buttons on his GPS to find a listing of different cuisines to choose from in the area. "What are you in the mood for, Soph?"

"You decide. I'm up for anything."

"You sure?"

She put her hand on his leg, squeezing just above the knee. "Positive. Surprise me." She paused and smiled. "Just no blindfolds."

"You got it." He pushed a couple more buttons, found a restaurant, and started driving.

The female voice gave periodic instructions, easily navigating the one-way roads, lane changes, and a series of unintuitive turns to a Japanese restaurant exactly six-point-three miles away.

"I know this place," whispered Sophie, half to herself, as she climbed out of the car.

"Oh yeah? Have you been here before?"

She bit her lip nervously as memories flooded her mind. "A long time ago," she said, her voice trailing off.

The restaurant was hibachi-style, with several highly skilled chefs who cooked the meals on the table right in front of the customers. Garrett thought it would be fun to try, but he could tell by Sophie's demeanor that something wasn't right.

After the hostess sat them at a table with a group of four other people, he quietly asked her what was wrong.

"This is the place," she confided, looking around at the walls and ceiling. "It hasn't changed a bit."

"What place?"

Picking up her chopsticks, Sophie tugged until they pulled apart. "It's where my parents took me for my ninth birthday.

We had our last meal together here." She turned and pointed to another large table where a chef was busy dousing a pile of chicken with teriyaki sauce. "At that table there."

Garrett rubbed her back lightly. "You want to go somewhere else?"

She let herself smile. "You're sweet. No, I'm fine," she said, looking around the room again. "Actually, it feels kind of good coming here. Maybe I shouldn't have avoided it for so long."

Their chef came a few minutes later and began his culinary show. It was entertaining, but the food wasn't as good as Sophie had remembered. "Maybe they're under new management," she told Garrett. "After all, it's been almost twenty years."

At the end of the meal, the hostess returned with a fortune cookie for everyone at the table. She started with the other four guests, going one by one as they chose a cookie from a stainless bowl. "I thought fortune cookies were Chinese," remarked Garrett, as he took the final cookie.

The hostess bowed her head politely. "*Asian* fortune cookie," she said in a thick Japanese accent. "China like cookie... Japan like fortune."

Garrett laughed. "I see. I'll have to remember that. And here I always thought they were just a Chinese thing."

The hostess snickered, and then leaned closer and spoke again, only without any accent at all. "Actually," she said, whispering, so as not to blow her cover with the other guests, "fortune cookies were invented by American immigrants in the early nineteen hundreds. They started off as biblical passages rather than fortunes, then after World War Two they morphed into a marketing tool by US restaurant owners. China and Japan had nothing to do with them."

"Seriously?" Sophie asked, intrigued by the history lesson.

"I may be faking the accent," the woman whispered with a wink, "but I don't fake the facts." Then she turned on the faux accent again and spoke more loudly so everyone could hear. "Asia share good fortune with you! Come again!" She bowed dramatically, and then left to tend another table.

Garrett was still laughing and imitating the hostess when they got back into his car. Sophie was more contemplative.

"Before we go home," she said, "do you mind if we head up this street a little ways?"

"Sure. What's up?"

She raised her eyebrows nervously. "Just something I want to show you."

Several blocks farther up the road, Sophie directed him to turn left onto a busy, four-lane arterial street, which they continued on for another mile. She stiffened as they passed her mother's favorite chocolate shop, the one she'd been so adamant about stopping at on her ninth birthday. Sophie clenched her teeth. *Nineteen years*, she thought, *and I still haven't gone in there to buy candy*.

A hundred yards beyond the candy shop she told Garrett to slow down and get into the far right lane. She saw the fire hydrant that she'd sat next to in the rain; it was approaching quickly along the sidewalk.

"Slow down!" she instructed. "We're here."

"Soph, if I go any slower I'll cause an accident. Where is *here*?"

She hesitated before answering, keeping her gaze on the yellow hydrant. "The accident."

There was no place to pull over, but Garrett tapped his brakes anyway and slowed to a crawl. Vehicles in the other lane continued to fly past on the left, while a few of the cars stuck behind him began honking. He turned on his hazard lights and waved them around as they continued inching forward.

"Right here?" he asked. Not only was he genuinely interested, Sophie could tell that he appreciated her opening up to him about it.

"I sat right here next to the fire hydrant for quite a while, just watching everything happen around me. The row of ambulances was down there, and our car was in the middle of the road, over there," she said, pointing. "I remember there was a UPS truck right up here, and the driver was just ahead of it on the ground." She kept talking as they moved slowly up the block. Garrett remained silent as she shared all the details she could remember—the number of fire trucks and ambulances, the pattern of flares along the road, how far the traffic was backed up, the police officers waving cars around the pileup.

When she stopped talking, Garrett was still quietly looking out at the road. "Garrett?" He turned to look at her. "What are you thinking?"

"Just... wow," he said softly. "That must have really been something." He kept looking at her. "I'm sorry you had to go through that, Sophie."

She smiled softly and touched his arm. "Let's go home."

Chapter 15

Your doubts about the future are easily explained: you're paranoid.

YOU ALL RIGHT?" SOPHIE ASKED GARRETT AFTER KISSing him good night. "You haven't been very talkative since we left the restaurant."

"Just tired, I suppose."

Sophie thought she saw a hint of something else flash across his face. "You sure? You're not having doubts, are you?"

He smiled faintly and wrapped his arms around her in a tight embrace. "No. It's just—seeing where your parents died. It's very sobering. Before tonight you hadn't talked much about it, and I guess seeing where it happened helped me visualize what it must have been like for you, and that touched a nerve. Makes me sad that you've carried those memories with you all these years."

Sophie kept him in the embrace, afraid that if she pulled back right then he might see in her eyes that there were worse things about the accident that she'd carried with her, which she hadn't shared with him. "Thank you," she whispered.

When they let go of each other, Garrett gave Sophie another little kiss. "I'll see you tomorrow, Soph," he said, and then went and got in his car.

WHILE DRIVING TO his own house in Tacoma, so many thoughts were running through Garrett's mind that he missed his exit. After passing it, he told himself he could just as easily take the next exit a mile farther, but he drove past that one, too. After all the Tacoma exits were distant blurs in his rearview mirror he stopped kidding himself.

Garrett wasn't going home. *Not yet.*

ELLEN WAS ALREADY drifting off to sleep when she heard the doorbell ring. She sat straight up in bed and listened. The three-chime ringer sounded again from the hallway a few seconds later. Jumping out of bed, she scrambled to throw on a robe, then poked her head into the hallway and yelled, "Knock once if friend, twice if foe."

There was no knock in response, only the chimes again from the doorbell. Ellen grabbed her holster and gun from her nightstand and carried it with her to the door, just in case.

"Hello?" she asked cautiously before unlocking anything. "Who's there?"

"It's Garrett Black," came the reply. "I'm sorry to bother you at this hour, Ellen, but I need to talk."

Garrett was the last person Ellen expected to show up late at night uninvited. The fact that it was less than two weeks from his wedding and that he sounded worried didn't give her a good feeling. She quickly unbolted the door and let him in.

"What's going on, Garrett?" she asked after she'd relocked the door. His face looked even more worried than his voice had sounded. "Is everything okay?"

"It's fine," he said, but his fragile smile said otherwise. "I really am sorry to bother you but...Sophie took me by the accident site tonight—the place where her parents died."

Ellen watched him briefly before speaking. "I see. I guess she must really love you as much as she says she does. She hardly talks about the accident, and has never—*ever*—taken anyone there. Not even Evalynn."

"I know," he said softly.

"So what's wrong?"

"Even while we were there, Soph didn't give me a lot of details, just a few mental images that she's kept locked away. But I'd like to get a better sense of what she actually went through." He paused momentarily. "I know it's too hard for her to talk about, but I want to know more about it, so I can support her more, and share the emotional burden a little bit. Does that make sense?"

Ellen smiled. "It makes perfect sense," she said. "And frankly, I'm relieved. It sounds like you care for her as much as she does for you."

He nodded. "I do. Ellen, I know you were there that night. Can you share what you remember?"

"I can do better than that. If you promise not to tell anyone, I'll let you see a copy of the police report from that night. I made a copy of it way back in the day. It's got every detail imaginable."

"Has Sophie read it?"

She shook her head. "I made a copy in case she ever came looking for details, but in all these years she's never asked. She doesn't even know I have it." She motioned to the sofa. "Have a seat. It'll take me a few minutes to find it."

Garrett did as instructed, but after she left he got up to look at the pictures on the wall. He'd been to Ellen's on several previous occasions but had never really had a chance to study them. Most were of Sophie and Evalynn growing up—school pictures, prom, graduation. But a small one, higher up on the wall, was of a young black couple holding hands. He recognized the woman as Ellen and guessed the man was her husband. Garrett knew that Ellen had been married, and that her husband had died, but that was all he'd been told.

While he was looking at it, Ellen came back in the room. "Found it," she announced.

Garrett turned. He didn't want to pry, but he knew she'd already seen him look at the picture. "Ellen, is this...?"

"My husband, Rick. Yes, that's him."

"He was a policeman too, right?"

She quietly nodded.

"Sophie said he was killed in the line of duty."

Ellen moved her head again, only it wasn't a nod. Nor was it a shake, but something in between the two. "That's... about right."

Garrett didn't want to intrude on her past any more than he already had, so he didn't say anything else. But Ellen could tell by his expression that he wanted to know more.

"He was off duty," she continued. "I've never told the girls exactly how it happened, because I didn't want them to worry about their own safety. Whenever they asked, I'd just say, 'He was a brave man, and he died doing his job.'"

He gave her a questioning look. "Why wouldn't they have felt safe?"

She exhaled. "Come have a seat." When they were both sitting down she continued. "Has Sophie ever told you what I used to tell her about there being purpose in everything, even the bad things?"

"Yes, she's mentioned it. Though to be honest, I don't think she shares your view."

"I know. Someday, I hope she will. Being a mother to Sophie and Evalynn has been such a blessing to me. But honestly, I'd have probably never known the joy of it, if I hadn't lost Rick. Sophie was my silver lining."

"Why is that?"

"It's... complicated. Do you have time?"

He nodded.

"Okay. Well, I guess I'll start with Rick. He and I met in the police academy, then we got hired on to the same precinct as rookies. We were both twenty-one at the time. We got married a year after we met, and then two years later, when we decided it was time to start a family..." She hesitated. "I found out that I couldn't. Apparently I'm not plumbed correctly for bearing children. Anyway, it was a huge disappointment. We went to specialist after specialist but were finally told there was no chance. So we weighed our options. We knew adoption was one route, and we seriously considered it. But because of our jobs we also knew that good, safe foster homes were in high demand. After a lot of talking and praying about it, we really felt that we could offer the foster system a great place to bring kids that needed a little extra love. We were in the process of getting qualified when Rick died."

Garrett looked at her curiously. "How does that relate to there being purpose in tragedy?"

Ellen's eyes dropped to the ground. Then she raised them slowly back up to meet his. "Some people might chalk it up to random coincidence, but I see more than everyday chance in the fact that Sophie became an orphan on my first night back on the job after becoming a widow. I believe it was meant to be."

He cleared his throat. "How so?"

Ellen grimaced. "Well I'd been on leave for two full months grieving, just trying to cope. It was hard losing him. I'd been working a double shift, covering for someone, so Rick had already left the precinct and gone home while I was still out on the beat. Near the end of my second shift I was listening to the radio chatter, and there was a call for all available units to an address in Seattle where an off-duty officer had been shot." Ellen paused and stared at Garrett. "It was *my* address."

Garrett gasped. "Oh my gosh, I'm so sorry, Ellen."

She smiled stoically. "I got there as fast as I could, but it didn't matter. He was already dead. Turns out he'd arrested a gangbanger earlier that evening, one of a handful that had robbed a store. The gang's sign was carved in our front door when I showed up. I guess one of the kids that got away at the store was waiting outside the police station when Rick left work, and followed him home. Shot him right in the doorway when he opened up, unarmed."

That explains Ellen's nervousness about answering the door, Garrett thought. "Geez. I don't know what to say. And I don't know how you're able to find a silver lining in that."

She shrugged. "After the initial trauma of losing him, and after I'd found a new place to live, I decided I still wanted to go through with being a foster mom. Rick had only wanted to take in boys, and so that's what we would have done if he hadn't died. But during my time off from work I decided a girl might be a better fit for a single mom. With that thought in mind I went back to work, and that very night I met a little girl who needed a mom more than anyone. During the months following Sophie's accident I kept making calls about her, letting the state know I was willing and able to care for her if the need should arise. Then one of her other foster situations fell apart when the husband died of a heart attack, and lo and behold, Social Service brought my silver lining right to my doorstep." She paused, and Garrett thought her eyes were getting moist. "I lost Rick, but I gained Sophie, and later Evalynn. I know that may not seem like a silver lining to them, but it's been everything to me."

Garrett exhaled slowly, taking it all in. "How come you've never told them what happened to Rick?"

She sighed again. "Mostly, I didn't want the girls to worry that someday a thug might show up at the door with a gun.

But also, I was heartbroken over what those girls had to go through, and I didn't feel like it was fair telling them that their greatest sorrows turned into my greatest joys. I feel guilty even thinking it, let alone telling them."

Garrett nodded that he understood, but he didn't say anything.

After a few moments of quiet, Ellen handed Garrett the police report. "Sorry, I'm talking your ear off. You still interested in this?"

In listening to Ellen's tale, he'd almost forgotten about it. "Oh. Yes." He flipped open the manila folder. It contained a ten-page report that included statements from eyewitnesses, details about the cars involved and the damage they'd sustained, names and ages of the people in each car, and an assessment of fault that said simply, "inclement weather, slippery roads, poor visibility."

Running his fingers quickly from one paragraph to the next, Garrett skimmed through the first few pages in under a minute. Then he slowed down, giving his full attention to the remaining pages, reading each sentence very carefully. He felt his face going flush and hoped that Ellen didn't notice. When he was done, he closed the folder and handed it back to her.

She tipped her head slightly. "You feel like you have a better sense of things now."

He nodded. "Yes. Thanks. And thanks for sharing about your husband. Sophie really is lucky to have you. I hope someday she recognizes what a great thing it was that your paths crossed." He stood up. "I better get going now so you can get some sleep."

She walked him to the door. "Good night, Garrett."

He turned and looked at her, and a strange sadness filled his face. "Good-bye, Ellen."

Chapter 16

If you thought things were looking up, you were upside down.

THE NEXT EVENING GARRETT CALLED SOPHIE AFTER work and explained that he needed to put in extra hours at the office so that he would be fully prepared to take time off for the honeymoon. Sophie understood completely, since she was in a similar situation with things at Chocolat' de Soph. With only two weeks to go, there were still a whole litany of things that needed to be set in order before she would feel comfortable leaving everything in Randy's hands for an entire week.

Due to one emergency or another, Garrett and Sophie hardly saw each other that entire week. Sophie missed him, but she reminded herself that in the very near future she would get to see him every day for the rest of her life, and that made the few days without him more tolerable. Besides, they still talked every night on the phone before going to bed, and that, for now, was enough to get her by.

After going to bed early on Saturday night, Sophie was

confused when her phone rang at one thirty in the morning. It took several moments before she was alert enough to recognize that it was Garrett's ringtone that she was hearing, and not a dream.

"Garrett?"

"We need to talk, Soph," he said. Sophie thought his voice sounded strangely distant, and it sent a warning chill down her spine.

"Now?"

"It can't wait."

"Umm. Okay. I'm listening. Are you all right?"

There was a brief silence on the phone before Garrett said, "I'm in my car out front. Can you come down?"

"Garrett... what's going on?"

"Just come down, Soph."

For Sophie, panic was already setting in. And dread. Whatever it was that Garrett wanted to talk about, she knew in her gut that it wasn't good. "I'll be right there," she whispered.

Getting out of her bed, Sophie peeked through the curtain at the driveway below. From her angle on the second floor she couldn't see Garrett's face, but she was able to make out both of his hands gripping the steering wheel. Although it was cold and drizzling outside, she didn't think to put on a robe or shoes; in her rush to find out what was going on she went downstairs in her satin pajamas and marched out to his car barefoot.

As she walked, Sophie tried to imagine all the different reasons why Garrett might wake her up in the middle of the night and call her down to his car for a chat. But for every external reason that she came up with, the voice in her head kept saying, *No... it's something about me.*

She was shivering when she slid into the front seat of his car, but she forced an optimistic smile. "This is a pleasant surprise. Good morning, handsome."

Garrett's hands remained riveted to the steering wheel. His face wasn't without emotion, but neither was it the look of someone who was happy to see her. As he turned his head, the light from Sophie's porch illuminated his face enough for her to see that he'd been crying. "Two hours," he said numbly. "That's how long I've been sitting here deciding what I should do."

Sophie retracted her arm swiftly, as though the tone of his voice had stung her. "What on earth is going on, Garrett? So help me... if you're even thinking about..."

Her words hung in the air.

"Garrett," she pleaded, "whatever it is, just put it out there so we can talk it through."

He turned away and whispered, "I'm sorry, Soph..."

"Sorry? Why are you sorry, Garrett? Talk to me!"

He dropped his gaze. "It's over."

Sophie wanted to vomit. She cupped her hand over her mouth just in case something was about to come spewing out. "What?" she finally managed once the gag reflex subsided. "What are you talking about? *Us?* We're over, just like that? Garrett, whatever it is, I'm sure we can work it out."

As she spoke, the rain and wind outside picked up, pelting the car in heavy waves.

"I'm sorry, Sophie," he said again, pulling his eyes from the steering wheel to look at her. His voice was much more sympathetic now. "If there were a way to avoid this, I would, but... some misfortunes just can't be fixed."

"You care to elaborate? At least tell me why," she demanded.

He shook his head once, slowly. "Does it matter? It's over, Soph. You told me a long time ago that good things don't last. Maybe you were right."

She didn't want to cry, but the impact of what he was saying—*the reminder that everything she'd ever loved had ended badly*—moved her to tears. "You lied to me!" she wailed. "You said you'd love me forever! You said that I could trust you! *I trusted you!*"

"Don't worry about the wedding arrangements," he said, as Sophie continued to sob. "I'll make sure everyone is notified. You don't have to do anything."

She heard him, but refused to look at him or respond in any way.

There were plenty of things he wanted to say to comfort her, but he knew if he said too much it would just lead to more questions. Questions that he wasn't willing to answer. "I need to go."

"So that's it? You're calling it quits and leaving, just like that?"

He tipped his head in response.

Sophie opened the door and stepped out into the pouring rain. By the time she shut the car door behind her she was completely soaked. But instead of running inside, she just stood there, barefoot in the rain, and watched as Garrett pulled out of her driveway and drove out of her life.

Once his taillights were out of view, she walked back inside. Dripping puddles across the floor as she went, she marched straight for the couch in the living room and, without bothering to dry off, flopped down, curled up in a ball, and cried until dawn.

Chapter 17

The world may be your oyster, but your oyster lacks the pearl.

"Open this door, Sophie!" yelled Evalynn for at least the tenth time.

"Go away!"

"Like hell! I'm just going to keep knocking, yelling, and ringing the doorbell until you let me in!" Evalynn pushed the doorbell five times in quick succession, then started pounding again. "The neighbors are watching! You'd better open before they call the cops!"

Thirty seconds later Sophie gave in and opened the front door. She stood there looking very pale, with fresh saline trails down her cheeks. Her eyes were puffy, her hair was a rat's nest, and it appeared as though she'd been wearing the same pajamas for days.

"Hi Sophie," Evalynn said softly.

"I just want to be left alone. Why is that so hard to understand?"

"I know. But you've already sequestered yourself for what—three days now? Enough is enough. Can I come in?"

Frowning dramatically, Sophie muttered, "Fine."

Evalynn stepped forward, opening up her arms to give Sophie a hug. "I won't lie to you. You look awful."

"Shut—"

"*Phew*...you don't smell so hot either. Have you showered?"

"Not since Sunday."

"Well then, it's time you did."

It took some nudging, but an hour later Sophie looked and smelled presentable. Not long thereafter, Ellen showed up in her squad car.

"You should have called me, Sophie," Ellen told her while they hugged. "I shouldn't have had to hear about this mess three days after the fact from Garrett's mom."

Sophie pulled back. "I know. I just...didn't want to face the reality of it."

Ellen hugged her again. "I know, Sweets. I know."

Halfway through her shift downtown, Ellen had gotten a direct call from the police dispatcher, Garrett's mother, telling her she was needed at the station immediately. Once she arrived, Olivia DeMattio explained how Garrett had just called with some terrible news. "He broke it off with her three days ago," she said hysterically, "but he didn't bother telling anyone else until today!" Olivia was mortified, especially because Garrett wouldn't provide any concrete reasons for what he'd done, only saying that Sophie had nothing to do with it and that it was his own fault.

As soon as Olivia stopped talking, Ellen started calling Sophie's cell phone, but it went straight to voice mail. Then she tried calling Chocolat' de Soph, but nobody answered there either. As a final resort, she called Evalynn, who was just getting off work in Tacoma. Ellen filled her in on what she knew, and told her to go straight to Sophie's house as quickly as possible.

With the whole foster family there, Sophie related the details of how she was officially dumped by Dr. Garrett Black. She was done telling them everything within a few minutes, which, as she explained to them, was about how long it took Garrett to call everything off and leave.

"And he wouldn't say why?"

"Nope. He said he had his reasons, but that it was better for both of us if he didn't elaborate."

"*Pfft*," Evalynn snorted. "Maybe better for *him*."

Sophie sighed. "Yeah. That's the thing that's been eating me up. I mean, sure, the whole thing sucks. And yes, I wish I wasn't going through this. But not understanding *why*? It's just unfair. I've been trying to call him ever since, but he won't answer."

"We should go to his house," said Ellen, as she stood up. "Right now. I'll drive, Soph. You deserve better than to be left in the lurch like this."

Initially, Sophie balked at the idea, but ten minutes later they were on the road, and fifteen minutes after that the squad car pulled up in front of Garrett's house. It was already dark outside, making it easy to tell that all the lights were off, but Sophie got out and walked to the door anyway. Nobody answered. She peeked through the window near the door, but there wasn't enough light to see anything, so she ran back to the car.

"Can you shine the floodlight on the front of the house?" Sophie asked Ellen.

"Of course, Sweets. You see something inside?"

"No. I just want to be sure about what I'm not seeing."

Sophie scuttled back up to the door and peeked through the window again. This time she could see everything perfectly. Only, there still wasn't anything to see. With the same urge to vomit that she'd felt three nights earlier, Sophie walked slowly back to the car and climbed in.

Ellen read the shock on her face. "Soph... what's wrong?"

"It's definitely over," she said, though the words were barely audible. "Everything... he's... there's... *nothing*."

"What?" asked Evalynn from the backseat.

Sophie felt numb. She turned her head slightly and with a hoarse voice said, "The house is completely empty. He's moved."

"Well, what about his office?" Ellen said. "We could go by there if you want. Either now or in the morning. He'll have to show up at work sooner or later."

"What's the point?" Sophie shot back. "Most people, when they're ready to move on, they just move on. He actually moved! If that doesn't send a message that he doesn't want to talk to me, then I don't know what would. No, if he doesn't want to see me, I'll leave him be."

"But Soph, what if—?"

"No! Ellen, it doesn't matter. I knew from the start that it would end this way. It's the story of my life. Let's just go. It's over."

Chapter 18

Your greatest success is your aptitude for failure.

TAKE ME TO THE STORE," SOPHIE SAID FLATLY FROM the front seat of Ellen's police cruiser. They'd been driving aimlessly around town for twenty minutes, using the time to mentally sort out where things had gone wrong with Garrett. But now that her fears of losing him had come true, Sophie wanted to find some other way to vent besides driving around in the dark and crying, and she had an idea that she thought might just do the trick.

"Huh?" replied Ellen

"Chocolat' de Soph. I need to go there to get ready for tomorrow."

Evalynn protested from the back. "Soph, you're smack-dab in the middle of a full-blown personal crisis. Work can wait."

She shook her head adamantly. "I can't let it stay closed another day. Besides, I think it'll be therapeutic."

"Making chocolates is anything but therapeutic," countered

Evalynn with a chuckle. "If you were *eating* chocolates, then maybe I'd agree."

"Just get me there. I have a new recipe I want to try, in honor of Garrett."

Ellen put the car into gear. "You're going to make something sweet, in honor of *him*?"

"Not exactly," replied Sophie quietly, the wheels already turning in her head about what ingredients to use for her new "treat."

When they arrived at the store, Evalynn volunteered to stay and help Sophie with preparations.

Ellen stayed just long enough to remind Sophie that everything was going to work out just fine. "God is at the helm," she insisted, "even when you think your ship is sinking. Just keep trusting that the Captain knows more about where you're heading than you do, and eventually you'll get where you need to be."

It was the first thing anyone had said all evening that made Sophie laugh. "If God's steering this boat, then I'm jumping ship," she'd responded. "Either that or outright mutiny. But God didn't break my heart. Garrett did."

"Give it time, Sweets," Ellen counseled softly. "Give it time."

After Ellen was gone, Sophie put Evalynn to work on fresh batches of fudge, along with a whole slew of hand-dipped items, while she embarked on her new creation. An hour later, just after 11:00 PM, Sophie had her first full batch of fortune cookies. The only things missing were the fortunes.

For that, she sat down at her desk in her office and pulled out a paper, which she cut into narrow slips with a pair of scissors. Then one by one she started filling the tiny papers with whatever words came to mind. The first one, she thought, was a gem. *Some people are lucky in love. You aren't one of them.* The second one made her smile, too. *Your life will fall apart in the blink of an eye. Don't blink!*

After that, the words just kept flowing until every paper had a unique misfortune. She slid the papers into the cookies and took them on a tray to show Evalynn, whose mouth was full of peanut-butter dough.

"Care to try?"

Evalynn swallowed. "Chocolate-covered fortune cookies? That's your new idea? I hate to break this to you, but I'm pretty sure that's been done before."

"Not like this," she said, smiling. "They aren't fortune cookies. They are Misfortune Cookies. I think you'll notice the difference."

Evalynn shrugged and picked up one. Watching her friend's expression as she bit into it, Sophie knew the recipe was a success. An instant later Evalynn was spitting and spewing the cookie out of her mouth. "It's horrible!"

"Like I said before…in honor of Garrett. Which message did you get?"

Evalynn reached into the crumbling mess and pulled out its paper. "*Like the cookie in your hand, your love life will eventually crumble and leave a very bad taste in your mouth.*" After reading it, Evalynn looked up and frowned. "It's…depressing."

"Yep."

"Makes me wonder a little bit about Justin."

"See," Sophie said, grinning again. "Therapeutic. Regular fortune cookies are too over the top with optimism. But these? A healthy dose of reality for those of us who've been around the block enough times to know that happiness is just an illusion."

"I don't know that I'd go that far," protested Evalynn.

Sophie just shrugged. "I would."

Part III

The End

Chapter 19

Accept something that you cannot change.
The way you look, for instance.

October 2009

THE POST OFFICE THAT HOUSED SOPHIE'S PO BOX WAS located just five blocks away from Chocolat' de Soph—close enough that she could walk there whenever she needed, but up a steep enough hill that she didn't bother going more than once per week. Any more than that would have been overkill anyway, since the only items that ever came were the occasional bills for her business, mixed here and there with catalogs or advertising from culinary and confectionary wholesalers. It had been a full three weeks since Garrett placed the want ad in the *Seattle Times*, and just as expected, she'd received no responses on her two previous trips to the post office.

As she finished her ascent up the hill on her weekly mail run, Sophie caught sight of a homeless man waving his arm on the opposite corner of the street. She gave a quick wave back, caught her breath while waiting for the signal to change, and then paced across the intersection to where he stood.

"Hello Sophie! How's my favorite customer?" The man cackled lightly. His greasy, graying hair hung in thick clusters, dangling past his forehead and ears, and curling up in the back above the collar of his red flannel shirt. Smudges of dirt covered the weathered skin directly below his eyes, while the rest of his face was covered with a thick beard that was tied beneath his chin with a rubber band. He held a cardboard sign that read: Vietnam changed me. You can change me too. GOT SPARE CHANGE?

"Is that what I've become to you, Jim? A customer? You make this sound like nothing more than a business transaction."

Jim had met Sophie nearly a year earlier, not long after Garrett dropped out of her life. She'd been on her way to send a small package of Misfortune Cookies to a man who owned a novelty shop in Portland and who was looking for potential new products, when Jim stopped her on the street to ask for food or money. Without any cash on her at the time, she told him he could have a Misfortune Cookie, but that he probably wouldn't like it. He took her up on it anyway, thanking her over and over for the kindness.

As it happened, Jim's taste buds didn't work so well, making him the only person Sophie had ever met who ate a Misfortune Cookie and loved it. He also loved the messages inside, and he swore up and down that he kept every one of them, and that one day they would all come true. After that initial encounter he kept a close eye out for Sophie, and eventually figured out that Monday was mail day, and so he planted himself there each week and waited for her to show up.

"Well I ain't out here for my health," he said wryly, his voice cracking as he spoke. "What do you call this, if it ain't my business? I'm luring customers with my uncommonly good looks and charm, just like you drive 'em into your store with the taste of your delicious cookies."

Sophie chuckled. "Most people think they taste awful."

"Exactly! Just like I'm no beauty queen, but somehow I still got people giving me cash."

She shook her head. "You're something else."

Jim scratched at his head and let out a hoot. "Ha! Precisely what my wife said before she walked out on me." He paused, moving his hand from the top of his head to the back of his neck, where something else apparently itched as well. "Well, enough small talk. You got another little something for me today?"

Sophie reached into her purse, retrieved a Misfortune Cookie wrapped in a napkin, and handed it to him. "It's all yours. Made fresh this morning."

Jim licked his cracked lips as he accepted it from her, then he lifted it to his mouth and took a small bite, savoring it. After a couple more small nibbles he retrieved the paper inside. "Hell yeah!" he hollered after silently reading it. "Another good one. Says me and the tires on my car will both be bald very soon."

Sophie shook her head again. "And why is that a good thing?"

He stopped and stared at her. "Why do I always gotta explain this to you? One day these fortunes are gonna come true. What a blessing that'll be. Bald tires or not, I don't got a car now, so sounds like things'll be turning around for me any day now."

"Always the optimist. Well, I've really got to run so I can get back to the store. Randy will be wondering what took me so long."

"You coming back next week, Miss Sophie?"

"I imagine so. If I don't get the mail, no one will."

He smiled, showing the purple-tinted gums where teeth should have been. "I'll be waiting."

As usual, there were only a handful of items in the PO box when Sophie opened it. But to her surprise, three of the letters had handwriting on the front, which wasn't normally the case for standard junk mail. She opened up one of the three and was floored to find that it was a response to the Happiness want ad. She quickly tore into the other two letters to discover that they, too, were happiness letters.

As she walked slowly down the hill toward Chocolat' de

Soph, Sophie read the brief notes over and over again, still surprised that someone—*anyone*—would respond to the want ad. Once she was back at the store she tucked the letters in the top drawer of her desk, and then took over for Randy at the register so he could do some much-needed cleaning in the back.

Not long after that, the phone near the register rang. "Chocolat' de Soph," Sophie said, as she lifted the receiver. "Can I help you?"

"Yes, may I speak with Miss de Soph, please?"

"Very funny, Garrett. What do you want?"

"Hi, Sophie. How are you?"

"I was fine until a few seconds ago," she said, her voice sounding strained.

"Oh c'mon, lighten up. Is it really so bad to talk to me? I'm just checking in to see how my ad is doing. Any takers yet?"

"Lousy," she said almost immediately. "Just like I knew it would."

"So I've paid for three straight weeks of that thing in the *Times*, and not a single response? Ouch."

"Well...it might have drummed up a response or two, but nothing really to speak of."

"Whoa. Really?" Garrett sounded suddenly very excited. "So there actually are happy people hiding out there. And apparently they read the classifieds."

"Apparently," she quipped.

"So was it just one response, or two?"

Sophie cleared her throat. "Three, actually. They just came today."

"Three! That's great. On average, that's one per week—not bad. At that rate, it'll only be, like, two years before I get my date with you."

"Hooray," she said with mock enthusiasm. "But keep in mind that just because three letters showed up doesn't necessarily mean that all three will count toward the hundred. They have to be legitimate, thoughtful, lasting examples of happiness. And since I'm the judge of that, they probably aren't."

The phone was silent for several moments. "You're really going to dig in your heels on this, aren't you?"

"I think it's only fair that I do whatever it takes to avoid you as much as possible."

More silence ensued, before Garrett eventually said, "So even if I get a hundred or more worthy responses, you're going to nix them all."

She laughed. "Not *all* of them. That wouldn't be fair. But enough to keep putting you off, yes."

"Well, in that case," he responded, "I think it's only reasonable that I get to read the responses, too, just so I'm in the loop. If I'm going to put out the money for this, I at least need to know that you're giving these things a fair shake."

Now it was Sophie who was silent. "You're seriously going to keep running the ad?" she finally asked. "It's going to get expensive, week after week."

"Hey, you made the rules, Soph. I'm just playing along. But one way or another I need to sit down with you and explain why I did what I did, and if this is what it takes, then so be it."

Sophie sighed. *Would one date hurt anything*, she wondered, *just to be done with it and move on*? She knew she was being stubborn and that the civil thing would be to just give in and let Garrett say whatever it was he wanted to say. But didn't the pain he'd caused her justify putting him off for as long as possible?

"It's your nickel," she said at length.

"Precisely."

"Huh?"

"It's my nickel, and I want to make sure I'm getting my money's worth. I'll be over in a little bit to read the first three letters. See you, Soph!" He clicked off before she could object.

True to his word, ten minutes later Garrett showed up at Chocolat' de Soph, wearing blue medical scrubs and a great big smile. Sophie was in the back gathering her things, hoping to get out the door before he arrived. Closing the front door behind him, Garrett waved cheerfully at Randy, then strolled around the counter and made his way back to Sophie's office.

"Leaving so soon?" he asked, as he poked his head in the room.

"Yes," she replied, picking up her umbrella, "but apparently not soon enough."

Garrett just kept smiling. "Well, don't rush off just yet. I want to see the letters you got today."

Sophie set the umbrella back down and opened the top drawer of her desk. "Fine. Here, have at it." She handed him the three topmost envelopes from the stack of mail.

Taking a seat on the front edge of Sophie's desk, Garrett began reading each of the letters. After he'd read all three he went back and studied each of them more carefully. One of them included a hand-drawn picture, another had a four-by-six photo, and the third was simply a letter. None of the correspondences were very long, but it was several minutes before he was through.

"Well," he started, as he stood up and turned to Sophie, "two out of three's not bad, right? Granted, it slows my weekly average a bit, but it's better than nothing."

Sophie let out a derisive laugh. "Two? I wasn't going to count any of them toward the hundred."

Chuckling, Garrett tossed one of the letters on the desk in front of her. "I knew right off you wouldn't count that one. And even though I can see how some people might enjoy the thrill of the hunt, I just don't think killing other living things for sport qualifies as lasting happiness."

"No," she agreed. "And I nearly gagged when I first looked at the picture of him standing next to that dead moose. Did you see how its tongue was hanging out of its mouth?" She shook like she had a sudden case of the shivers.

"So we're agreed on that one," he said with a laugh, then held out the other two envelopes. "But how come you're tossing out these?"

She crossed her arms and stood up, separated from him by the desk. "The letter from the woman is simply too generic.

She wrote more than the others, but all she really said is that happiness is watching your kids grow up, which isn't true."

He tilted his head to the side. "Why not?"

"Well, first, what about the people who don't have kids—who *can't* have kids. That sort of happiness would exclude them. And kids are, potentially, fleeting, sad as that sounds. If your kids don't make it to adulthood, then you haven't watched them grow up. You've watched them die. Is that happiness? And—"

"There's more?"

"Hush," she said. "You wanted my reasoning, and I'm giving it to you. Just look at my parents. By this woman's definition, they weren't happy because they didn't see me grow up—they didn't make it that far."

"You're tough," he said softly. "How about the other one? From the kid?"

"Oh geez," she said, sounding almost offended. "A crayon drawing of a cat? Really?"

"Well to a little girl, a pet can be something that brings happiness, can't it?"

"It's a *cat*, Garrett. As in shedding all over the furniture, and coughing up hair, most of which they've licked from their own body. Does that sound like happiness to you? And the drawing? If it weren't labeled as a cat, I'd have guessed it was a hippo."

Garrett smirked. "So that's a definite no?"

Sophie nodded. "Now then, is there anything else I can do for you? I really want to catch the next bus back to Gig Harbor."

"No," he said, smiling as he turned to leave. "Go catch your bus." He paused momentarily, then asked, "When are you checking the PO box again?"

She cocked her head to the side. "Next Monday. Why?"

Grinning playfully, Garrett turned on his heels and whispered, "Perfect. I'll see you then." He quickly darted out through the office door before she could put up a fuss.

Chapter 20

Some say that life is a play, and the world is their stage.
If you say that, then I hope you have a very good understudy.

"WHERE HAVE YOU BEEN!" EVI DEMANDED WHEN SOPHIE finally answered her cell phone. "I've been trying to get a hold of you for an hour but it went straight to voice mail."

"Sorry," Sophie said apologetically. "I just turned my phone back on a few minutes ago. Garrett kept calling earlier and I was tired of listening to his ringtone, so I shut it off. What's up?"

"Ugh. So you didn't talk to him today?"

Sophie could hear the worry in her foster sister's voice. "No, we haven't spoken since he showed up at the store a couple days ago. Why?"

"Well he was probably trying to reach you for the same reason as me. I take it you haven't seen the evening news?" Evi asked.

"You know I avoid it. Half of what they report on is just plain depressing."

Sophie heard Evi breathe out quickly through her nose, like she was suppressing a laugh. "Too true. Listen, if you're not dressed to be in public, then put on some clothes. I'm picking you up in ten minutes. There's some depressing news you need to see."

"Is it something...*bad*?" Sophie asked reluctantly.

"Not bad, just—Hold on a sec. *Justin! Don't you dare change the channel, until you're absolutely sure it's recorded on the DVR!* You still there, Soph?"

"Yep."

"So, it's not *bad*, it's just something you need to see for yourself. Okay? I'll be there soon."

With a heavy sigh, Sophie mumbled, "Can hardly wait."

Not quite ten minutes had passed when Evalynn's car pulled into the driveway and she honked for Sophie to come out. Shortly thereafter they were back at Evi's. Justin was screwing in a lightbulb in the kitchen as they passed through to the living room, where the plasma TV was paused on a close-up of the Geico gecko with its mouth wide open.

"Have a seat," instructed Evalynn.

"Hey Sophie," said Justin a few seconds later, as he walked in and plopped down in an empty armchair. "Did Ev tell you yet?"

"Not a single word."

Justin rubbed his hands together. "Ooh, then you're in for a real treat. We've already watched it like ten times and—"

"Shut it," Evalynn said, cutting him off. "Just let her see for herself."

Sophie looked back and forth between them. Evi was biting her lip to keep from outright frowning, but Justin was grinning impishly. She didn't know what to make of their disparate expressions, but the sinking feeling in her stomach told her that whatever she was about to see on TV would leave her feeling sick.

Evalynn took her place on the couch next to Sophie and pointed the remote at the screen. "Here we go," she whispered to herself, as her thumb pressed the Play button.

The Geico gecko became immediately animated, offering a few last words in its thick Cockney accent before the commercial ended. Then the screen jumped to the seven o'clock news broadcast—now almost two hours old—zooming in on the primped face of the Channel 2 anchorman.

"Welcome back to Channel Two News," he said confidently, maintaining a polished smile. "I'm Kip Waverly." As if on cue, the anchorman's steady grin become suddenly more contemplative, bordering on somber. "For tonight's special segment on news of local interest, we go now to Lori Acres in Tacoma. Lori?"

A chill shot up Sophie's spine as the man mentioned Tacoma.

The scene cut to a sharply dressed woman in her late twenties, perfectly manicured, standing outside the post office that Sophie frequented every week. Her blondish hair was blowing gently in the breeze. *"Thank you, Kip,"* she said very seriously. "In these challenging economic times—with so much high-level focus on unemployment rates, business failures, and mortgage foreclosures—it can be easy to lose sight of the fact that behind the numbers, at the very heart of all the facts and figures, there are people. Ordinary people who are just trying to get by, following their American dream in the pursuit of happiness." Lori paused dramatically to purse her lips. "But what happens," she continued, "when that dream no longer seems possible? When happiness feels like an unachievable pursuit? Some of us might lean on family or friends for support. Others turn to religious advisors or spiritual mentors. But how many of us would turn to the public at large? Probably not many...but at least one individual in the greater Seattle area is yearning for a glimmer of hope from others."

Sophie dug her fingers into the couch as the news correspondent held up a copy of the *Seattle Times*. "Thanks to one of our viewers, who tipped us off to a most unusual advertisement, I am here to report tonight that a desperate cry for help has been issued to all of us."

Kip Waverly jumped in. "I'm sorry, Lori. Did you say advertisement?"

"That's exactly right, Kip. For the past several weeks an anonymous want ad has been running in the classified section of the *Seattle Times*. Allow me to read its brief—yet poignant—plea." Lori paused again as she lifted the paper into a position where she could see it without blocking her face, and then she read each word from the ad slowly, adding dramatic inflections everywhere possible. "'Wanted: Happiness. Please help me find what I've lost. Send suggestions to PO Box three two nine seven, Tacoma, Washington, nine eight four zero two. Lasting happiness only, please. Nothing that fleets.'"

"Wow," piped Kip from the newsroom. "I'd have never thought to turn to the want ads to find happiness, but I guess when you really need help, you've got to seek it out wherever you can."

"Wow indeed, Kip. I'm standing outside the post office where our anonymous advertiser's PO Box resides, and where, hopefully, he will receive the answers—from all of us—that will help him get through what we assume to be a difficult time. Our hope is to find out who this person is and see if there's more we can all do to help, but in the meantime if you wish to write a response to this ad, you'll find the address at our website, given at the bottom of the screen. Let's let him know that the pursuit of happiness is alive and well here in the heart of the Puget Sound. Reporting live from Tacoma, I'm Lori Acres. Back to you, Kip."

"Thank you Lori." Kip nodded thoughtfully, and then turned to the nearest camera. "And to the nameless person who created that most unusual want ad, if you are watching, may I add that our thoughts are with you, and we hope you find what you are looking for." After another quiet pause,

Kip's entire demeanor changed on a dime. Suddenly he was all smiles again. "Now, moving on to other local news. The Seattle Supersonics learned today that—"

Evi clicked off the television.

Sophie sat staring at the black screen, stunned. "'Yearning for a glimmer of hope from others'?" she said finally, repeating Lori's words. "'Happiness is alive and well in the heart of the Puget Sound'? This actually passes for news? They're concocting a news story where none exits."

"That's pretty much what they're paid to do," observed Justin.

Sophie ignored him. "I don't know whether to laugh or cry."

"Neither did we," admitted Evalynn. "Justin laughed. I'm still on the fence."

As she stood up and paced across the room, Sophie's mouth tightened into a knot. "You know what? I'm not sad about this. I'm furious! 'Thanks to one of our viewers,' she said. No doubt in my mind who that was."

"You think it was Garrett?" Evi asked.

"Of course it was Garrett! What a conniving little—oh, he makes me mad. I told him he could only place the ad in the *Times*, so he found a way to skirt that little rule."

Justin chuckled. "It's actually quite brilliant."

Evalynn shot Justin a look, warning him to stay out of it.

"I'm just saying," he muttered.

While Evi was giving Justin another nonverbal warning, Sophie turned her phone back on and saw that she'd missed ten calls and six new text messages. She didn't bother to listen to the voice mails. Instead, she dialed Garrett's number.

He answered after the first ring. "Did you get my messages?" he said immediately, sounding slightly panicked.

"How could you do this to me?" she groaned, and then started on a small tirade. "Even if nobody knows it's me, it's still hugely embarrassing! That news lady talked about the ad like it was the work of some despondent lunatic who's hanging on by his very last thread. Unbelievable. Of all the rotten things you've done to me, this one takes the cake!"

"Sophie!" he said, raising his voice to compete with hers. "Go back and listen to my messages. I'm as surprised about this as you are. I tried to call you as soon as I saw it, but I couldn't get through."

"I was ignoring you...and for good reason. You just cause me problems."

"I worried you'd think it was me, so I called as soon as I could."

She wasn't listening to him—or if she was, she didn't believe what he was saying. "What if they find out it's me? What if the follow-up story has my face plastered all over television? What then? Did you think about that before you peddled the story to the evening news? Well, what if I tell them it was really *you* who placed the ad? You think your patients would like to know that Lori Acres says their doctor is the most unhappy person on the planet?"

"She didn't say that," he countered.

"Well she might as well have! Seriously, Garrett, what if they trace this to me?"

He waited before responding. "Might be good for business," he offered.

"Oh, you're unbelievable!"

"I'm joking, Soph. Honestly, nobody is going to find out it has anything to do with either of us. I've already called the paper and cancelled the ad, and I made it very clear that if the identity of the person who placed the ad is leaked to anyone they'll have a very painful lawsuit on their hands."

Sophie was still pacing around Evalynn and Justin's living room. She breathed out slowly, trying to calm herself. "I just...I can't believe you did this. The deal is off, Garrett. No date. Not after this."

When Garrett spoke again, his voice was much quieter, as though hoping that by changing his tone he could better gain her attention. "Sophie," he said softly, "I'm going to repeat this as many times as it takes for you to understand. *I had nothing to do with it.* Frankly, it would have been very clever for me to do. Deceitful and wrong, but clever. But I swear it wasn't me. You know, there *are* people out there who read the newspaper. A lot of them, in fact. And any one of them could have latched on to the happiness ad and decided to share it with the media. But I didn't do it."

Sophie was reeling. She wanted him to be the culprit, the bad guy she could blame everything on. She wanted another reason to hate him after everything he'd done to her. But she knew he was telling the truth. Still, she kept quiet after he finished speaking.

"Sophie?"

"I'm here," she eventually muttered.

"Do you believe me?"

"Why should I?"

"Because it's the truth."

"Well...I don't want to," she replied honestly.

"But?"

"I'm still deciding."

"So...our deal. It's still on?"

"Fine," she said reluctantly. "But only because I keep my promises. Unlike some people I know."

"Ouch, that stings a little."

"Darn," she said, relaxing slightly for the first time since Lori Acres opened her mouth. "It was supposed to sting a lot."

"Well, thanks for calling. Even when you're yelling at me, I enjoy hearing your voice."

She wished he could see her rolling her eyes. "Good night, Garrett."

"'Night, Soph."

Chapter 21

Compel yourself to do something you wouldn't normally do, because what you normally do doesn't seem to be working.

U been online lately?

The text message from Garrett popped up on Sophie's cell phone just as she was preparing to go to bed on Sunday evening. It had been four days since they'd talked on the phone in the wake of the Channel Two News debacle. Sophie slid under her covers and stared at the short note, then decided she wasn't interested in texting at the moment—at least not with Garrett. She set the phone down on her nightstand just as another message popped up. Frustrated at being bothered, she flipped the phone open quickly to see what it said.

It's gone viral!

The odd message caught her attention and she thumbed a quick response. *What has?*

IT! The want ad. It's everywhere!

Sophie's breathing picked up as she typed again. *R U kidding??*

Get online. I just sent you an e-mail with a few links... uuuggghhh.

Snapping the phone shut, Sophie jumped out of bed and hurried downstairs to her computer. Her Gmail account was loaded to the gills with spam, but it didn't take long to filter through them. Garrett's e-mail had the subject line "Uh Oh…don't blame me." The body of the message had no text, simply URLs to various Internet sites.

The first link was to YouTube, where Lori Acres's newscast had already been viewed by nearly 500,000 people worldwide. But other media outlets across the country had picked up on the story, too, and at least a dozen other TV stations had aired their own versions of the story, which were also posted on YouTube, each of them retelling it as though they were the first to report on what one overly dramatic anchorman described as the "epically sad, heroically unhappy, mystery want-ader in Tacoma, Washington, who has gripped our hearts, and made us all pause to reflect on what happiness is, where to find it, and above all, how to hold onto it."

"You've got to be kidding," said Sophie out loud. "This is absolutely absurd." She cringed as video after video flashed her PO box on the screen, urging viewers to respond.

Other links in Garrett's note sent Sophie exploring chat rooms, Facebook, Twitter, and MySpace. On one site, a group calling themselves H-Cubed, short for "Happy Helping Hands," had raised enough money among themselves to run Sophie and Garrett's want ad for four weeks in the twenty largest US newspapers.

After an hour and a half of poring through web pages, with each new link taking her to at least ten others, Sophie finally gave up and turned off the computer. Her head was pounding from staring at the screen for so long. Slowly, she made her way upstairs and climbed back into bed, but it would be another hour before she fell asleep. As she laid in bed, the one thought that kept cycling through her mind was, *Why didn't I just let Garrett have one stupid date?*

* *

THE NEXT DAY, as soon as Randy arrived at Chocolat' de Soph, Sophie gathered her umbrella, purse, and a spare Misfortune Cookie and began her weekly trek up the hill to pick up the mail. She wondered, as she walked, if there would be a noticeable uptick yet in the number of responses to the want ad.

Jim was waiting in his normal spot in front of the post office, carrying his ragged sign about Change. He seemed to sense that Sophie had other things on her mind, so he kept his comments to a minimum when she handed him his cookie. However, he did take time to thank her once again for her kindness, and then shared his fortune with her.

"Hot dang!" he chirped, his cracked lips turning up at the corners. "Says my fifteen minutes of fame will be cut down to five, at best." He winked at Sophie before she left. "That'll be five minutes more than I ever expected. Thanks again, Miss Sophie."

By government standards the work day was already well over, so only the post office's lobby area, which housed two walls of PO boxes, remained open to the public. As usual, there were a handful of people around, likely stopping off on their way home from work like Sophie. As soon as she stuck her key in PO Box 3297, however, the atmosphere in the post office changed.

Whispers started erupting from all over, especially from a group clustered together on the opposite wall. At first Sophie tried to convince herself the growing chatter had nothing to do with her. But ignoring it turned out to be impossible once she heard someone whisper too loudly, "Hurry up! Get the cameras in here while she's still got the box open."

Frozen by the comment, Sophie was instantly aware that all of the hubbub was about the "mystery want-ader" who, it seemed, had just been discovered. She had been sure a fluff story like hers would have been old news by now, but she should have realized from all those websites and videos that it wasn't. The only part of her that she knew was still moving was her heart, which felt like it had been flipped into high gear, pounding against her chest as though it were trying to escape.

She was stuck, and she knew it. After doing nothing but stand there for what felt like eons, while the noise behind her continued to grow, Sophie finally accepted the fact that sooner or later, she would have to turn around. With a giant gulp of air she inflated her shoulders until they were straight, pulled a single yellow slip of paper from her PO box, closed the door until it latched, and then calmly spun around.

Flashbulbs began popping from every direction as soon as her face was in full view. In an instant she was surrounded by a throng of news reporters shoving microphones and recorders in her face, maniacally trying to get the full scoop on the "heroically unhappy" woman standing before them.

"Can you tell us what prompted you to place the want ad?" asked one slender woman with blondish hair, whom Sophie recognized as Lori Acres.

"You don't appear to be down on your luck," commented another. "It this a publicity stunt of some sort?"

Then things really started to heat up, and it quickly became apparent that everyone was working the story from some predetermined angle, each of them hoping to drum up controversy. As the chaos escalated, Sophie was unable to tell who was asking what, because they were all firing off questions in rapid succession. "What's your full name?" "How long will the ad run?" "How many responses have you received?" "Are you doing this for the attention, or do you really expect to find happiness through the classifieds?" "What type of happiness doesn't fleet?" "Are you taking any kind of antidepressants?"

Sophie was too mortified to say anything, so she just stood there listening to everyone talking at her, blinking periodically when the camera flashes caught her straight on. She thought she should try smiling for the pictures, but she couldn't get the muscles in her face to move. After a minute or two of the unceasing barrage, a small tear escaped Sophie's eye. The warmth of the moisture running down her cheek seemed to melt the barriers that were holding back her emotions, and Sophie realized that the dam was about to burst. She hated the thought of crying in front of these people—not to mention the thousands of people who would see videos and pictures of the episode later—but she knew there was nothing she could do about it.

Just as a giant wave of despair was washing over her, when she was sure that she was only moments away from cleaning the floor with tears, a loud voice shouted from somewhere at the back of the crowd, "What in the hell are you all doing to her!"

The gathering fell silent almost immediately, the inquisition turning as one body to locate the source of the outburst.

"It's me you're after!" the voice bellowed. "Leave her alone, or so help me I'll take every last one of you to task right here and now!"

There were stunned looks from everyone in the media crowd, but no one was more surprised by what had just happened than Sophie. To her utter disbelief, standing a few feet inside the glass doorway of the post office was Jim, his greasy, bearded head held high.

Lori Acres was still the closest person to Sophie. She quickly turned back to her original target and asked what the indigent man was talking about.

Good question, she thought. "Why don't you ask him?"

Jim overheard the exchange and immediately pushed his way through the pack to get to Sophie. Once there, he extracted a beat-up wallet from his back pocket and withdrew a wrinkled twenty-dollar bill from its folds. Making sure that everyone could both see and hear what he was doing, Jim held the bill up in front of Sophie and said, "Here you go, miss. As promised, twenty bucks for your effort. And I apologize for getting you mixed up in all this ruckus." As he handed her the money he coyly turned his back to the crowd and whispered, so only she could hear, "Here's my five minutes." He winked.

"Umm...thanks," she said, as much to the reporters as to Jim. "It was no trouble. Well, aside from, you know...being mobbed. But I only did it to help. You don't have to pay me." Sophie handed the money back, then slithered out of the limelight and took up a position at the back of the crowd, being careful not to look anyone directly in the eyes lest they recognize her bluff and call her on it. The smart thing to do, Sophie knew, was to leave right then and not look back; but even though she risked being discovered, she desperately wanted to know what Jim was about to say to the reporters.

Up front, Jim cleared his throat, licked his lips, and then addressed the reporters with surprising confidence. The savvy with which he spoke, combined with the fact that everything he was saying was a sham, made Sophie think that with the proper attire, a clean shave, and a nice set of dentures, Jim would make a good politician—insofar as politicians can be considered good. "First," he said, "let me answer what I know you're all wondering. Is this guy homeless?" A few people snickered. Jim didn't seem to mind. "The answer is, yes. I live on the street. It's a hard life. Lonely. And with plenty of time to think."

"How can you expect us to believe a homeless person placed this ad?" someone shouted, then a few others started mumbling similar doubts.

Jim calmly raised his hands to quiet them. "If you'll let me speak, I'll tell you. Whether you choose to believe it is...well...that's your problem. I'll just tell you what I know, and then you can go do with it what you want. Last year about this time a little girl and her mom walked up to me one day and gave me five bucks. But before they left, the girl asked me if I was happy living like I do. And that got me thinking. Am I happy? And what is happiness, anyway? I see people every day in their shiny cars, driving to their big, warm houses. Are they any happier than me? I dunno. But I decided I wanted to find out. Now, it took me awhile, because, as you might guess, I'm not exactly swimming in cash. But I scrimped and saved, just like anyone would who wants something bad enough. And then about a month ago I had enough money stored up to get myself a PO box and a want ad in the paper. I wanted to know what the rest of you think happiness is. Seems like everything I ever had in my life that brought me happiness eventually went away. My job. My house. My savings. I was dying to know if you people—the ones that seem to have it made—know anything more about happiness than me. Someone out there must know, right?" He paused and looked around. "So there you have it," he added. "Now you know my story."

There was a brief silence, and then one of the reporters asked, "If it's your PO box, then why did you send the woman in here to open it?"

Jim stroked his beard thoughtfully. "You think I don't read the papers? Hell, I sleep on them every night. I've seen all the editorials the last couple of days, and I was worried the media might start snooping around, trying to find out who was behind the ad. When I saw more people loitering in here than normal, I approached her on the street. She's shown me kindness in the past and I know her to be a very generous woman; she agreed to come in here on my behalf. Of course, I didn't expect the sort of feeding frenzy that happened. If I'd seen the news vans parked around the block I wouldn't have put her up to it." He looked directly at Sophie. "Again, ma'am, sorry for your inconvenience."

Sophie waved, as though it had been nothing. She was still worried that someone was going to ask why she still had the key to the box in her possession, and why she hadn't given him the single piece of mail that she'd retrieved, but nobody did. Apparently, they were all too caught up in the victory of uncovering the story to wallow in such details.

When Jim asked if there were any more questions and they responded with things like, "How long, exactly, have you been on the street?" and "How old, would you guess, was that precocious little girl who triggered your quest for happiness and journey of self-discovery?" Sophie knew that it was safe to leave. Without drawing any further attention to herself she quietly slipped out the door.

Once she was a safe distance from the post office, Sophie found the yellow piece of mail that she'd taken from her box. It was a notice from the postmaster that her recent volume of mail far exceeded her box's capacity, and that she would have to pick it up at the counter during business hours. Not wanting to risk being seen collecting all that mail, she decided to have it forwarded instead. Any other time, she might have been upset to learn that she was on the verge of being inundated with responses to the want ad, but at that moment she was simply grateful to be out on the street, her anonymity intact, and on her way back to Chocolat' de Soph.

Four hours later, with Evalynn and Justin beside her on the couch, it was all Sophie could do to keep herself from crying, through repeated fits of laughter, as they watched, rewound, and watched again, the top story from the ten o'clock news. It was an inspiring piece about a homeless man in Tacoma whose humble petition in a newspaper want ad was, as Lori Acres explained, "Compelling people everywhere to reflect more carefully on what things matter most in life; urging them to seek out happiness, wherever it may be. Back to you, Kip."

Chapter 22

When you speak honestly and openly, others truly listen. They don't believe you, but at least you have their attention.

SEVERAL DAYS PASSED BEFORE THE POST OFFICE PROcessed Sophie's request to have her mail forwarded directly to Chocolat' de Soph. By then, nearly two weeks had passed since she'd picked up the first three letters. With all the media attention it had received, she knew the next wave of responses would be considerably larger.

She couldn't have imagined how much.

The postal worker who pulled up in front of the store on Saturday afternoon came inside first to ask if there was someplace special Sophie wanted him to deposit her mail.

"You can just leave it here on the counter," she told him. "I'll sort through it while I'm tending the register."

The man chuckled dryly. "I don't think that's gonna work. Is there anywhere *else* you'd like me to leave it?"

"There's that much?"

He chuckled again. "You got room in the back, maybe?

I think I can maneuver my hand truck back through there."

"Yeah... oh... umm, sure. The back would be fine."

The man nodded, then went out to his mail van and opened up the tailgate. Sophie watched with disbelief as he stacked four plastic bins full of mail on a dolly and wheeled them in through the front door.

"Ho-ly crrrow," she said slowly, as he rolled past her to get to the kitchen. "It'll take me days—*maybe weeks*—to get through all of this."

The mailman gave another dry laugh. "Not done yet." After setting the stack against the wall near her office door, the postman went back out and filled his hand truck twice more. On his fourth and final trip, he brought in a large box full of assorted small packages that wouldn't have fit well in the plastic mail bins. "That's the last of it," he told her after he was through. "Good luck with that, ma'am."

She nodded vacantly, but her eyes remained glued to the stacks of mail in front of her. The postman let himself out while Sophie continued to stare at the mesmerizing sight.

Several minutes later she heard the bell on the front door ring, followed by Randy's familiar steps pacing through the store. He stopped walking as he came around the dividing wall into the kitchen.

"Dude!" he exclaimed. "This is like... *dude!* You got some serious postage."

Sophie ran her fingers through her hair. "Tell me about it. How am I ever going to read all of this?"

"Just like a vulture chomps down the rotting flesh of an elephant carcass, I guess. One piece at a time."

She turned briefly away from the mail and glanced at her quirky employee. "Thanks for that very visual—and slightly disturbing—description."

He nodded. "'Course, some vultures don't mind sharing

with the flock, long as there's plenty to go around. Saw that on Discovery, I think."

She eyed him again. "Is that your way of volunteering to help me take a bite out of this rotten pile of mail?"

Randy shrugged. "If you need help, I'll do whatever I can."

Approaching the nearest stack of bins, Sophie dug her hands into the letters, scooped some out, and then let them slip through her fingers like enormous grains of sand. "You know what? I'll take you up on that. Let's make sure we're all set on candy and cleaning to cover the rest of tonight and tomorrow, and then we'll dig into this nightmare. I may even make some calls to see if I can round up a couple more turkeys to join our flock."

"Vultures," he corrected.

"*Turkey* vultures," she shot back.

Randy thought about that for a second, taking another long look at the ridiculous hoard of letters and packages. "You're probably right," he said, then turned around to tend the front of the store.

Sophie went into her office and made phone calls to Evalynn and Ellen to see if they were willing and able to help sort through the mail. Not only were they free, but they were excited to be a part of it. Ellen, in particular, said she was hoping she'd get a chance to see what kinds of things people had sent, but didn't want to be too nosy.

While Sophie was in the back sprinkling cashews on a fresh batch of caramel apples and mixing pralines into a thick fudge sauce, Randy was counting cash in the register to do a quick inventory against sales for the day. He lost track of the count when the phone rang.

"Chocolat' de Soph," he answered. "This is Randy."

Just then Sophie came barreling around the corner. "If that's Garrett," she whispered frantically, "I don't want to talk to him. Tell him I can't come to the phone." He'd been leaving messages for two days on her cell phone to see if any more mail had arrived, but so far she'd managed to avoid direct contact with him.

Randy stuck the phone under his armpit to cover up the receiver. "It is," he whispered back. "What should I say?"

"Anything! I don't care, make something up."

Clearing his throat, Randy extracted the phone from beneath his arm and pressed it to his ear. "Oh hey, Garrett. I'm sorry, dude, what did you say?"

Sophie watched with keen interest, searching his face for any clues about what was being said. Randy nodded his head up and down twice in response to whatever Garrett was saying on the other end of the line.

After a few long pauses, Randy spoke up. "Yeah, sure. Understood. The only thing is, she... she can't really come to the phone right now, 'cuz she's, like, swamped with mail and stuff from that want ad. Bummer, right?"

"No!" Sophie shouted, not caring that Garrett would probably hear her. "Anything but that!"

Randy's eyebrows shot up at Sophie's rebuke, but he couldn't respond to her right away because Garrett was apparently speaking again. A few seconds later he said, "Yeah... okay. I'll... yep, I'll let her know. Later." Then he set the phone back down on its base.

Randy didn't speak right away, but he didn't have to. His expression said it all.

"He's coming here, isn't he?" Sophie said. It was as much a statement as a question.

Randy nodded.

Her shoulders sagged. It was bad enough having to spend the entire evening wading through miles of unwanted letters from strangers, but to do it with Garrett hovering nearby, prodding her to accept one hundred responses so he could earn his date, sounded to Sophie like a cruel and unusual punishment, though for what crime she wasn't sure. She let out a giant sigh. "Do you happen to know what vultures do to each other when the flock gets too large?" she inquired.

He shook his head.

"Well whatever it is, I'm sure it isn't pleasant." Sophie frowned, then went back to finish her preparations for what was shaping up to be a very long night.

"HELLO?" EVALYNN CALLED out, after she and Justin entered Chocolat' de Soph to find the front of the store empty.

"We're back here," shouted Sophie.

Evalynn and Justin rounded the final corner to find Sophie, Ellen, Randy, and Garrett sitting on the floor, swimming in a sea of paper.

"Holy crap," remarked Justin.

"I know," Sophie said quickly. "I didn't invite him—he just showed up."

Garrett laughed, even though her comment was directed at him. "I think he was talking about the mail. How are you, Justin? Haven't seen you in a while."

"I'm keeping out of trouble. You?"

With a wry grin plastered on his face, Garrett said, "I'll be better after tonight, I think. I'm on the cusp of winning this little game we've got going."

Sophie pretended like she didn't hear him. Given the flood of responses, she knew that he was probably right, but she wasn't willing to roll over and let him declare victory just yet. She was, after all, the sole judge of the responses, and therefore in complete control over the outcome. *No*, she told herself, *if I'm going to have to suffer through a date with him, I'm at least going to put up a good fight*. But even as that thought popped into her head, she knew it wasn't really the date that she wanted to avoid. More than being alone with the man who had destroyed her heart, her single biggest fear—and the thing that kept her up at night—was the worry that she might still have feelings for him. She'd already decided that it was safer just to avoid him altogether, rather than risk being emotionally chewed up and spit out all over again.

Evalynn's voice pried Sophie from her own thoughts. "Sorry we're late, Soph. We stopped to get takeout for everyone. Chinese okay?"

"Oh...yeah. Thanks. Just set it on the counter there and folks can grab what they want."

"Is there a method to the madness?" Justin asked, eyeing the stacks of letters.

"Umm...not really," replied Sophie. "But I was thinking maybe if everyone could start by sort of screening everything, and them lumping them into piles, that might be easiest. One pile for the definite nos, another for maybes, and then one for the responses that have real promise." She paused and glanced at Garrett. "Assuming that there are any, of course. How does that sound?"

"Sounds reasonable," Ellen replied. She was sitting on a chair against the wall with a plastic bin full of letters on her lap, and she was rifling through them as though she were looking for something in particular. "Oh, wait, Sweets. Do you have any guidance on what constitutes a no, a maybe, and a 'has promise'?"

Garrett let out a little laugh. "Ooh, this should be good," he mumbled.

Sophie glared at him before answering her foster mother. "Yes, I do. Essentially, anything that is crude or base goes in the No pile. Along with anything about men or romantic relationships. Oh, and anything that is obviously perishable is a no as well. Beyond that, use your own judgment. I trust you—well, most of you anyway—to be able to filter out the junk."

"And the maybes?" asked Ellen. She held up a letter, inspected the return address, and then set it off to the side in a growing pile of unopened letters near the base of her chair.

"Just anything that doesn't strike you as junk but also doesn't necessarily jump out as something terribly insightful. Then if you happen to find some that you think are really good responses, they can go in the third pile." She paused, looking around at everyone. "Any other questions?"

Garrett raised his hand and waited until Sophie addressed him.

She rolled her eyes. "Mr. Black?"

He smiled sheepishly. "Yes, umm... is that a new blouse? I was just noticing how great it looks on you."

She looked away and forced a frown, hoping that would be enough to camouflage her cheeks, which suddenly felt flush. "Any questions related to the mail or how to sort it?"

Justin and Garrett both chuckled.

For the next hour the group waded through letter after letter, patiently sorting them into piles per Sophie's instructions. It didn't take long before everyone became adept at speed-reading, scanning for key words that might tip them off about each letter's overall theme. The only person who wasn't doing much reading was Ellen, whose pile of unopened letters was getting very big very fast as she scanned the return addresses on the envelopes and then, if she didn't like what she saw, dropped them at her feet. Sophie saw what Ellen was doing and considered asking her what she was looking for, but decided it didn't matter—if it was important enough, eventually Ellen would tell her anyway.

Not surprising to Sophie, most of the responses had nothing to do with finding or experiencing true happiness, but rather leaned toward what she described as "momentary fits of pleasure." Bobby, for example, a woman from Louisiana, described happiness as "a Harley, a helmet, and a tank full of nothing to do but ride." Amy from Boston wrote that happiness is "a week on Bermuda's pink sandy beaches," while a man from Idaho, who identified himself as Uncle

Rico Incarnate, asserted that "true happiness is that magical point in time where *Napoleon Dynamite* finally starts to make sense."

No one was surprised at the number of letters that mentioned the word *family*, but Sophie dismissed them all, offering her own lack of living relatives as proof that families are too temporary to meet her criteria. Ellen seemed hurt by Sophie's vigorous claim that she had no family, but said nothing about it.

"I assume," said Randy, as the night wore on, "that hour-long massages are not going to count, right?" He was holding an egg roll in one hand and a letter in the other.

"Depends on who's giving the massage," Justin said flippantly.

Evalynn was sitting close enough to her husband to slug him in the arm. "You'd better be thinking about *me*," she warned, "or you're in serious trouble."

"No," confirmed Sophie. "Massages are definitely out."

Randy's eyes lit up. "Sweet," he drawled. "Then can I keep this coupon? A spa in Seattle sent you a complimentary one-hour hot rock session."

Sophie smiled and held out her hand to take the coupon. "It's not happiness, but that doesn't mean it's not extremely enjoyable."

A little while later Justin found a note from a woman in Texas that he thought was worthy of at least the Maybe pile. "Here, Ev," he said, handing her a small piece of paper that was clipped to a wallet-size photo of an infant. "I think you could use this. It says happiness is the love and pride one feels for their children."

Evalynn turned instantly red. When she stood up in place, Sophie noticed that a vein on the side of her neck was sticking out abnormally. Leaning down directly in her husband's face, Evi whispered something through gritted teeth that nobody could make out but him, and then she turned and left. A few seconds later they heard the front door of the store slam behind her.

Everyone sat in stunned silence.

"What was that about?" Garrett asked eventually.

"It's complicated," said Justin, obviously upset with himself. "I shouldn't have mentioned it in front of all of you. She's not mad at what I said—she's just upset that you all heard it. She doesn't want anyone to know."

"Know what?" Sophie asked.

Justin smirked. "I'm not sure I should say. She's told me to keep it between me and her, but I keep telling her she needs to share her worries with her family."

Sophie looked back and forth between Justin and Garrett, and then her eyes landed on Ellen, who was holding three letters in her hand and looked like she wanted to cry.

"I already know," Ellen whispered. "I've known for a while now."

"I wondered," replied Justin, "but I didn't want to come right out and ask, just in case you didn't. Did she tell you?"

Ellen shook her head. "Not directly. But she's said enough here and there for me to infer."

"Know *what*?" Sophie asked again. "What's going on?" Though she already had a pretty good hunch of what was bothering Evalynn, she still wanted either Justin or Ellen to confirm her suspicion.

Justin looked at Ellen and nodded, as if giving her permission to enlighten the others.

Swallowing a lump in her throat, Ellen said, "Evi just... isn't sure she wants to be a mom. And given that she's four months pregnant, that puts her in quite a jam."

Justin nodded. "It's been rough. I thought she'd see it different once she was pregnant, but if anything it's gotten worse."

"Is she afraid of the labor pains or something?" Randy asked.

"No, nothing like that," said Ellen.

"Then what?" Randy asked.

At first, nobody spoke. Then Ellen sat up in her chair and tried to smile. "Ever since she was left in my care, she's had this notion that her mother just up and abandoned her—that she wasn't loved. I told her time and again, until I was blue in the face, her mother did what she did out of love. But that concept never took root. Eventually I decided that even if I couldn't convince her that her natural mother had loved her, I could at least show her that *I* loved her. I hoped that would be enough. And to some extent, it was. But now that she's pregnant, she's worried that maybe she'll be more like her natural mother and less like me. She's afraid that she won't love her child."

Justin gave a confirming nod.

Ellen fidgeted with the three letters in her hands, then continued speaking. "I could tell Evi was struggling by the way she skirted around the fact that she was pregnant. So for the past couple months I've been trying to find a way to *prove* to her, once and for all, that she was wrong about her mother not loving her. Because her mom died a number of years ago, I couldn't go straight to the source, but I think I've found an eyewitness, of sorts, who agreed to send a personal account of Evi's mom. That's what I was looking for in this big mess tonight, but I haven't stumbled across it yet."

Now Sophie, Justin, and Garrett looked as confused as Randy had just a few minutes earlier.

"What?" asked Justin.

Ellen handed him the three letters she was holding. "They're all from a woman's prison about thirty minutes northeast of here. I did some digging into Evi's mother's past and found her best friend from high school, a woman named Carly. I met with her last month and explained who I was, and she said she'd help out any way she could. So when the whole want ad thing took off, I figured Evi would be reading the responses, too, which made this an easy way to get this woman's story to her without anyone knowing I had a hand in it." She paused and looked at Sophie. "I know how you girls hate me meddling. Anyway, several other inmates decided that they wanted to send letters, too, just as a way to pass the time. I've found a few of them, but I haven't found Carly's yet."

Justin stared at the letters. "And you think what Carly has to say will help Evalynn?"

Ellen shrugged. "Can't be sure, but I like to think so."

"Then we should all look for it," suggested Garrett. He looked directly at Sophie and added, "Together."

Everyone agreed. It took twenty minutes of concerted effort, but finally Sophie stood up excitedly and declared, "Found it!"

As much as she wanted to open it, Sophie knew it wasn't for her. She handed it to Justin.

"Thanks," he said. "I'd better go track her down. Hopefully she's had enough time to cool off. I think we'll just head straight home once I find her. You guys gonna be okay here without us?"

Sophie nodded. "Actually," she said, looking around at the mess, "we've probably all had enough fun for one night. We'll just clean up a bit and then call it good for now." She thanked him for all their help, and then Justin took off in search of Evi.

"How you doing?" Justin asked, as he sat down next to his pregnant wife on a bench two blocks up the road. "I was getting worried about you." He could tell she'd been crying.

"Been better," she said, refusing to look at him.

He put an arm around her, half-expecting her to swat it away. "I'm sorry," he offered. "That was a stupid thing for me to say back at Soph's."

She didn't disagree.

"I brought you something," he continued. "It came in with Sophie's mail, but it's really for you."

"It's not even opened," she replied, as she took the letter from him. "Why do you think it's for me?"

"Just a hunch," he said. "Call me psychic."

"Psycho, maybe."

Justin chuckled. "So, you going to read it?"

Now Evalynn turned her eyes to meet Justin's stare. "You honestly think this letter is for me?"

He smiled. "Only one way to find out."

"If it's for me, then why did it come to Sophie?"

"I'll explain later," he promised. "Just read, Ev."

Evalynn didn't say anything more. Flipping the letter over, she carefully slid a long fingernail beneath one edge of the adhesive flap, just behind the stamp, until the paper tore. Then she ran the same nail along the full length of the envelope, carefully pulled out a stack of folded papers from within, and began to read.

Chapter 23

To shoulder the responsibility for a mistake is noble.
Less noble, of course, than not messing things up in the first place.

October 26, 2009

To Whom It May Concern:

I recently saw your ad in the Seattle Times, in search of happiness. I have to say, it made me laugh. Thank you for that—I don't often have good reasons to laugh. I have even fewer reasons to be happy. But that's not to say I don't know a thing or two about happiness. If you saw me, you'd probably think I was the most miserable woman alive. My life is not grand. It is not even fulfilling, in the typical sense. It is what it is, and I have accepted that. But along the road to the 12×12 cell that I currently call home, I have had glimpses into what happiness is, and I'd like to share.

I think to fully appreciate where I'm going with this, you need to understand my past. It's a colorful past, to say the least. Not to lean on excuses, but my childhood was far from ideal. No—that's being too generous. It was crap, pure and simple. My parents were dirt-poor, so we had next to nothing growing up. That alone would have been fine.

I didn't need material things (though three meals a day would have been nice), because they don't last. Let's face it, even the fanciest designer jeans can only be worn a few times before they start to fade or rip up the back. What I wanted was something that remained—something permanent.

I wanted love.

Do I think my parents didn't love me? Who knows. They cared for me, I guess, at some level. But I wasn't their first priority. That distinction belonged solely to "Mary Jane and the hero," which is who they said they were going to visit whenever they wanted to get stoned (which was pretty much any time that they weren't already high). My parents wasted almost every penny they got on drugs; heroin mostly (the hero), but they dabbled in everything, so long as it buzzed.

I was just a hair older than ten when Mom and Dad invited me to join them to smoke pot (Mary Jane) for the first time. Before that I'd settled for the euphoria that came from breathing the air around them. From then on, they gave me an "allowance" of illegal substances, but only if all my chores and homework were done. It was all very twisted. The two people who should have been protecting me from harm were using drugs as a carrot to get me to do things. But it worked—I made sure the house was spotless, and my grades were always solid, and I was "rewarded" for it.

I never really had close friends as a little girl, because other parents were smart enough to keep their kids far away from our family. No birthday parties with other children, no sleepovers—nothing really that resembled a normal childhood. My first real friend didn't come along until I was a freshman in high school. She was a good student—very smart—and pretty. She wasn't really the type who should have been hanging out with the likes of me, but I didn't question why—I was just glad to have someone to talk to during lunch.

In time, I came to understand that she faced trials that were far greater than my own. Unlucky her. I won't burden you with the details, but her stepfather should have been skinned alive for what he did to her.

Between our freshman and sophomore years, while my parents were at work, I invited my friend to my house, and did something to her that I have always regretted. Ignoring the obvious fact that she had enough problems to worry about already, I stupidly added to them by sticking a joint in her mouth and teaching her how to properly inhale. I thought it would help dull the pain of other things in her life. Unfortunately, it did. She took to drugs like a maggot to a turd, and soon everything else in her life became crap as well.

Before long, she was paying me to steal drugs from my parents. Later, when my family's leftovers were not enough, she would steal things from stores to earn money to buy her own smack from dealers on the street.

I've always struggled with what I did to my friend. I knew that drugs wouldn't really help her, but I gave them to her anyway. Still, I couldn't have imagined back then that I was kick-starting a habit that would one day kill her.

By now you're probably asking yourself what any of this has to do with happiness. Like I said, I've had glimpses–thanks to my friend, who showed me that happiness is sometimes the saddest thing in the world.

A few years after high school my friend became pregnant. She loved her daughter like crazy. Only problem was, she couldn't ditch the drugs that I'd introduced her to. She tried, believe me. She sought all sorts of help, and would go clean for periods of time, but she always relapsed. Eventually she landed in jail on drug-related charges, and her daughter wound up in foster care. It tore my friend apart. She wanted to be with her daughter so bad. Four months later she got out of jail and was told she had to stay clean for another two months to get her daughter back. Physically, it nearly broke her, but she stayed clean so she could see her daughter. I was with my friend when she went with the state's social worker to pick up her daughter from the foster mother. We were to meet them at a park. But when we pulled up, my friend saw her daughter playing on the playground with another little girl, just as happy and healthy as can be.

"She's the best girl in the world, isn't she?" she asked me. I agreed one hundred percent.

Other than her daughter, my friend hadn't had much happiness in her life. While she watched that little girl of hers on the swing, she started to cry. "She deserves better than me," she said. "She needs someone who will keep her out of trouble and give her a future." Then my friend looked right at me and asked, "How much do you think I love my Little Angel?" That was what she called her; or sometimes, "Angel Ev."

"A hell of a lot more than my parents loved me," I told her.

"That's a fact," she said quietly. Then she promptly told the social worker to go see what the foster mother would think about making the foster situation more permanent.

The biggest tears I've ever seen cried were those of my friend when we pulled away from that park without her little girl. But they were tears of happiness. She was glad to be able to give her daughter a gift. A gift of stability and safety. A life free from her own demons.

That was almost twenty years ago. I hope to God that that little girl, "Angel" Evalynn, knows how much her mom loved her.

I've thought a lot about happiness since reading your ad in the paper, and I can't think of greater happiness than this: Having the courage, like my friend Marion, to do the hard thing for those you love, even if it breaks your heart.

Carly Gibbs

Chapter 24

Life will throw you an unpleasant curve.

THE DAY IMMEDIATELY FOLLOWING THE GROUP MAIL-sorting session, Garrett stopped by Chocolat' de Soph uninvited, over lunch, to help continue the effort. Sophie tried hard to convey how annoyed she was by his presence, but for all her frowns, glares, rolling eyes, and sideways glances, he wasn't dissuaded. In fact, he managed to keep smiling the entire hour he was there, politely deflecting her occasional gibes. And if that weren't enough, he had the gall to show up after work for more of the same.

Randy was busy in the evening for long periods of time helping customers, which left Sophie alone with Garrett longer than she would have liked. But the more time they spent alone, the more she remembered how much she enjoyed his company. On more than one occasion she caught herself admiring his dimples or relishing the sound of his voice. She quickly scolded herself in each instance for the lack of self-restraint.

Their conversation lingered mostly on impersonal topics related to the mail that they were sorting, but occasionally Garrett would start a sentence with, "Remember when...?" which immediately sent Sophie's mind spiraling back to much happier times—times when she would never have felt self-conscious for stealing second glances at Garrett when he bent over to pick something up off the floor. After the third *Remember when*, Sophie told herself she'd better take control of the conversation or risk losing control of her emotions.

"So did you catch any of the news coverage of me at the post office?" she asked while tearing open a pink envelope from St. Louis.

"I have it recorded," he responded with a laugh. "I can't believe they bought that guy's story."

"Yeah, thank heavens for Jim. He saved both of us a lot of unwanted attention."

Garrett leaned against a counter. "Is he really homeless?"

Sophie nodded, then explained how she'd met the man a year earlier and how they'd established a weekly Misfortune Cookie rendezvous.

"Do you know how he knew what was going on with the whole want ad frenzy?" he asked.

She dropped a letter on the No pile. "I do. He came by yesterday and explained the whole thing. Turns out that was about the only truthful thing he told reporters that day. He really did read about the want ad in the newspapers he was using to sleep on. He knew which post office was listed in the ad, so when he saw the group of reporters hounding me he made the connection and jumped in to help."

"Thank goodness. He deserves a reward, if you ask me. He really threw you a lifeline."

"I know. I told him yesterday he can have chocolates for life any time he comes in the store. But you should have seen him when he came in. The only way I recognized him was from the toothless grin. He's all cleaned up, new clothes and everything. Since his little press conference, people all over are sending in donations to a fund that Channel Two set up for him. He's already got an apartment and a part-time job, and he says a car dealership has offered him a free used car in exchange for helping them at a promotional event."

"You're kidding."

She shook her head.

"Unbelievable." Garrett smiled affectionately at Sophie.

Sophie returned the smile, but when she realized what she was doing she immediately wiped it away, fearing that he might take it to mean that she was enjoying being with him—which she wasn't. Was she?

Around eight o'clock Garrett and Sophie each opened one last letter, quickly scanned what was written, and then dropped them on the No pile.

"Mine was from a guy in Pennsylvania who said happiness is a roll of toilet paper when you're lost in the woods," quipped Garrett. "Yours?"

"Waking up every morning next to the same man for thirty-six years... and counting."

He gave her a funny look. "And you don't think that qualifies as happiness?"

"What?" she said, shrugging.

"Seriously, you're not going to count that? I'd give anything to have... someone... that I could rely on to be there every day, and to have that kind of love and trust for so long."

"Oh, really," she fired back, trying to keep her emotions in check. "Well I'm sorry to remind you, but you could have had that, and you walked away from it."

He dropped his gaze. "I know."

She waited to see if he was going to say anything else. "But I think you're misinterpreting what she wrote. If you boil down the words, all she really said was that happiness is 'waking up.'

And I'm not really a morning person, so...no, definitely not happiness."

Garrett lifted his gaze and chuckled. "You're a hard nut to crack, Sophie Jones."

She crossed her arms and shot him a look, miffed at the way her name rolled causally off his tongue, as though things between them had never been better. "Hard to crack, maybe. But of the two of us, I'm not the nut."

He laughed again, then looked around at the piles of mail. "So what now?"

Sophie followed his attention to the mounds of envelopes on the kitchen floor. The largest, by far, was the No pile, followed by a modest amount of maybes. The letters deemed promising were fewest in number, but Sophie guessed that even that stack totaled well over two hundred pieces. And there was still one more mail carton full of letters they'd not yet opened.

A little farther away was an unofficial fourth pile of random items that had been set aside during the sorting process. These were things that Sophie would never count as examples of happiness, but everyone wanted to keep them out so they could easily see all the strange objects that people had sent in. On top of that pile was a well-worn Birkenstock sandal, its cork mostly gone near the heel, which had sparked a lengthy discussion the night before when Garrett, ever the podiatrist, argued that it should be lumped in the Promising pile because "the road to happiness is best walked with happy feet." Among other items in the pile were a wooden spoon, ticket stubs to the circus, a Neil Diamond CD, a catalog of gourmet-roasted coffee beans, a picture of Bill and Hillary Clinton, and a handful of unopened packets of Taco Bell hot sauce.

"Now," she replied, "I'll take these home and see how many pass my judgment." She straightened and put a rubber band around the smallest pile of letters. "The nos can be tossed in the trash right now. We can leave the maybes in my office until I've had a chance to go through the first stack. And I guess I'll take some of these, as well." She sighed as she grabbed a thick handful of unopened letters from the bin.

Garrett nodded once. "Fair enough." He looked at his watch. "The last express to Gig Harbor has already left," he said. "Can I give you a lift? Might beat carrying all this mail around on an hour-long loop through the city."

Sophie really didn't want to be alone with Garrett in the car. The last time she'd sat in a car with him had been in her driveway on the night he nixed the wedding and drove away. But he was right—taking all that mail on an hour-long bus ride would be a pain. And if she hurried home, there might still be time to go see how Evi was doing. "Fine," she said unenthusiastically. "But only out of convenience."

He smiled generously. "Great."

Sophie turned away and began gathering her things. "Oh, stop flaunting your dimples," she muttered quietly to herself.

ON THE DRIVE to her house, Sophie dialed Evi's number on her cell phone. She hadn't talked to her foster sister since she'd stormed out of the store the night before. She would have called sooner, but she wanted to give Evi some time to digest whatever the inmate from the penitentiary had written in her letter.

"Hey Soph," Evi answered. "I was wondering when I'd hear from you."

"You sound good. Everything okay?"

There was a brief pause. "Actually...yeah. More than okay."

"So...the letter? What did it say?"

"Why don't you come over, and I'll let you read it. Got time?"

Sophie turned to Garrett and whispered, "Can you drop me

off at Evi's instead?" He nodded. "Yep," Sophie said into the phone. "I'll be there in a few."

Fifteen minutes later Sophie was seated on the couch in the Macks' living room reading the letter from Evi's birth mom's best friend. When she was done, she brushed away a tear that had run all the way down to her chin and said, "Crap. I think I'm going to have to count this toward Garrett's hundred." She looked back and forth between Justin and Evalynn. "So... Ev. Do you think this will... I mean... are you going to be okay? With the whole mom thing?"

Evalynn bit her lip and looked at Justin. Then she squeezed his leg with one hand and rubbed her belly with the other. Looking at Sophie once more she replied, "The letter answered a lot of things for me—questions that have plagued me for a long time." She looked at Justin again and smiled. "I think things are going to be fine."

"You're going to be a great mom," Sophie assured her. "I have no doubt."

"I've been telling her that forever," Justin chimed in, "but it took a letter from a convicted felon to get her to listen to reason. Go figure." He winked playfully at Evalynn, then addressed Sophie again. "Well, before we have to send the prego lady here off to bed, did you want some more help with the letters?"

The corners of Sophie's mouth curled into a frown. "I hate to be a burden. I'm likely going to reject them all anyway, so no sense wasting your time."

"Oh c'mon," Justin prodded. "What can it hurt? Just let us give our opinions on them before you make your final decision. That way, if nothing else, at least you can tell Garrett there were accomplices in the process, and that you gave each response a fair shake."

Sophie considered the offer. On the one hand, she didn't want the decision making to be fettered by her friends' input, especially since neither of them would have to suffer through a date with her ex-fiancée should she find one hundred good responses. But on the other hand, she was enjoying their company, and the thought of spending the rest of the evening alone picking through sappy letters from strangers was not altogether appealing. "Fine," she said. "But only until Ev starts looking tired."

With that, Sophie began going one by one through the letters. Regardless of length she read the notes aloud in their entirety, gave Evi and Justin a chance to weigh in, and then made her final decision. Besides the letter from Carly Gibbs, the first letter to meet Sophie's highly subjective criteria was from a man in Wichita, Kansas, who offered sound reasoning, backed by examples from his own life, to support the claim that happiness is "the consequence of exercising one's right to choose between good and bad, and choosing the good."

After another thirty minutes, only a small handful of letters had received Sophie's reluctant stamp of approval, and she was rapidly gaining confidence that she would be able to coast guilt free through the stack without coming even close to the number of acceptable responses needed to meet the terms of the deal.

By five minutes to ten Sophie had finished with the ones they thought had promise, and was working on the stack of unopened mail. She grabbed the next envelope from the pile, noting that it had been sent from Bellevue, Washington, about thirty minutes northeast of Tacoma. Of all the envelopes she'd read, this one was by far the lightest in weight; as she lifted it, she wondered whether there was anything in it at all, or if, perhaps, someone had sent an empty envelope. Ripping the top seam, she observed that there was, indeed, something in it, albeit very small. Her brow furrowed as she carefully tipped the envelope up at an angle, sending its contents fluttering onto the floor in front of her.

Looking at the paper that had fallen out, Sophie's brow shifted instinctively from furrowed to frightened. For one who worked with them on a daily basis, there was no mistaking the small, rectangular shape of a fortune cookie message. She knew right off that it wasn't from Chocolat' de Soph because she'd always written hers by hand with a fine calligraphy pen, and this one was typed. It was also clear that this fortune had seen better days. The paper was wrinkled and worn, and the letters were smeared and somewhat blurry.

With a strange sense of foreboding, Sophie picked it up and read the tiny message, gasping aloud as recognition set in. She flipped it over and then froze. The only thing that moved as she stared at the back of the fortune was a small tear that worked itself free from her eye and trickled down her face.

At length, Sophie brushed away the dampness on her cheek and closed her hand around the paper, then looked up at the perplexed faces of Justin and Evalynn.

"Soph? What's wrong?"

Sophie's gaze narrowed on Justin. "I need to talk to Evi alone," she said in a hoarse whisper.

"Of course," he replied, standing up immediately. He put his hand on his wife's shoulder. "I'll just be down the hall if you need anything."

"I need you to be totally honest with me, Evi," said Sophie, once Justin was out of sight. "And this may sound a little strange, but...do you know how my parents died?"

Evalynn shot her a confused glance. "Of course. In a car accident."

"I know, but do you have any idea what caused it?"

Another questioning look. "The weather, right?"

"Have you ever talked with Ellen about it in private?"

"Maybe. Probably."

"Well did she ever mention that something...or someone, was partially to blame for what happened?"

"No. Sophie, what are you getting at?"

Sophie glanced down at her clenched fist. In her mind, she recalled having clutched the paper like that once before. "I want to tell you something, but you have to swear not to ever tell anyone else."

"I promise."

"Not even your hubby?"

Evalynn looked back over her shoulder and whispered, "Trust me, there's plenty that Justin doesn't know."

Sophie took a deep breath. She'd wanted to share her secret with Evalynn for years, but had never built up the nerve. Knowing that she would need her foster sister's help to figure out why the old fortune had mysteriously shown up in the mail—and who had sent it—she decided it was time to share her burden. For the next twenty minutes Sophie retold, in terrifying detail, the sequence of events on the night of her ninth birthday that led up to the deaths of her mother, father, and grandmother.

Evalynn sat mesmerized, at times looking like she might burst into tears herself.

Sophie gave extra attention to her own role in the birthday nightmare, explaining how silly she'd been for believing that the fortune would come true.

When she was done, Evalynn scooted over and put her arms around Sophie in a giant hug. "You can't blame yourself for what happened. There's a reason that they're called accidents. It wasn't your fault, Sophie." She pulled back. "If you've held this inside for so long, why are you telling me now?"

Sophie pursed her lips. "Because," she replied slowly, staring once more at her hand, "even though it was an accident, I *do* own most of the blame." She let her fingers fall open. "And somebody out there knows it."

Evalynn took the fortune from Sophie's hand and read the message. *"Happiness is a gift that shines within you. The wish of your heart will soon come true."* She looked up. "It was twenty years ago—how can you even remember it? Maybe your message was just similar. Besides, they print these things by the thousands. This could just be a coincidence."

Sophie rolled her eyes. "The only thing coincidental is that it got back to me by way of Garrett's stupid happiness want ad. But the creepy part is that it really is my fortune from that night. Not just the same message. *It's the same piece of paper!*"

Evalynn gave Sophie a look of doubt. "How can you be sure?"

"Flip it over," Sophie said, her voice ringing with dread.

Evalynn gasped so hard when she saw what was written on the back that she nearly choked. In faded pencil were the words, *Sophia Maria Jones, September 21, 1989*. "No! This is some sort of a joke! It has to be."

"If it is, I don't see the humor."

"The only person you told was Ellen?"

"That's all I remember. Well, maybe I told the shrink about it when I was a kid, but no one else."

"So you think Ellen had something to do with sending this to you?" Evalynn asked.

Sophie shrugged. "I don't know. I mean, I'd like to think that she wouldn't, but she did dig in your past to get that letter sent from Carly, so who knows?" Sophie hesitated, trying to sort it out in her mind. "Still... something doesn't add up."

"What?"

"I threw it away! I wadded it up and threw it away, and Ellen was right there with me and watched it float away."

"Exactly," Evi replied. "She was there, and she was the only person who even knew you had it. Plus, it came to your PO box, and only a few of us knew the responses were coming to you. So she must have something to do with this." Evalynn checked her watch, then grabbed Sophie by the hand and stood up. "C'mon, Sophie."

"Where are we going?"

"For your sanity, I think we need to go pay Ellen a little visit."

"But it's after ten o'clock," Sophie protested. "It'll be eleven before we get there, and she goes to bed early."

Evalynn gave Sophie her *Don't argue with me* look. She asked if Sophie thought either of them would be able to sleep until they got a little more information.

Sophie sighed. "Probably not."

"Well if we can't sleep tonight, then our dear foster mom shouldn't get to sleep, either."

Chapter 25

Happiness rightly eludes you.

YOU OKAY?" EVALYNN ASKED, AS SHE AND SOPHIE GOT out of Evi's car in front of Ellen's apartment on the outskirts of Seattle's east side.

It was ten minutes to eleven, and the cold evening wind was starting to whip around. Sophie zipped up her jacket to just below the chin and nodded, but kept her eyes fixed on the four-story building. It looked as beat-up and run-down as ever. The bricks that covered the exterior of the first two floors were dirty and worn, with small vines creeping in and out of the cracks and fissures in the mortar joints. The top two floors were solid concrete, painted a bland color that approximated the gray of the mortar. Large patches of paint were peeling off, especially near the top of the west end, where a broken gutter had allowed excess water to run down the side of the building for the majority of the previous fall and winter.

Sophie had always wondered why her foster mother chose

to live there when she could have afforded something a little nicer, especially after Sophie and Evalynn moved out. When Sophie asked about it a few years back, Ellen explained that all her best memories were there. "My little chicks may have flown the coop," she added, "but the coop still suits me fine."

"Welcome home," Evalynn whispered softly, leading the way through the building's exterior door.

The inside of the complex wasn't as dilapidated as the outside, simply because the tenants cared enough to keep it up. Whereas nobody, including the landlord, wanted to cough up the big bucks for new bricks or paint on the outside, the building dwellers didn't mind spending a few dollars here and there to keep the hallways neat and clean.

Both Sophie and Evalynn had keys to apartment number 309, but since the clock was encroaching on Ellen's typical sleep schedule, they chose to ring the bell.

There was a small delay before a faint, "Who is it?" came from one of the back rooms. "Knock once if friend, twice if foe." That was Ellen's standard response whenever someone rang the doorbell or knocked unexpectedly. Sophie and Evalynn both knew that was just her way of stalling to make sure her firearm was nearby.

Sophie knocked three times.

"Evalynn? Is that you? Or is it Sophie?"

Evalynn and Sophie exchanged brief glances as they listened to the sound of footsteps moving quickly from the kitchen, across the main room, and up to the door. The deadbolt clicked as it was twisted, and then the door flew open.

"Both of my chickadees!" Ellen nearly leapt out of her police boots, which she still wore following an extended shift at the precinct downtown. She grabbed Sophie in a giant hug and pulled her into the apartment, then did the same with Evalynn. "What on earth are you girls doing here so late at night? Never mind. When was the last time we were all in this apartment at the same time? Seems like a year or more. What a treat!" She gave Sophie another little squeeze, but as she did so Ellen couldn't help noticing that neither of her visitors were as excited as she was.

The three women moved together through the living room to the kitchen and took seats around the small, circular dining table. Ellen glanced nervously between Sophie and Evalynn, as though she sensed that the news they'd come to share so late at night was not good.

Sophie ran her hand along the table's wooden surface. She could still make out engraved letters and words from where she and Evalynn had pressed too hard with their pens while doing homework as teenagers. Following the contour of her own name in the surface of the wood with her index finger, she looked up at Ellen and forced a smile, but didn't speak.

"I had fun going through all that mail last night," said Ellen softly, as soon as the silence became uncomfortable. "Have you found any good ones yet?"

"A couple," Sophie replied.

As more silence ensued, Sophie's eyes walked around the room that she'd spent so much time in during her youth. It felt smaller than it had when she was little. Even though the family room was the biggest space in the apartment, the kitchen had always been their gathering place. They ate there, talked there, studied there, and watched TV there, and sometimes they managed to do all of those things there at the same time. Sophie wondered how many hours of her childhood had been spent sitting in the very chair she now occupied.

Invariably, thoughts of her youth rewound all the way back to the day she first arrived at the home of Officer Ellen Monroe. Sophie recalled how hard it was raining outside; even harder than the night she'd first met Ellen on the side of the road in

Seattle. The water fell in heavy sheets that day, pelting the side of the apartment building at a forty-five-degree angle. The social worker had an umbrella for herself, but didn't offer to share, so by the time Sophie dragged her suitcase from the back-seat of the social worker's car to the front door of the apartment building, she was drenched from head to toe, her blonde curls plastered like wet noodles against her forehead.

Sophie remembered the reluctance with which she carried her suitcase up the stairs to the third floor. The social worker was in a bit of a hurry, but Sophie took her time. It was already her fourth trip to a new foster home in the short span of five months, and she was in no hurry to meet her next "family."

The first home she'd been placed in was intentionally brief; just a week or so to allow her caseworker time to find a good, long-term match, perhaps even an adoptive situation. When no such match was found, Sophie was moved to the home of a single mom named Marion Mason, who was taking in children as a way to milk the state for a little extra cash. Social Services eventually figured out that the woman was using the money to support a drug habit, so seven weeks after arriving there, Sophie and another foster child, plus the woman's own biological daughter—a precocious little girl named Evalynn—were picked up in a white van and delivered to new locations throughout northern Washington.

Sophie's stop was the last of the day, way up north in Everett. She landed with some very nice empty-nesters, the Bards, who took in children from time to time out of the goodness of their hearts, simply because they knew there was a need. Unfortunately for Sophie, the husband's heart was good only in the metaphorical sense; Mr. Bard suffered a major heart attack right around the two-month anniversary of Sophie's arrival. Sophie watched in horror from a stool in the kitchen as emergency workers used a defibrillator in the middle of the living room to try to jump-start his heart before they wheeled him away. Mrs. Bard was crying hysterically. Nobody ever came right out and said how Mr. Bard's trip to the hospital ended up, but based on the fact that nobody ever said, Sophie assumed the worst.

Later that night, in the middle of a rainstorm, Sophie's caseworker showed up and told her to pack her things. They drove south for a while along the interstate, took a Seattle exit, and eventually pulled up in front of Ellen's building. After a brief walk in the drowning din, followed by a slow climb to the third floor, a dripping, shivering Sophie knocked for the first time on door 309.

"Knock once if friend, twice if foe," called a friendly voice from within. Sophie looked up at the caseworker, puzzled, and shrugged. The woman told her to knock once. A moment later the door peeled open, and there, to Sophie's very pleasant surprise, was a familiar face staring back at her. Ellen, the police officer who'd first approached her in the aftermath of the accident, and the same woman who had showed her kindness at her parents' funeral, was standing in the doorway, beaming. She had her arms open wide, and scooped Sophie up in a giant hug. With Ellen's big, black arms around her, Sophie's heart felt warmer than it had in months.

"I have a secret," Ellen said, smiling, as she squatted down to Sophie's level. "Don't tell anyone, but it's three knocks for family. Okay? If you ever have to knock, that's your number now." Sophie nodded as Ellen hugged her again and pulled her the rest of the way into the apartment.

Evalynn arrived about a month later, right after her mom was sent to prison on multiple drug and fraud charges. The state had approached Ellen about taking in a second child because she and Sophie were so close in age. It was supposed to be a short-term deal, six months at most, but Evalynn's mother kept running into problems, and eventually it became a permanent situation. Since then, the black woman, white girl, and half-white Latina had been, in principle, a family.

"Sophie?"

The question from the other side of the table drew Sophie back to the present. She tilted her head and tried to smile. "Huh?"

Ellen smirked nervously. "You seem troubled, Sweets. Was there something you wanted to talk about?"

Sophie nodded, but didn't say anything further.

Ellen shifted uncomfortably in her chair. "You found out, didn't you?"

Evalynn and Sophie responded in unison. "Found out what?"

"That I called Channel Two about the want ad?"

"You!" exclaimed Sophie. "Why on earth would you do that?"

"Because," she said carefully, "I wanted you to have that date with Garrett, Sweets. Whatever else happens, I think you need to hear what he has to say. He wouldn't just show up after a year, unless it was important. You know me—I'm nosy. I want to know what he has to say as much as anyone, so I went to the news hoping to help the process along. But heavens, I couldn't have imagined the kind of response it's received." She hesitated. "Is that why you came?"

Sophie shook her head emphatically.

Ellen looked puzzled. "What then? You can tell me anything, Sophie. You know that, right?" She redirected her focus to Evalynn. "Is it serious? Does it involve both of you?"

"Not me," Evalynn responded. "I'm just the designated driver." She turned to Sophie. "You need to show her, Soph."

Nodding again, Sophie unzipped her purse and pulled out the envelope from Bellevue. "Ellen," she started, sliding the envelope across the table. "Do you recognize this address?"

Ellen squinted at the print. "Downtown Tacoma. Your PO box, right?"

"No, the return address. Who lives in Bellevue, Ellen?" Sophie was curter than she wanted to be with the woman who had done so much for her over the years, but she couldn't help it.

A look of confusion settled in Ellen's features. "Bellevue? I don't know anyone in Bellevue. Why? What is this, Sophie?"

"Open it up."

Ellen slid two fingers into the already-torn envelope and let the small paper fall out. It landed upside down, such that the handwritten words were facing up. "What the—?" she said, as she read the name and date. There was no questioning that she knew what day that was. A lightbulb seemed to flip on in her mind, like she'd just figured out what she was holding. She turned the paper over quickly and gasped. "Sophie," she said, looking a little ill. "I swear to you, I don't know anything about this."

Something inside Sophie broke loose. She pounded her fist on the table. "Then who? You were the only one, Ellen! The only one who knew about that fortune! Other than my parents, but they sure as hell didn't send it to me!"

"I don't...I mean...I'm just as surprised by this..." Ellen was caught off guard by Sophie's outburst and was fumbling for the right thing to say.

"Who did you tell? Just one person, or were there more? Did you tell people about the ad as well?"

Ellen was deeply hurt by the accusation. Her eyes got moist, just like they had on the first night she'd found Sophie sitting along the side of the road. "Sophie, I've *never* mentioned that fortune to a single soul. I can't begin to imagine how it ended up in your mail, let alone coming to the PO box, but I swear to you, I had nothing to do with it."

A moment of silence gave Evalynn an opportunity to speak

up. She wanted to turn the conversation around before Sophie said something she might regret later. "Thanks, Ellen. It's good to hear it straight from you."

Neither Sophie nor Ellen spoke.

"I know I'm the odd man out here," Evalynn continued, "seeing as I didn't find out about any of this until tonight, but I think we should—"

"You told her?" Ellen interrupted.

Sophie nodded. "I needed to tell someone. And I needed to find out if she'd already heard it from you."

"Good. I've told you for years: the more you share your burdens, the lighter they become. But I *never* told anyone, Sophie. I promise you that."

Evalynn spoke again. "I believe you, Ellen. Soph?"

Sophie's eyes darted between Evalynn and Ellen. Then she whispered, "Me too."

"Okay," Evalynn continued, breathing a sigh of relief. "Now that that's settled, I think the key is to figure out who sent it, and how they got it. Personally, I was kind of hoping that Ellen did have something to do with it. At least that would explain things. But now? It's sort of spooky."

Ellen picked up the envelope again. "I agree, Ev. And I think that's something I can help with. Give me a few minutes to make some calls." She stood up and left the kitchen.

"You okay?" Evalynn asked, once Ellen was out of the room.

"I'm fine," she replied, chuckling sardonically. "I haven't yelled at Ellen like that since she did a background check on Tom Potter before the homecoming dance our sophomore year."

Evalynn laughed. "Poor Tom. After that, I don't think he asked out another girl until he was well out of high school." She paused. "Well I thought you handled yourself very well tonight, given the circumstances."

"Thanks. I'm not any closer to knowing who sent it, but I'm at least relieved to know Ellen had nothing to do with it. She's the closest thing I have to a mother, and I'd have been crushed to think I could no longer trust her."

"Any other ideas about who might have sent it or where they would have gotten it from?"

"None whatsoever. But you know Ellen. If she says she can get the information, then I'm sure she will."

As promised, a few minutes later Ellen strode proudly back into the kitchen. "Got it!" she announced.

"That was fast," said Sophie.

"This one was easy-peasy. All I had to do was call up an old—"

Sophie didn't want to hear every little detail about the data chase. All growing up she'd listened to Ellen's lengthy explanations about the intricacies of tracking down perps, and she wasn't in the mood for that now. "Who sent it, Ellen?" she pressed diplomatically. "Cut to the chase."

"Fine," she responded, only slightly put off. "The return address on your envelope is the home of one Jacob Barnes. Ring any bells?"

Evalynn and Sophie both shook their heads.

Ellen grinned. "Well, it did for me. As soon as my guy downtown said the name, I knew who it was. But just to be sure, I checked a copy of an old police report that I keep in my desk. Anyone care to venture a guess as to what report that is?" She waited for responses, but all she got from either of her visitors was blank stares. "*The accident*, Sophie. He was listed as one of the people who sustained injuries."

"Jacob Barnes?" asked Sophie. "Do you remember him from that night?"

"Sweets," Ellen said as she took a seat next to Sophie and draped an arm around her shoulder. To Sophie, Ellen suddenly sounded more like a mother, and less like a cop. "The only thing I remember from that night is that I met you. The rest of the details are just a blur, along with the thousands of other accidents I've had the misfortune of witnessing in my twenty-three years on the force."

"Jacob Barnes," Sophie repeated, familiarizing herself with the name. "So if this Jacob Barnes was there, then he must have found my fortune after I tossed it. But how did he know that it was *my* fortune? It could have been anyone's."

"It's tough to say," remarked Ellen, as she withdrew her arm from Sophie's shoulder and placed it on her own lap. "But at least we know he was there, which explains how he got it."

"I'm no detective," quipped Evalynn, "but I think I know how we can find out how he knew it was yours, and why he wrote your name on the back. We know where the guy lives, right? I think we need to take a little trip to Bellevue. Sophie, are you game?"

Sophie nodded.

"Ellen?"

Ellen winked. "Me and my nine-millimeter would be happy to give you a police escort."

Chapter 26

If good people have good luck, and bad people have bad luck, why is it that you have dumb luck?

EVALYNN AND SOPHIE PICKED UP ELLEN SHORTLY AFTER lunch on the following Saturday, which was the first day that worked with all of their schedules. It meant that Sophie had to get Randy to cover a few extra hours at Chocolat' de Soph, but he was more than willing to help out. Justin had purchased a plug-in GPS unit for Evalynn on her last birthday, so finding the home of Jacob Barnes was a cinch. The device's female voice directed them off of the interstate after twenty-five minutes, and from there it was almost a straight shot up 150th Avenue to a development full of beautiful homes at the top of the hill near Saddleback Park.

"Wow," Ellen commented. "Jacob Barnes is doing well for himself."

"Destination on the…left…in point one miles," said the electronic female voice after Evalynn made a turn onto 54th Place.

Evalynn slowed the car and pulled to a stop near the curb. "You sure you're okay doing this, Sophie?"

"Yeah, Sweets," Ellen added from the backseat. "You're looking kind of flush."

Clutching the envelope that had been sent from the house across the street, Sophie tried to smile bravely. "I wasn't nervous until we pulled up. But now...?"

"I'm sure there's nothing to worry about," Evalynn said reassuringly.

Again, Sophie tried to grin. She turned to look at Ellen, and then again at Evalynn. "I know. It's not meeting Jacob Barnes that has my stomach in knots. It's more the thought of facing my past. It's just...weird, you know? After twenty years, to suddenly find out that some stranger has known all along that I played a part in the accident."

"You don't know that's what he's thinking."

"I know—I can feel it. Why else would he have sent that fortune back to me? He must have seen me on the news and somehow recognized me and figured out I was the one who placed the ad."

Ellen reached forward and rubbed Sophie's shoulder. "I've told you since you were nine that you can't blame yourself. Maybe meeting Mr. Barnes will help that to finally sink in."

"Maybe," Sophie said, but sounded doubtful. *Or maybe he'll blame me, too, and reinforce my worst fear.*

With Ellen leading the way, the trio got out of the car and crossed the street. Sophie tried to ignore the woman in the house next door who was watching them like a hawk from her front window as they walked up the steep driveway. She also noticed that no cars were in the drive, and silently hoped that meant nobody was home.

Ellen marched straight up to the door without a moment's hesitation and rang the doorbell. Sophie and Evalynn took a fallback position a few feet behind her.

Several moments later, a stout little man with a large round face opened the door. He had almond-shaped eyes and a grin that stretched from one earlobe to the other. "Hello," he said with a funny accent. "Visitors. I love visitors. I don't get too many of them, though." He paused before adding another, "Hello."

None of the three women needed to be told that the young man staring back at them had Down's syndrome. His happy demeanor put them instantly at ease. "Hi," Ellen said. "We're looking for Jacob Barnes. Is he around?"

The man scratched at his thick blond hair. "Is it really important?" he asked, smiling. "He's my dad. Maybe I can help you instead. I'm Alex." Alex glanced at Evalynn's sweatshirt and read the purple screen-printed words. "Washington State Dawgs."

Evalynn laughed with amusement. "That's right. Are you a fan?"

"No. But I like the word. D-A-W-G-S," he said, stretching out the sound of each letter. "But I don't think it's spelled right."

Sophie was watching the man intently. Something about him felt strangely familiar. "Alex, have we met before?" she asked.

He shrugged. "I don't know. Have you ever shopped at Albertsons? I work there. Lots of people shop at Albertsons. They buy groceries." He pointed at the mascot on Evi's chest. "And dog food." He paused once more to think. "And magazines with Britney Spears or Oprah on the cover."

Sophie chuckled. "Maybe that's it."

Ellen laughed, too, as she opened up her police badge that was clipped to her hip. Even when she wasn't in uniform, she always carried her badge, just in case. On more than one occasion it had saved her from getting a speeding ticket after being pulled over. "Alex, my name is Officer Monroe, and I work with the Seattle Police department."

He seemed fascinated by the badge, reaching out to run his fingers over its shiny surface. "Cool. A cop."

"My friend here," Ellen continued, pointing to Sophie, "got a letter this week in the mail that has something in it that came from your dad."

Alex stared at Sophie quizzically. "*You're* the one looking for happiness? Cool."

"So you know about what was sent?" Sophie asked, holding up the envelope in her hands.

He looked at it briefly. "Uh-huh."

Sophie exhaled. "I'd like to talk to your father about it. Is he at home?"

"Nope."

"Will he be back soon?"

Alex's bright smile dimmed a little. "Nope."

Evalynn had been largely silent but finally spoke up. "Do you know where he is? If it's not too far, maybe we could pay him a quick visit."

Alex scratched his head again. "I know where he is. I don't know the address, but I could take you there."

Evalynn and Ellen looked to Sophie to see what she wanted to do. Having taken half the day off of work to meet Jacob Barnes, she wanted to make good use of her time, but she wasn't sure how she felt about involving Jacob's son. Before she could make up her mind, another person showed up at the house.

"Can I help you?" asked the woman, as she walked up the front steps. "I'm Meredith Sloan, from next door."

The hawk from the window, thought Sophie.

Ellen smiled. "No, I think we're okay. We just came to visit Mr. Barnes."

Meredith's demeanor shifted. "Well I'm not just Alex's neighbor. I'm also paid to look after him and help with his...special needs. So if there's something specific that you require, I'm probably the right person to work with."

Before Sophie, Ellen, or Evalynn could say anything further, Alex piped up. "It's okay, Meredith. She's a police officer."

Meredith straightened. "Oh my. Whatever happened, I'm sure Alex had nothing to do with it. He's a good kid."

"It's nothing like that," Ellen reassured. "This isn't official police business. More of a personal courtesy call."

Sophie stepped forward. "I was in an accident when I was a little girl, and Jacob Barnes was in it, too."

"Ah," Meredith said. "Probably the accident that took his fingers."

An image flashed in Sophie's head of a man lying on the ground staring up at his hand while an EMT worked to stop the bleeding where his fingers had been severed. "Yes," Sophie replied softly, "that's the one. We came today looking for a little more information about the accident, and Alex said—"

"They want to go visit my dad," Alex interjected. "Can I take them?"

Meredith looked more puzzled than ever. "You want to visit Jacob?"

All three women nodded. "If it wouldn't be a bother," said Sophie. "Alex says he knows how to get there."

"Yes, he knows quite well. Goes as often as he can." She looked at Alex, and then searched the faces of the visitors. "But I don't see what you're going to learn at the cemetery about a decades-old car accident."

"Cemetery?" Sophie blurted out, trading worried looks with Ellen. "Why on earth would we go to the—?" She stopped and stared at Meredith, confused. "Is Jacob Barnes...*dead*?"

Now Meredith looked confused, too. "You didn't know?" she said. "He passed away a few months ago. Lost a good fight with leukemia."

"Of course not... we... I mean, I got a letter in the mail and I just assumed..." She turned to face Alex again, and a new wave of recollection set in. "Which cemetery?" Sophie asked.

Alex looked to Meredith for the name. "Evergreen," she said. "It's up there off of—"

"Aurora Avenue!" said Sophie excitedly. "That's where I saw you! About a month ago, on my birthday. Sunglasses, right?"

"I always wear sunglasses there," Alex acknowledged.

"In case he cries," Meredith said under her breath. "So other people don't see."

Sophie remembered the brief but odd encounter with Alex in the moments before Evalynn showed up that night, and suddenly became concerned. "Alex, were you following me at the cemetery?"

He stuck his hands in his pockets. "I was there first. I don't think the first person can follow. Can they?"

Good point, she thought. Tucking a strand of hair behind her ear, Sophie stepped closer to Alex, who was still standing in the doorway of the house. Her expression was serious, but her tone was soft and gentle. "Alex, when I saw you, you weren't visiting your father. You were staring at the grave of *my parents*. What were you doing there?"

Everyone was silent, waiting for Alex to reply. "Reading," he said, matching Sophie's quiet voice. "'Husband and Father. Wife and Mother. Loved their daughter and each other fully and forever.' It's very nice. I memorized it. Dad showed it to me every time we went there. He said he met that daughter once." He looked at everyone in turn, his eyes landing on Sophie last of all. His voice dropped even further, but his face still shone with an innocent happiness. "I guess you must be her. Sophia Maria Jones."

Chapter 27

A poor conclusion is simply the place where you got tired of thinking.

Everyone on the Barnes front porch stood in awkward silence.

Everyone, that is, except Alex. "Are we still going to visit my dad?" he asked. "Or do you want to come inside my house? Inside is warmer than outside, and I like warmer better."

"That's a good idea, Alex," Meredith said, taking a small step toward the door. "Maybe we should all go inside and sit for a bit. Would you ladies care for something to drink?"

Evalynn and Ellen both looked again to Sophie for direction. "That would be fine," Sophie said politely. "Thank you."

The house was even more spacious on the inside than it looked on the outside, with tall, vaulted ceilings and an open floor plan that made every room feel big. In the living room, most of the walls were lined with custom cherry cabinets, almost all of which were filled with books. To Sophie it looked like a small library. The only empty space was the end cabinet on the far wall, which was only half full.

"Wow," Sophie said, impressed. "Someone likes to read."

"Me!" Alex exclaimed proudly. "I've read every book here. Some more than once. Some even *more than* more than once."

"You're almost out of shelf space," commented Evalynn. "What are you going to do then?"

Alex gave Evalynn a funny look, as though trying to decide if the question was a joke. "Get more shelves," he said finally, without a hint of irony.

Sophie and Ellen laughed in unison. For her part, Sophie was beginning to feel a giant sense of relief. She'd been dreading facing Jacob Barnes, simply because she didn't know how he would react. Had he held deep animosity toward her for the past two decades? Was his life in shambles because of her selfish impatience as a child? But in place of the grumpy old man that she imagined she'd be meeting, there was Alex, whose happy disposition and innocent friendliness was about as threatening as a purring kitten.

Meredith went to fetch coffee, while the rest of the group took seats in the living room. Sophie and Evalynn shared the leather sofa, Ellen sat in the love seat, and Alex plopped down merrily in a thick suede recliner.

Once everyone was settled, Sophie was the first to speak. "Alex, I'm really sorry to hear that your father passed away. Just meeting you, I can tell I would have liked him."

Alex fidgeted with his fingers, but kept smiling. "Are you going to ask a lot of questions about him?"

"I'd like to ask a few, if that's all right with you."

His eyebrows jutted up and he scratched nervously at his ear. Then, without saying a word, he got up from his chair and shuffled over to a curved console in the entryway. In the top drawer was a pair of dark sunglasses. He put them on and then returned to the recliner. "Okay."

Sophie smiled warmly. "Okay, you said your dad took

you to the cemetery to visit my parents' grave. How often did you go?"

"Every year. The day after my birthday."

"Oh? When is your birthday?"

"September twenty."

Sophie made eye contact with Ellen on the love seat. "That's... the day before my birthday. So you went to the cemetery every year on September twenty-first?"

Alex leaned forward slightly in his chair and nodded. "On my birthday we always had a big party. Dad said the day I was born was the very, very most important day of his life. And the next day was the very most important one—*just one 'very.'* There were other important days too, but I can't remember them all. Except for Christmas. And Easter." He paused to smile. "And Valentine's. I remember those."

Evalynn smiled.

"Did he ever talk about the accident?" Sophie asked.

Meredith returned from the kitchen a few moments later with five coffee mugs and an assortment of herbal teas. "I forgot, we don't keep any coffee stocked here—it doesn't sit well with Alex. Is tea okay? If not, I can run over to my house and put a pot on."

"This is fine," Ellen said. "Thanks."

Meredith set everything on the coffee table and invited them to help themselves.

"What was your question?" Alex asked Sophie, once Meredith was seated.

"The accident that your father and I were in. Did he talk about it much? Maybe when you guys went to the cemetery?"

He shook his head. "Nope. Dad just said it was a day he would never forget. Mostly we just went there to take the stones."

Sophie sat up as she recalled the beautiful stones she found annually on the corner of her parents' gravestone. She saw out of the corner of her eye that the comment had caught

Evalynn's attention as well. "The rocks on the grave? That was you and your dad?"

"Uh-huh."

"Is that what you were doing there two weeks ago? Dropping off another rock?"

"Yes. Dad told me before he...*left*, that it would be nice to keep taking rocks each year. Now I leave them for Tom and Cecelia, Jacob, and Katherine, but not on the same days." Alex fiddled with his sunglasses to make sure they were still adequately covering his eyes. "A few years ago we figured out that if we went late enough in the day, we would find a piece of chocolate waiting there for me. Dad said that was my treat for taking the stones."

Ellen stopped stirring her cup of tea. "Who is Katherine?"

Alex didn't respond.

"Maybe I can field that one," offered Meredith. "In fact, since your family was obviously important to Jacob, perhaps a little history is deserved. I can't tell you much about the accident that you were involved in, but I knew pretty much everything else about the Barneses."

Evalynn and Sophie fixed themselves cups of orange spice tea while Meredith spoke. Alex sat listening behind the safety of his dark lenses.

"Jacob and Katherine Barnes were both lawyers," she continued. "Partners in a big firm downtown. When Katherine became pregnant they started searching for a full-time nanny who could help out once the baby arrived." Meredith smiled and took a sip of her tea. "They chose me just a week before he was born. Unfortunately," she glanced at Alex, as if looking for permission to continue, "it was a difficult labor. There were...*complications*. Katherine didn't make it."

The room was silent, except for the sound coming from Alex, who was fidgeting again with his ear.

Meredith shrugged. "So my role expanded somewhat for

those first few years, until Alex was old enough to go to school during the day. But when he was little, I did almost everything to keep the family going."

"And you've stayed on all these years?" Ellen asked.

She nodded. "The workload varied, depending on Alex's needs and Jacob's schedule. But Alex has always been such a joy to be around, I couldn't think of a better job. Eventually I got married and started my own family. I have two teenagers—and if I know them, they are probably fighting right now over the Wii at home—but I've always been able to balance my own life with the Barneses' needs. Once Jacob developed leukemia, he purchased the house next door so my family and I could be closer, basically to avoid having to move Alex to an assisted-living home once he was gone. I'm still technically an employee—I'm paid monthly from a trust—but I hardly feel like one. Alex is family, and that'll never change. My whole family adores him." She paused and looked directly at Alex, grinning proudly. "Everybody adores him."

Alex slid four fingers beneath the rim of his glasses to rub at his eyes.

Sophie stared at the tea bag that was still steeping in her cup. She thought about the old paper fortune she'd wanted to discuss with Jacob. Then she pulled her eyes from her warm drink and looked at Alex, considering all that he must've gone through in his life, starting on day one with the loss of his mother, followed by years of struggling with a disability, and recently losing his father to a terminal illness. A new sense of guilt coursed through her for the additional pain that she'd caused this family.

Without thinking about it, Sophie put her cup down and took a giant breath. She looked at Alex and Meredith. "This wasn't exactly why I came here today, but now that I'm here, I want you to know the truth. *I... am somewhat to blame for the accident twenty years ago that cut off Jacob's fingers.*" After adding a few details about how she was distracting her father while they were driving in the rain, she quickly pulled out the envelope with the old fortune-cookie message and held it out for them to see. "This was my fortune from my ninth birthday. I threw it away that night at the crash, right after I told a police officer—Ellen—that it was my fault. But somehow Jacob found it." Sophie took another moment to breathe while Meredith examined the fortune. "I can only assume that he overheard what I told Ellen, and then kept it all this time so he wouldn't forget who was responsible for crippling his hand. Anyway...I...I know I should have apologized to Jacob while he was still...around. But until this very moment, meeting both of you, I never had the nerve. So, I'm...very sorry."

Everyone let the words settle before making a sound. Meredith was the first to speak. "Ms. Jones, thank you for that. But honestly, I'm sure that Jacob did not blame you for what happened to his hand." She snickered. "Jacob was a good and honest man, but...well, let's just say he was a lawyer. If he'd thought someone was responsible for that accident, I can assure you there would have been lawsuits involved."

"Then why keep the paper all this time? And why write my name on the back of it?" She turned to Alex. "And as a sidebar—who mailed this out last week, anyway?"

Alex raised his hand and let his glasses slide to the end of his nose so everyone could see his eyes again. "I sent it. I saw the thingy on YouTube—Meredith sent it to me—about the newspaper ad, and I wanted to help. Dad always told me that happiness is a gift, and so I thought his paper might help someone—you, I guess—find it. Sorry."

"Oh, don't be sorry," Sophie said, backpedaling. "I just want to understand." She smiled warmly at Alex. "I'm actually really glad you sent it. Of all the things that people sent me, this is my favorite, because it led me here to meet you."

Alex adjusted the glasses that covered his eyes, but nothing could cover his giant smile.

"And as for why he kept that fortune all this time," Meredith said to Sophie, "I don't think you need to worry. Maybe he liked the message. Perhaps it gave him hope or lifted his spirits. But I can assure you that he didn't harbor any animosity toward you, Sophia."

"Can I ask something?" said Evalynn after a short span of quiet. "I'm still curious about the rocks on the grave. Is that like a religious thing?"

Meredith chuckled. "I don't think anyone would ever label Jacob Barnes as a religious man. But he had faith. He believed that he would see Katherine again, that she wasn't just gone. When I asked about the stones he always came up with a different answer. 'Just for decoration,' 'Because flowers wilt,' 'I like rocks,' that sort of thing. But on one occasion he said something that I thought was a little closer to the truth—'Rocks and memories last forever.' I think the rocks were just his way of memorializing the woman he loved."

Evalynn nodded, but Sophie looked puzzled. "Then why did he put them on my parents' grave?"

Meredith just shrugged. "Out of respect? I don't know. Alex, any ideas?"

He shook his head. "Nope. I just know we took them, put them on the graves, and then he would tell me about Sophia Maria Jones. That was all." Alex focused on Sophie. "And sometimes he would say that he'd like me to meet you, and..." His voice trailed off, and he looked to be thinking very hard.

"Alex?" said Meredith. "Is everything okay?"

A few seconds later Alex reached up and yanked his sunglasses from his face. There was an obvious excitement in his eye. "I'll be right back!" With that, he jumped up out of his seat and ran down the hallway, returning a couple minutes later looking slightly dejected. "I can't find it," he announced.

"What were you looking for?" Meredith asked.

Alex sat back down. "I remembered. When he was sick,

Dad said he was writing a letter for Sophia Maria Jones. Said he would put it in my favorite place, and told me that after he...you know—after he..."

"Died," Meredith said softly.

Alex frowned. "Uh-huh...after that, he said if I found it I should mail it to her, and that maybe someday she'd come knocking on the door."

Sophie waited a few seconds to see if he was going to say more, and then remarked, "Well, then, looks like I'm early."

Shifting in her seat, Meredith asked Alex where he'd looked for the letter.

"In my room," he replied. "My favorite place is my bedroom. I like sleep, so I looked under the bed, under the mattress, under the sheet—even under the pillow, but I couldn't find it." He turned to Sophie. "I'm sorry, Sophia, I don't know where it is. But I'll keep looking."

"Thank you, Alex. That's very nice of you. Can I give you my phone number, in case it turns up?"

His eyes lit up. "Yes! I like to talk on the phone. Can I call you?"

"Of course," she said with a slight giggle. "If you ever want to talk, just give me a ring."

Sophie wrote down her cell number and handed it to him.

Alex turned to Meredith and grinned like a hyena. "Now your sons can't tease me that I don't talk to girls!"

Everyone laughed out loud.

Everyone, that is, except Alex. He just smiled and turned a light shade of red.

The group chatted for a few more minutes before Ellen decided it was time to go. Sophie kept stealing glances at Alex during the conversation, marveling at his genuine optimism, especially given his circumstances. *Fitting,* she thought, *that he should want to respond to a want ad for happiness. Lives by himself, lost both of his parents, and he still manages to keep a smile on his face.*

Chapter 28

Your temper must be tempered, before someone gets hurt.

EVALYNN TURNED ON THE IGNITION AND LET THE CAR idle. "So? Where to now?" She was looking at Sophie, who was twirling her hair around a finger in the other front seat.

But Sophie wasn't looking back at Evalynn. She was still staring out the window at the home of Jacob—and Alex—Barnes. Alex was waving from the front door. Sophie smiled and waved back.

When Sophie didn't answer Evalynn's question, Ellen spoke up from the backseat. "You know what I think, Sweets? I think that did you a boatload of good."

"Oh yeah?" Sophie asked, twisting around in her seat so she could see her foster mom better. "What part do you think was best? Hearing that I single-handedly lopped off Jacob's fingers on the day after his wife died, or finding out that now he's dead, too?"

"Single-handedly," snickered Evi. "That's terrible."

Ellen rolled her eyes. "I meant the part where you heard that he didn't blame you."

"*Pfff*. Meredith was speculating."

"Sophie," Ellen said, slipping into her motherly voice. "When is it going to sink in that it wasn't your fault? It was just an unlucky circumstance."

Sophie's eyebrows jutted up. "Oh, c'mon, let's be fair. I've dealt with this pretty well over the years, if you don't count my moodiness on birthdays. We wouldn't even be having this discussion if the fortune hadn't shown up in the mail."

Ellen gave a sympathetic smile. "You're right, you've done well. And it really is unbelievable that that fortune made it back to you. One might almost go as far as to say it's—"

"Here we go," mumbled Sophie.

Evi laughed.

Ellen ignored both of them. "*Divine providence*. Gotta be."

"Oh yeah," retorted Sophie sarcastically, turning again to look out the window. "God *made* Alex get on YouTube and then forced him to reply to the want ad. I'm sure stirring up my past is at the top of His omnipotent list of things to do." Sophie chuckled out loud at her own comment. She always found humor in, and frequently poked fun at, Ellen's longstanding assertion that life's little coincidences were evidence of God involving Himself in the affairs of mankind.

Evi chuckled once more.

"Laugh if you want," commented Ellen, "but I'm telling you, this is providence."

Sophie and Evalynn shared a sideways glance, but let the debate die. Since Alex was still on the front porch waving good-bye, Evalynn decided it was time to actually go somewhere. She put the car into gear and pulled into the street. It was a cul-de-sac, so thirty seconds later they passed by the house again, and Alex was still there smiling and waving. All three women waved back.

Once they were clear of the Barneses' neighborhood, Evalynn adjusted her rearview mirror so she could better see Ellen's face. "Now would someone like to tell me where we're heading?"

Locking eyes with Evalynn in the mirror, Ellen dismissed the question with a look that said, *Darned if I know.*

"Sophie?" Evalynn asked.

There was more silence, but only for a moment.

"I want to see your copy of the police report from the accident," Sophie told Ellen without turning around. "You said you still have it, right?"

"Yes," she replied. "But not if anyone else asks, okay? It's not exactly protocol to copy such things and take them home. You want to read through it?"

Sophie nodded.

"Mind if I ask why?"

Now Sophie turned around again. Her expression was calm and resolute, like things had suddenly become clear. "Because you were right. Going there today was good for me. I should have done it a long time ago." Right then, Sophie's phone rang. She looked at the number but didn't recognize it. Initially, she considered not answering, but by the fifth ring she got curious and flipped it open. "Hello?"

The voice on the other end was loud enough that even Evalynn and Ellen could hear most of what was being said. Sophie had to hold the phone several inches from her ear to keep it from hurting. "Hello! Is this Sophia Jones?"

"Alex?"

"Yes! It's me. I'm calling. Hi!"

"Alex, can you talk a little softer? I'm getting static."

"Sorry, Sophie. I don't talk on the phone a lot. Is that better? I know you're in the car. Can you still hear me?"

Sophie put the phone up to her ear and smiled. She liked the melodic quality of his voice. "Yes, Alex. That's much better.

And I can still hear you just fine. To what do I owe this pleasure?"

"Huh?"

Sophie suppressed a laugh. "What can I do for you? Is everything okay?"

"Oh. Yes. But after you left I remembered some things."

Sophie lifted one eyebrow and shot a look to Evalynn, thinking perhaps she was about to learn more details about either the accident or Jacob Barnes. "Really? Do you want to tell me?"

"Yep! I remembered that there are lots of reasons to be happy, and I wanted to tell you, so you don't have to have an ad in the newspaper anymore."

Sophie couldn't help but smile. "I see. That's very thoughtful, Alex. Can I put you on speakerphone so Evalynn and Ellen can hear, too?"

There was a pause, and then Alex said, "Okay."

While Sophie pushed several buttons on her phone, Evalynn whispered, "Where are we going?"

"To Ellen's," Sophie whispered back, and then she told Alex they were ready.

"Sophie?"

"Yes?"

"I've never been on speakerphone before."

"I see," she said soothingly. "Are you nervous? I can turn it off if you want."

Alex took a few second to consider that. "No," he said finally. "I'll just pretend like I'm talking on the microphone at Albertsons. Sometimes I get to do that. And sometimes they call my name on the speakers and everyone hears. *Alex to customer service!* The speakerphone is fine."

"Okay. Fire away," said Sophie, thoroughly amused.

For the next two minutes Alex rattled off a litany of things that to him were happiness. The three women in the car just sat and listened, grateful for his insights. Later they would try to remember everything that he'd said, but the list was too big to capture them all. Happiness, he told them, is watching the sun break through clouds, or watching it rise in the morning. "If the sun didn't come up tomorrow, I think I'd be pretty sad. And," he added, "it would be really dark." He also explained that happiness is eating dinner with your family—even the teenage boys who like to tease—and talking about what happened during the day. It is working hard at a job, even if you don't always enjoy it, because it feels good knowing you did your best. Talking was on his list, plus reading a good book, or reading a good book aloud so you can talk and read at the same time. Then there was waking up in the morning.

"Waking up in the morning?" Sophie asked, making sure she'd heard him correctly.

"Of course. When was the last time you didn't wake up in the morning?"

She let out a laugh. "Never."

"See. If you didn't wake up, I don't think you'd be very happy about it."

Everyone in the car laughed. Alex wasn't sure he saw the humor, so he continued: "And happiness is helping people when they need help, and smiling at other people, even if they don't smile back." He stopped for a second. "Or even if they laugh at you. And happiness is looking at pictures of your family…and remembering." He paused once more, this time longer than before, and Sophie thought she heard him put the phone down and then pick it up again. "That can be sad, too. But more happy than sad."

"Did you just put on your sunglasses, Alex?" she asked.

"Yes. How did you know?"

"Just a hunch."

When he was through, everyone in the car thanked him for

calling and sharing his thoughts. Sophie reiterated that he was welcome to call her any time he wanted.

"I'll call if I think of more happy things," he told her.

"I can't wait."

"Or if I find the letter."

"Thank you Alex."

"Or... maybe if I just want to talk."

"That would be nice."

"Bye, Sophia Jones!"

Sophie smiled at the phone. "Good-bye, Alex."

Evalynn took her right hand off the steering wheel and poked Sophie in the side. "Somebody's got a new boyfriend," she joked.

"Yes," Sophie responded proudly. "I think you're right."

"So are you going to tell us why you want to see the police report?" asked Ellen from the backseat.

Loosening her seat belt so she could maneuver more easily, Sophie twisted around and smiled at her foster mother. "The best part of meeting Alex and Meredith had nothing to do with what they told me. It was what I told them. Simply acknowledging my role in the accident and apologizing for it was... liberating." The look of resolution returned to her face. "I want to put this behind me once and for all. It's been my little black cloud for too long, and I'm tired of the rain. So if there's anyone else in the report that warrants a visit, I want to know."

Ellen nodded. "It's in my desk at home."

Fifteen minutes later they pulled up in front of Ellen's aging building, then walked up together to the third-floor apartment. Sophie and Evalynn sat at the kitchen table while Ellen retrieved the police report from her desk in the bedroom.

Sophie spent a good twenty minutes quietly poring through the old pages of the report, familiarizing herself with the names of people in the other cars, reading their accounts of what happened, and studying the words of eyewitnesses who'd watched the disaster unfold. It was like a walk down memory lane in her mind, only the memory seemed slightly askew—her own version of what had happened that night had always been from the perspective of a scared nine-year-old girl. Now, through adult eyes, she was reading the accounts of other adults, none of whom recognized that a spoiled little kid in the Volvo had anything to do with the deadly incident.

When she was done reading, Sophie closed the report and slid it on the table toward Ellen.

"Please don't tell me you want to contact everyone who was in the accident," Ellen said.

Sophie shook her head. "No..."

"It sounds like there's a 'but' coming," said Evi.

Sophie smiled faintly. "But...one family really deserves a visit."

Ellen frowned. "The family of the other guy that died?"

With a nod, Sophie said, "Tim McDonald. He was a UPS driver, and he died from his injuries a few days after the accident. I just...Reading the report was good for me. I think they might like a copy too, if that's okay. And when I take it, that'll give me a chance to explain a few of the details that didn't make it into the report. To me, it's important that they know."

Ellen sighed, then pushed her chair away from the table. "I can't let them have a copy, Sweets, but if they keep it under wraps, I'll let you take this one for them to read." She shook her head, like the whole thing was a bad idea. "I'll go make a few calls, see if I can track down the family." She picked up the report and left.

Ten minutes later Ellen retuned holding a yellow Post-it note. She dropped the police report on the table and then stuck the note to it. "The closest living relative is Tim's mother, a woman named Lucy McDonald. She lives on the other side of the state, near Idaho, in a little suburb of Spokane called Millwood. There's the address."

"Millwood," Sophie repeated. "How many hours is it from here to there?"

"About eight hours round-trip," Ellen answered.

Sophie grinned. "Looks like I'm definitely going to have to brush up on my driving."

"You can't go all that way by yourself, Sophie. Let Evi go along. Or I can go too, if you want, but that's too much time behind the wheel for you. Besides, you don't even have a car."

Sophie tapped her fingers on the table while considering what she wanted to do. When she'd turned sixteen, Ellen had forced her to get her driver's license, but Sophie hated it, mostly because she was afraid that she might cause a collision like the one she'd experienced as a child. So although she knew how to drive and had a license, she'd always chosen to either ride the bus or bum rides off of friends. "You're right. It's high time I get a car."

"And you'll let me come along?" asked Evalynn, though the tone she used made it sound like she was coming whether Sophie wanted her to or not.

"It's up to you. But if you do, you'll have to help me finish going through all that stupid mail. I'm sure I'll have even more by then. One of us can read letters while the other is driving."

Evi grinned. "Great...sounds like a thrilling road trip. I'll read letters, then you'll dismiss them and throw them out the window."

Sophie laughed. "Exactly! Hey, whatever it takes to avoid a date with you-know-who."

Chapter 29

Your lingering melancholy is intertwined with your outlook on life.

DURING THE NEXT WEEK, GARRETT CALLED ALMOST DAILY to see how things were going with the mail. Though Sophie had chosen to take a brief hiatus from the piles of letters that were building up again in the back of the kitchen, she promised him that she would give them proper attention during her Sunday trip.

"Oh?" he asked. "Where are you going?"

"None of your business."

"Well, who are you going with?" he pressed.

"A friend," she said, and left it at that.

"Not a guy friend though, right?"

Sophie was laughing inside, but she didn't let on. "Does it matter?"

"Well... no...," he stammered. "It's just... mind if I ask what the purpose of the trip is?"

Sophie was thoroughly enjoying the fact that she was getting under Garrett's skin. "Well, let's just say I'm going to meet someone's parents."

Garrett became very quiet. "I see," he said finally. "Well then, have a good time...I guess." He hung up.

When Friday rolled around, Sophie left Chocolat' de Soph as soon as Randy arrived. With less hesitation than she'd expected, she boarded a bus, rode it three stops to a pawnshop in Tacoma, and carried out an idea she'd been toying with for a year: she rid herself of the engagement ring that Garrett had given her. When the deed was done, she walked out with a wad of cash, which she promptly spent on a seven-year-old Ford Explorer at a used-car dealership two blocks away. It wasn't the prettiest car around, but it had low miles for its age, the price was right, and, above all, it felt safe to drive.

Sophie eased the Explorer out of the car lot very slowly, and for the entire ride home she never came close to reaching the posted speed limit. *Safety first*, she told herself, when faster cars honked their horns at her.

After work on Saturday she spent several hours driving around the local highways, just to make sure she felt completely comfortable behind the wheel. The more time she drove, the better she felt, but her speed remained uncommonly slow.

"You drive like an old woman," commented Evalynn the next morning, after Sophie picked her up for their long drive to Millwood.

"Well, that's a sexist thing to say," observed Sophie.

"And ageist, too. I don't care—it's the truth. If you don't pick up the pace we won't get there until next week."

With white knuckles clenching the steering wheel, Sophie pressed a little harder on the gas, but still didn't keep up with traffic.

After an hour on the road, Evalynn demanded that Sophie

take the next exit so they could switch places in the car. Sophie gladly obliged and was relieved to take over opening the responses to the want ad from the safety of the passenger seat.

Halfway through the drive Sophie's cell began ringing. She picked it up to find Garrett's picture staring back at her. "Should I answer?" she asked Evalynn.

"Up to you."

"I shouldn't."

"Okay."

"But he'll just keep calling until I do."

Evalynn laughed. "Oh, just pick it up, already. You obviously want to."

Sophie scowled back, silently mouthing the words *I do not!* at the same time as she picked up. "Hello?"

GARRETT WAS SITTING at home in the living room. "Hey, Soph!" he said. "It's Garrett."

"I know who it is. What do you want?" She sounded completely disinterested.

"Just checking to see how your trip is going. You're traveling today, right? Who'd you say you're with?"

"I didn't," she replied flatly.

"Oh, that's right," he said, amused at her unwillingness to divulge information. "Well how are the letters coming? Are we getting any closer to our date?"

"I'm going through them now," she said, "but I have to say, it's still not looking good."

"Well, there are a lot of crazy people out there," he joked, "who wouldn't know happiness even if they were talking to it on the phone."

"Huh? What's that supposed to mean?"

"I'm just having fun, Soph. But seriously, what's the tally at now? Seventy? Eighty?"

"Twelve," she chirped, sounding a bit smug. "But I've got

about two hundred letters on my lap right now, so by the end of the day we might make it to thirteen."

Garrett laughed again. He was about to make another joke, but Sophie spoke first.

"Hold on, Garrett, I'll be right back. Someone else is calling in." He heard the line click off. Thirty seconds later it clicked back on. "You still there?"

"Yep. Telemarketers?"

"Ah, wouldn't you like to know."

"Actually, I would."

"Well sorry to disappoint, but I have to take this call, Garrett. I can't leave him waiting too long."

Garrett clenched the fist that wasn't holding the phone to his ear. "*Him?* Him who?"

"His name is Alex."

There was a long silence. "And how do you know Alex?"

"Oh, our paths crossed recently, and we just sort of hit it off. He's the sweetest guy in the world."

Garrett could feel his temperature rising. "Seriously? You're like...seeing him? Just like that?"

"Just like what?"

"I dunno. But I could've sworn you said you were done with men."

"Sorry, Garrett. I can't keep him waiting any longer. Bye." Sophie clicked off.

LUCY MCDONALD LIVED at the end of a dusty road on a one-acre parcel near the edge of town. The home had all the charm of an old country farmhouse, but if there had ever been a working farm there, it was long since gone. A patchwork of unmowed grass and weeds surrounded the gabled house, and the edge of the property was lined with thick maple trees that had already lost their leaves for the winter.

After four hours of driving, Evalynn turned into the

McDonalds' drive. As they pulled to a stop, Sophie quickly scanned the row of windows along the front of the house, looking for any indication that someone was home. Her stomach did a somersault when she saw that two lights were on.

"You want to come in with me?" Sophie asked.

"Really? You sure you want me there?"

Sophie exhaled to calm her nerves. "Actually, I think I could use the support."

Both women got out of the car and made their way to the large covered porch that wrapped around three full sides of the square-shaped structure. Sophie rang the bell, and moments later the door swung open slowly. Standing in front of them was a little old woman, slightly hunched, and smiling. "Can I help you?" she asked.

"I hope so," said Sophie. "Are you Lucy McDonald?"

The woman winked. "Last time I checked." Her words came out slow, but were clear and articulate. "Have we met?"

"No, ma'am."

"You sure? I swear I've seen your face somewhere." She waved a bony finger. "I have a real knack for faces. Can't remember names to save my life, but I don't forget a face..." Lucy's voice trailed off as she studied Sophie's hair, then her eyes, followed by her mouth and chin, and finally back to her eyes.

Sophie tried to ignore the examination. "I'm sorry to bother you, Mrs. McDonald. My name is Sophie. I was hoping I could talk to you about your son, Tim. Do you have a few minutes?"

"Tim? Oh my. Dear sweet Tim. You know he's passed on, don't you?"

Sophie grimaced. "Yes. That's what I wanted to talk to you about."

"Well then," she cackled, "don't just stand out there in the cold. Come in. Come in."

Lucy led the way through the house to a sitting room that connected the formal dining room with the main living room. A small fire burning in the fireplace made it feel cozy. Lucy held onto the armrests of a tall chair with both hands to lower herself down to sit. Evalynn and Sophie sat next to each other a few yards away on a burgundy-colored, Victorian-style sofa that was a near-perfect match in color to the room's deep red wallpaper.

"Did you know Timmy personally?" she asked, but then immediately answered her own question. "No, you would have been too young."

"You're right, I didn't know him. But I saw him once. On the day of the accident."

Mrs. McDonald's expression had been all smiles up to that point, but the smile quickly deflated in a heavy sigh. "I see," she said, as much to herself as to Sophie. "On the day of the accident, or at the accident?"

Sophie cleared her throat. "At the accident. Before he was taken to the hospital."

Lucy nodded, and then turned to Evalynn. "You too? Did you see my Timmy at the accident?"

Evalynn shook her head without speaking.

Fixing her eyes once more on Sophie, Lucy said, "He was a good boy. Had his struggles, like everyone, I suppose. But he was a good boy." She continued looking in Sophie's direction, but her mental focus shifted as she recalled the past. "I'll never forget the day I found out. A mother never wants to hear that her boy was killed, and I swear I wanted to die myself when I got the call." Her face curled up and she shook her head gently from side to side. "He'd been in the hospital for three days already, and nobody bothered to tell me. Why wouldn't they tell me? I didn't hear anything about the accident until after he was gone. I'd have sure liked to pay him a visit before he passed, but I never had the chance." Lucy blinked, helping her to focus once more on Sophie. "How was it that you saw him? Did you see the accident happen?"

Sophie grimaced. "From very close range, I'm afraid. I was in one of the other cars. After it happened I saw the paramedics working to help your son." She paused. "I know it's been a very long time since it happened, but I'm really sorry for your loss, Mrs. McDonald."

Lucy may have been old, but she was sharp as a tack. "Well I can't imagine that you looked me up and drove all this way just to tell me that you saw my son on death's door." She tilted her head and leaned forward in her seat. "I'm not one for pussyfooting. What's really on your mind, Miss Sophie?"

Sophie tried to smile but couldn't. She handed the old woman Ellen's police report. "I came across this recently. It's the report from the accident, and I thought you might like the official account of what happened that night."

With a cockeyed glance, Lucy said, "That's sweet, dear. But you didn't have to go to the trouble." She took the report from Sophie and flipped through it. After scanning the main parts about her son, she looked up and said. "It says just what they told me back then—more or less. You really came all the way out here just so I could see this?"

"Yes."

"And that's it?"

"Well...not quite. Lucy, I don't quite know the right way to say this. I guess I could start by pointing out that the term *car accident* can mean different things. Mechanical failures sometimes cause accidents, or poor weather, like the report says there. What I mean is, circumstances from one accident to the next are never identical."

Lucy leaned back and cackled again. "Now you're not just pussyfooting. You're beating around the bush too. What's the punch line, dear?"

Sophie glanced momentarily at Evalynn, whose wide eyes and pursed lips encouraged her to press onward.

"Okay, here's the deal. Although everyone chalked the accident up to the rain, that doesn't quite tell the whole story. I want you to know the whole truth about what happened. That night, before the cars started sliding into each other in the rain, a person made a costly mistake."

Lucy blinked hard. "Oh dear," she said with a heavy sigh. "I always wondered if maybe Tim was responsible. Is that the news you've come to share?"

"What? Oh, no, that's not it at all. It was…someone else. Someone who's always felt terrible about what she did."

Now Mrs. McDonald closed one wrinkled eyelid so she could narrow her focus. "Don't tell me you think you were responsible," she said dismissively, guessing at Sophie's unspoken implication.

"But," stammered Sophie, "I was."

"Oh really? Were you driving?"

"No, but—"

"No buts. You were a little girl. How old back then? Six? Seven?"

"Nine."

"Well, there you go. Nine-year-old girls who aren't driving the car don't cause accidents." She raised an index finger again and pointed. "That's a fact, mind you, so don't try to argue."

"But—"

"Shush! No arguing!" She put her finger down and smiled. "Sophie, I miss my son. Loved him like…well, like every mother loves their child. But you needn't carry the weight of what happened on your back, no matter what you think happened that night. And I don't hold you or anyone else responsible. It was an accident in the rain, end of discussion."

"But I—"

"Shush," she said again, smiling.

Evalynn chuckled.

Sophie tried to frown, but it didn't stick.

"Now then," continued Lucy, "I just can't stop thinking that I've seen you somewhere. Are you sure we haven't met before today?" She took another visual tour of Sophie's facial features.

Sophie was in the middle of telling her that she'd never previously been to either Millwood or Spokane, when Lucy's wrinkled eyes lit up.

"Good Lord! What did you say your name was?"

"Sophie."

"Yes, but Sophie what? Jonas?"

"Jones. Sophie Jones."

"Sophie, or Sophia?"

Sophie stared back at the old woman nervously. "It's Sophia," she responded slowly. "How did you know that?"

"Good Lord!" Lucy repeated excitedly. "I *have* seen you! By golly, I was right!" She extended a hand. "Help me up, dear. I need to show you something."

Sophie and Evalynn stood up together, and Sophie took Lucy's arm. As fast as her legs could go, Lucy led them back to the kitchen the same way they'd come in. She stopped near the large island countertop and pointed to the refrigerator. "There," she said, using her entire hand to direct their attention to countless odds and ends affixed with magnets to the refrigerator door.

Sophie didn't speak. Her eyes were glued to a sage green envelope right in the middle of the mess. She paced slowly forward.

"What the heck?" Evalynn whispered, when she saw what Sophie was staring at.

When she was close enough, Sophie lifted the magnet that kept the envelope pinned against the black refrigerator surface. She ran her hand over the seal on the back of the envelope, remembering how its embossed doves felt to the touch. She already knew what the envelope contained, but she separated the top seam and pulled out the contents anyway.

Inside was a picture of her and Garrett, taken more than a year earlier, along with an invitation to the wedding.

"Who sent this to you?" Sophie asked, her voice shallow, racking her brain to remember if the woman's name was on the guest list.

"I have to believe that you did. Or perhaps it was Garrett," Lucy replied with a twinkle in her eye.

"But... why? How do you know Garrett?"

"Sophie, dear, I don't just know Garrett. I'm his grandmother. Tim McDonald was his father. Looks just like him, too."

Sophie covered her mouth with her hand.

"We don't talk much, he and I, but I send him a birthday card every year, and once in a while I'll get something from him in the mail. Graduation announcements, change-of-address notifications, that sort of thing. I was pleased as punch when I got that announcement; hadn't heard from Garrett in several years, and I was looking forward to coming to the wedding. Then a week or so before, he called me on the phone and said it was canceled. I haven't heard anything from him since then."

Sophie's mind was reeling as Lucy spoke. Garrett had hardly told her anything about his father. When she'd asked, he said there wasn't much to tell, because his father had never played much of a role in his life. The fact that he'd grown up with his mother's maiden name instead of his father's last name had never been a topic of discussion. Her thoughts quickly raced back to all the times Garrett had asked Sophie about the accident. She recalled with clarity the consternation on his face when he'd learned that her parents died on September 21, 1989; it was the same look of worry that flashed across his eyes when she pointed out where the accident had taken place.

Her face went white. "Oh my gosh," Sophie whispered, as she fit the pieces together in her head. "He knew. All this time, he knew."

"Soph, you don't know that," Evalynn said.

Sophie glanced at Lucy, and then stared blankly at Evalynn. "Yes. I do." The grimace that formed on her face was just a symptom of the nausea she suddenly felt in her stomach. Locking her eyes onto Lucy's, Sophie said, "You can't tell him, Mrs. McDonald. Please promise you won't tell Garrett that I was here. If I decide he needs to know, I'd rather he hear it from me."

Chapter 30

Your determination to move slowly will bring about a speedy disaster.

ON THEIR RIDE BACK FROM MILLWOOD, SOPHIE MANAGED to convince herself that Ellen must have known more about Lucy McDonald—and, by extension, Garrett and his family history—than she'd ever let on. How could she not? She'd been on the scene the night Tim McDonald died. She'd kept a copy of the police report for decades. She even worked with Garrett's mother at the police station. And wasn't Ellen the snoopiest mom in the world, with detectives at the ready to do her investigative bidding? Those thoughts, along with an awful sense of betrayal, began festering the moment they'd pulled out of Lucy's dusty driveway.

Sophie could hardly contain her emotions when she finally reached the third floor of Ellen's apartment complex and rang the doorbell.

"Knock once if friend, twice if foe!"

Sophie looked sideways at Evalynn before knocking loudly

three times. She hesitated, then continued pounding until the door finally opened up.

The safety chain was still attached on the inside of the door when Ellen poked her nose into the opening to see who was there. "Sophie? Ev? What are you girls doing here?" She unlatched the chain and opened the door the rest of the way. "I thought you were spending the day out near Spokane."

"We're back," Sophie said abruptly.

"Was the woman not home?"

"Oh, she was home all right," snapped Sophie. "And she had a little surprise waiting for us."

Ellen could read the emotion in Sophie's voice. "Let's sit and talk, Sweets." She motioned to the empty seats in the living room. "Now then, what's got you all worked up?"

An awkward silence followed Ellen's question. Evalynn looked like she wanted to speak up, but she refrained; this was Sophie's bone to pick with their foster mother.

When she was ready, Sophie's response came out as an explosion. "I know you like to meddle in our lives, but this is going too far! After everything I went through with Garrett, how could you not tell me? It honestly makes me sick to my stomach."

Ellen took half a step backward. "Sophie, I have no idea what you're talking about."

"Oh save it. Don't pretend like you don't know who Lucy McDonald is."

"Who is she?" gasped Ellen.

"Did you know before Garrett called off the wedding, or after?"

"Huh?"

Sophie's already pink face turned bright red as another possibility hit her. "You probably knew right from the beginning, before I went on that first date with him!"

"Stop it!" screamed Ellen. "Stop it right now! I have no idea what you're talking about, and I refuse to be treated like this until you explain what it is you think I've done."

Sophie clenched her fists. "Just answer me this, and I swear if you lie to me you'll never see me again. When did you first learn that Garrett was Tim McDonald's son?"

Ellen's hand shot up and covered her mouth. "The UPS driver? That was Garrett's father?"

Sophie and Evalynn exchanged puzzled looks. "You mean you didn't know?" asked Sophie suspiciously.

"On my life, I swear I had no idea. I mean, I heard it mentioned way back when that he had a son, but that was all I knew about the man. The detectives on the scene and the sergeant handled most of those details, and they were the ones who notified Mrs. McDonald. I swear, Sophie, with God as my witness, I had no idea that there was a connection to Garrett."

Sophie sat down on the couch and slumped back against the cushions, holding her stomach with her hands to quell the sick feeling that was forming there once more. "Well, Garrett knew," she said with a groan.

Ellen sat down beside her. "How?"

"I think he started piecing it together when I took him to the cemetery and he saw the date that my parents died. Then just about a week before he dumped me I showed him where the accident had happened, and even pointed out the spot where I'd seen the EMTs working on a UPS driver. He couldn't have *not* known. Tim died when Garrett was twelve, so I'm sure he at least knew what his dad did for a living, and how and when he died." She paused. "Finding out that our parents died in the same accident must've flipped him out."

Ellen clasped a hand over her mouth again. She said something, but it came out too muffled to understand.

"What?" Sophie asked.

Lowering her hand, Ellen repeated what she'd just said. "He read the report."

Sophie sat straight up. "What! When?"

"About a week before...I'm so sorry, Soph. I should have told you before. He came by one night and said he wanted to read it to better understand what you'd gone through. I thought he was being sweet. And it was far enough before he called things off that I didn't think it was related. And I...I didn't want to mention the report, unless you came looking for details about the accident of your own accord. I didn't want to stir up the past without cause."

Ellen's words hung in the air.

Sophie flung herself back against the cushions. "He knows," she lamented. "That has to be why he called off the wedding. It says right in the report that the first cars to collide were the Volvo and the UPS truck. So he knows that my family killed his dad." She groaned loudly. "Rain or not—*accident or not*—he knows who struck who." She paused, wanting to double over and puke. "I don't blame him for leaving. I'd have probably done the same."

Ellen touched Sophie gently on the leg. "No, you wouldn't have. You'd have talked to him about it. And you'd have worked it out."

Sophie let out a painful laugh. "I doubt it. Just think of the position he was in. Would you want to be married to someone, knowing her family killed your dad? How would you even start that conversation?"

Ellen looked like she was mulling Sophie's comments over in her mind. When she spoke, it was with her motherly voice, and she smiled warmly. "Do you remember what I said after he left?"

"Yes."

"What?"

"Oh, the whole 'God is steering the boat, and everything has a purpose' bit."

"Exactly! Maybe we're seeing that unfold right before our

eyes. What are the odds that you would grow up and fall in love with someone who shared the same tragedy as a child?"

"Not great, I guess."

"Not great? The odds are so infinitesimally small that it's not worth speculating." She paused. "It's providence, Sweets."

Sophie laughed off the comment. She knew Ellen was going to say that; it's what she always said. But Sophie wouldn't allow herself to believe it.

"You have to talk to him," Ellen added.

Sophie knew she should do exactly what Ellen was suggesting and talk to Garrett about everything. Part of her even wanted to, if only to come clean so she could get on with her hopeless, tragic life and forget all about him. But this wasn't just a faceless stranger that she would be confronting, like Jacob Barnes or Lucy McDonald. This was the boy who'd lost a father twenty years ago, who grew up to become the man who'd stolen her heart. This was *Garrett*. "I know," she said, as tears began to trickle down her cheek again. "But I don't think I can."

Chapter 31

The one you love is closer than you think.
If you were smart, you'd start running.

For more than an hour that night Sophie paced her living room nervously, eyeing the cell phone on the coffee table. Periodically she would pick it up, stare at it, and then set it back down. It occurred to her that she was probably experiencing the same trepidation that had kept Garrett away for so many months. *Sometimes living the lie is easier to bear than confronting the truth,* she thought.

Sophie twirled her hair with one hand while biting the nails on her other. When all the nails were shorter than she preferred, she decided it was now or never. Grabbing the phone in one swift, fluid motion, she pushed send and shoved it against her ear, then focused on controlling her breathing as she listened to it ring.

It kept ringing. And ringing. Nobody answered. Eventually Garrett's voice mail kicked in.

Sophie flipped her phone shut in frustration. *He always picks up! After all that time building up the nerve, he doesn't even answer?*

She dialed again. This time he answered on the fourth ring.

"Sophie?"

"Garrett! I just tried calling."

He didn't reply immediately. "I...wasn't expecting your call. Can I call you back, Soph? I'm sort of in the middle of something."

"Oh. Umm...what sort of something? Because this is kind of important."

More silence. "I've got someone on the other line," he said.

Now Sophie needed a moment before she responded. "Oh. Work-related?"

"No, Soph. Listen, can I call you back in a little bit? I've been talking to her for a while already. I think another five or ten minutes and we'll call it a night."

"*Her?*" Sophie said immediately, flummoxed. "Is this a social call?"

Garrett paused for the third time. "I'll call you back, Sophie. Don't go anywhere."

The line went dead.

Sophie looked at the digits on her cell phone that showed how long the call had lasted.

One minute and three seconds? After all my waiting I got a lousy one minute and three seconds?

It wasn't the amount of time that bothered her. She knew she had no claim on him, but the thought of Garrett spending time with another woman didn't sit right. How could he do that when they still had unsettled business? Didn't he know that he first had to settle the score with the old flame before lighting a new fire? How could he walk into her store one month ago and swear that for all his faults, he'd never stopped loving her, and now suddenly he's loving someone else? She hated that she felt like she'd just lost something that was very important to her, even though, technically, she'd lost it more than a year earlier. Sophie closed her phone and threw it against the couch, then went and sat down next to it.

Almost exactly ten minutes later, her phone rang. She answered immediately.

"We need to talk," Sophie said curtly without bothering to say hello. She didn't intend to sound unfriendly, but knowing that he'd just finished talking to—*or flirting with*—another woman, she couldn't seem to help it.

"I figured," he said with a chuckle. "Why else would you have called, other than to talk?"

"Funny. But I mean...*we need to talk*. As in, I want to have the conversation you've been pestering me to have. I've decided that I shouldn't make you wait any longer, and I want to hear whatever it is you have to say."

Garrett spoke softly into the receiver. "You mean the discussion that involves us going on a date?"

"Yes."

He chuckled again, louder. "Wow, do I sense a bit of jealousy here? As soon as you hear I'm talking to another woman, suddenly you're ready to give me a chance?"

"That has nothing to do with it," she asserted firmly. "I just...we need to talk. Forget our deal. It's done. It was stupid, anyway. Let's just get together somewhere so we can sit down and chat. It doesn't even have to be a date. You can even come here for all I care. We just...need to talk. In person."

"Hmmm," he said thoughtfully. "I don't know how the woman I was talking to would feel about that. Can I bring her along?"

Was he purposefully trying to tick her off, she wondered? "Absolutely not!"

"Then I don't know, Soph. I'm not sure it's such a good idea."

Sophie could hardly believe what she was hearing. "But just

a month ago you were dying to have this discussion with me."

"I know," he replied coolly. "And I'm willing to. Just not right now." He let the words settle. "You know, we've already got this deal worked out with the want ad and everything. Why don't we just stick with it, and we'll get together as soon as you've found one hundred acceptable responses."

"You're serious?"

"Of course. Why wouldn't I be?" He paused. "You've got thousands of letters to choose from, Soph. And I just want you to admit that happiness really does exist out there. So you show me one hundred happy letters, and then we'll talk."

Sophie felt her face heating up; this wasn't at all how she'd expected the conversation to go. Was it that woman he'd been talking with on the phone that suddenly made him less interested in their date? It galled her that she even cared, but she did. And then to be coerced into acknowledging happiness, when all she wanted to do was give him a little closure by telling him she understood why he'd left? That was too much. She kicked herself for having listened to Ellen's advice that she should call him. "Fine. Forget it. We don't need to talk. I was trying to do you a favor, but never mind." She pulled the phone away from her mouth and groaned. "Closure is probably overrated anyway."

"You okay, Sophie? You sound a bit out of sorts."

"I'm great," she lied. "Good-bye, Garrett."

Sophie slammed her phone shut and threw it against the couch for the second time. Then she laid down next to it and allowed her emotions loose in a flood of tears. For the first time since Garrett had called off the wedding, her crying had nothing to do with anger, resentment, or remorse for what he'd done to her. Rather, they were tears at the unexpected sense of loss that came from knowing that Garrett had another woman in his life, and there was nothing she could do about it.

At his home in Tacoma, Garrett closed his phone as well, frustrated that the conversation with Sophie hadn't quite gone the way he'd hoped. He pitched his phone like a fastball toward the stone fireplace mantel, breaking it into several pieces.

He didn't care.

Chapter 32

No matter what your past has been, your future is bleak.

SOPHIE TOSSED AND TURNED ALL NIGHT. IMAGES OF Garrett schmoozing on the phone with hordes of faceless women littered her dreams, causing her to wake up periodically in a cold sweat. The third time she woke up she decided it wasn't worth going back to sleep, so she crawled out of bed and got ready for work.

When Sophie arrived at Chocolat' de Soph an hour later and started the daily preparations, her Misfortunes seemed to come much easier than normal, and she wasn't at all surprised that most of them had something to do with miseries of the heart. Her final message, she decided, was specifically for Garrett. *"Sure, there are other attractive fish in the sea,"* she read aloud to make sure it captured what she was feeling. *"Too bad you're swimming in a shallow pond full of piranhas."* A wry grin crept across her face as she slid the paper into an empty cookie. *I hope she eats him alive.*

After the store opened, but before any customers arrived, Sophie got an unexpected call on her work phone.

"Chocolat' de Soph," she said.

"Sophie?" asked the distinctive singsong voice. "Is that you, or is that someone else?"

"Alex? Why didn't you call my cell?"

"Because you're at work, and I thought you might not answer it at work, because my boss doesn't let anyone talk on cell phones while we're working at Albertsons, and maybe your boss wouldn't let you either."

Hearing his voice relaxed her, and brought a peaceful smile to her face. "*I'm* the boss, Alex. But I appreciate your thoughtfulness. How are you? Aren't you supposed to be at work right now, too?"

"It's break time. I can call anyone on break time. And so I looked up your candy store in the phone book."

"I see. So what can I do for you?"

She heard him tap the receiver, trying to remember why he'd dialed. "Umm…oh yeah. I found something."

"Oh? What is it?"

"The letter."

Sophie was quiet, collecting her thoughts. "From your dad?"

"Uh-huh. To you."

Sophie went quiet again.

"Sophie?"

She cleared her throat. "Are you sure it's intended for me?"

"Yep. It has your name on it. Sophia Jones. And your address. And it has a note on the outside, telling me that when I find it, I should mail it. It's a yellow note, the sticky kind. And the letter even has stamps on it already."

"Where did you find it, Alex?"

"To Kill a Mockingbird."

"The book?"

"Uh-huh. I should have thought of that when you were here. My bedroom is my favorite room, but that book is my favorite place. I really like its happy ending. And I really *really* like the name Boo. I read it at least one time every year. Dad knew that. I think that's why he put it there."

"Wow. Did you read the letter?"

"Nope. It's closed. Do you want me to send it?" He paused. "Or maybe...do you want to come get it?"

Sophie thought briefly. She wanted to see Alex, but wasn't sure she could get there before the mail could deliver it. Plus, there were other things on her mind that also needed some attention.

"Sophie?"

"Sorry, Alex," she replied. "I'm afraid I can't come over this week. Would you mind putting it in the mail?"

"Okay," he said.

Sophie could hear the disappointment in his voice. "But I promise to come over real soon," she said quickly. "As soon as things calm down a little bit."

It was several seconds before Alex said anything else. "Sophie, have you found your happiness?"

"Sadly, no," she answered with a sigh.

"Any more letters from your newspaper ad?"

"Many. But none that I think are really happy."

"That's what I thought, because even though I can't see your face, I can tell your voice isn't smiling as much as other days."

"You're very perceptive, Alex. But even if it doesn't sound like it, I promise that my heart is smiling right now from talking to you."

There was another long silence before Alex said, "Sophie?"

"Yeah?"

"My break is over, Sophie."

He said good-bye and clicked off.

Chapter 33

There is a fine line between success and failure,
and you've crossed that line.

SOPHIE GLANCED AT THE CLOCK ON THE WALL AS SHE handed a customer a skewered apple, loaded an inch thick in all directions with a semisoft mixture of white chocolate, milk chocolate, caramel, chopped cashews, and crumbled Oreos.

"Beautiful," he whispered, salivating as he felt the weight of it in his hands.

She checked her wristwatch to make sure the clock on the wall was correct. Both sources confirmed that it was already five minutes to five, which meant that the mailman was officially late. Normally, she wouldn't care when the mail arrived, because it just meant that there would be more bills to pay, but it had been three days since she'd last talked to Alex, and as each day passed Sophie grew more and more interested—*and nervous*—to see what Jacob Barnes had written in his letter.

Jacob was the only other person from the night of the accident who would have had any inkling about her involvement, and their brief encounter along the side of the road had affected him enough that he'd remembered who she was, literally until the day he died. Though Alex's caregiver had sworn up and down that Jacob didn't harbor any ill feelings toward her, Sophie couldn't help but worry that maybe Meredith was wrong. Why would he bother writing a letter, she wondered, if not to blame or accuse? The thought had her on edge.

"I don't recommend eating that all at once," Sophie told the man, as he turned to leave with his apple, "unless you've got someone to share it with."

"You kiddin'?" he shot back, grinning. "It's *an apple*. Practically health food. No, this baby's all mine." He lifted it to his mouth and took his first bite, then left the store looking very satisfied.

Ten minutes later the mailman finally arrived and dropped off a box of mail inside of the front door. Sophie would have loved to sneak over right then to check for the letter, but she was too busy passing out samples to a family with five kids who wanted to taste everything in the store before making a decision. By the time all seven of them had made up their minds, there were another three customers waiting in line. Sophie breathed a giant sigh. Jacob's letter would have to wait, if it was there at all.

Randy arrived shortly thereafter and picked up the box of mail while Sophie was ringing up a woman in her eighties who wouldn't stop talking about how her great-grandchildren were going to love the peppermint truffles in their stockings on Christmas morning. "That's almost two months away," said Sophie. "You'll probably want to come back for fresh ones as it gets a little closer."

The woman turned up her nose and waved her hand dismissively. "Hogwash, dear. The best sales are on right now, before the holiday rush. I'll just put them in the freezer, and the kids will never know the difference."

Sophie decided it wasn't worth telling her that the truffles weren't on sale. "Well, then... Merry Christmas."

The woman smiled happily and waved good-bye.

"Randy?" Sophie called to the back once all of the customers were gone. "Where'd you put the mail?" She was glancing out the front windows at the busy traffic as she spoke, and as she watched, a familiar Mercedes pulled into one of the metered parking spaces in front of the store.

"Oh, crap," she muttered.

As quickly as she could, Sophie scrambled to the back of the store, pulled off her apron and tossed it on a dirty countertop. "I'm leaving early, Randy. Where's the mail?"

Randy looked up from a vat of fudge. "On your desk, like I said." He cocked his head at an angle. "You okay?"

"I'm fine," she lied. "But, if a *certain someone* happens to come in the store in, like, the next thirty seconds, do your best to stall. I need him to stay here long enough for me to slip out the rear exit." Thoughts of Garrett had been festering ever since she found out that he was seeing—or at least talking to—another woman. How dare he? And after all his previous pestering, when she called to give him a chance at talking to her, he'd turned her down! No, she was not fine. She was frustrated, ticked off, perhaps slightly jealous, and she didn't even have words for how what she'd learned about his father made her feel. With all of those emotions swimming around in her head and heart, the last thing she wanted right then was to talk to him.

Randy nodded like it was no big deal, and then went up front to tend the register. Sophie hustled to her office, threw on her coat, and was rifling through the box of mail when she heard the front door open.

"Hey, Randy," she heard Garrett say.

"Wassup, bro?"

"Is Sophie around?"

Sophie stood motionless, listening. There was a long pause before Randy said, "Umm...maybe? I mean. She was. But now...I'm not sure. Well...yeah. She's here, but like, in the john...or something."

"Oh," Garrett said diplomatically. "I guess I'll just wait."

Sophie grinned, pleased that he'd bought Randy's fumbling lie. Quietly, she continued sorting the mail. The letter from Jacob Barnes was near the bottom of the box. She left the rest of the letters on the desk, grabbed her purse and umbrella, then tiptoed to the back door and out into the alley.

Although she still rode the bus on most days, Sophie had figured out that owning a car and driving herself to work had a few benefits, such as being able to sleep in longer in the morning. This morning had been one of the days that she'd needed a little extra time to wake up, and so she drove her Explorer from Gig Harbor to Tacoma and parked it in a pay-per-day garage two blocks away from Chocolat' de Soph.

Sophie popped open her umbrella to repel the rain and started walking quickly toward the parking garage. By the time she got there, found her car on the fourth level, and paid the fare to leave, she assumed that Garrett had long since left her store. Either that, she thought, or he was growing very worried about the nature of her business in the bathroom. She pulled out onto the road, making a hard right turn, then hung a left at the next light. A few minutes later she was cruising along the highway, headed home, at her maximum rainy-day speed of forty-five miles per hour.

As usual, plenty of cars were annoyed by her tempo, but the only ones that bothered to honk were those that got stuck in her wake, or the occasional Good Samaritan who wanted to wave at her with one finger. She ignored them all. Sophie was almost to the Narrows Bridge when one pulled alongside her, slowing just enough to get a good look at the driver of the snail-paced SUV.

Unlike other cars, the one to her left didn't pass. It just stayed there, keeping pace. Sophie was sure that the driver was staring at her, but she refused to turn and look, because that would require diverting her focus from the increasingly wet road ahead, so she just kept driving.

A few moments later Sophie's phone began ringing inside her purse, playing Garrett's new honky-tonk ringtone, "Don't break my heart, my achy breaky heart..." He must have finally figured out that she wasn't in the bathroom, but even if she hadn't been driving right then, she wouldn't have answered, for the simple reason that she didn't have anything to say to him.

The song played through twice, then the phone went quiet. A few seconds later it started up again. Sophie wondered how many times he was going to call before he finally got the hint. She wished she could take her hands off the wheel long enough to put it on silent.

After the song ended for the second time, the car in the next lane over, which was still keeping pace, started honking loudly. It kept honking for fifteen seconds. Eventually, the sound of it became such a distraction that Sophie glanced over at it out of the corner of her eye.

The sight of Garrett's dimpled face staring back at her sent her into an instant panic. She gasped in surprise, but as she did so she inadvertently punched the accelerator, causing her V8 engine to leap forward. The sudden shift in speed also scared her, so she instinctively hit the brakes to correct the situation.

Then things went very wrong.

The man in the car behind Sophie, who'd been stuck on her bumper for almost two miles because nobody would let him get around, followed her lead when she sped up. He was still on her tail, accelerating quickly, when her brake lights flashed.

Sophie felt the car jolt unnaturally as she was hit from behind. The next thing she knew she was sliding down the road out of control, tires screeching, heart pounding, and mouth screaming. Her Explorer twisted just enough that it crossed over into Garrett's lane, but that didn't matter. He'd watched the whole thing unfold, and had already slammed on his own brakes, resulting in another rear-end collision between him and the car behind him. Eight other vehicles that were traveling in tight formation also got caught up in the melee, stacking up end to end in one loud, momentous crash.

Chapter 34

Open your heart a little, and it will end up hurting a lot.

When Garrett's car finally came to a stop, the only thing on his mind was Sophie. The car she was driving was thirty yards farther up the road, just shy of the bridge, wedged snuggly at a ninety-degree angle between another car and the guardrail. Checking to make sure it was safe to get out, he threw open his door, ran to the shoulder, and darted up the highway to her.

The passenger door was unlocked when he got there. He yanked it open to find Sophie hunched behind the steering wheel's deflated air bag, with her head buried in her hands.

Garrett exhaled, relieved to see that she wasn't seriously hurt, at least not outwardly. "Sophie, are you okay?"

She kept her face covered, hiding her tears.

The car was still running, so Garrett climbed in and turned the key. Sophie continued to cry, refusing to acknowledge him.

"Soph?"

Not knowing what else to do, Garrett reached out and put his hand on her back. She flinched, then dropped her hands from her face and sat up, wiping her nose on the back of her hand.

"I'm fine," she said finally.

"You sure?"

She nodded.

Garrett turned to look out through the car's rear window. "Listen, I should go and make sure everyone else is okay. You gonna be all right here for a little bit?"

"I'm going with you. I need... to see what I've done."

Garrett helped her out of the car, and together they took off at a trot, going from car to car to check for injuries. Most of the people were already out along the shoulder talking, trying to sort out what had happened. One man in his fifties was complaining of minor back pain, and a woman in a pantsuit had a large bump on her forehead where she'd hit the steering column, but everyone else seemed fine. Only when they were sure that nobody needed immediate medical attention, did Garrett and Sophie make their way back to the Explorer to get out of the rain.

"Well at least everyone's okay," ventured Garrett, once they were inside.

Sophie stared through the window toward the Narrows. She seemed to be focused on a spot near the other shore where she'd once taken Garrett to skip a stone. She didn't speak, or even acknowledge that she'd heard him.

"Soph? You alright?" He touched her gently.

When Sophie was ready to speak, her words came in whimpered spurts. "You... should have... told me."

"Told you what?" Garrett drew his hand back.

Emotionally, Sophie had reached her capacity. For a full year she'd struggled with not knowing why Garrett had abandoned her. And for nineteen years before that she'd been hampered by the loss of her family, their deaths feeling like lead bricks that weighed down all hope of ever being truly happy. And now, after so much time, to find out that the two greatest tragedies of her life were inexorably connected? Adding all of that to the immediate stress over the accident she'd just caused was too much. Sophie's emotions erupted. "You should have told me!" she repeated, this time screaming the words. She began sobbing loudly and swatted at his leg with an open palm. "You knew, and you had no right to keep it to yourself! *I deserved to know!*"

From the look on his face, that wasn't what he'd expected her to say in the immediate aftermath of a ten car pile-up. He corralled Sophie's hand to keep her from swinging it at him again, gently interlocking her fingers in his and pulling it close. "Soph," he said softly, "what should I have told you? I'll tell you anything you want."

A man outside the car rushed up to Sophie's window, holding a cell phone against his ear and blocking his eyes from the rain. "You guys okay?" he shouted.

Garrett nodded.

The man held up a thumb. "Excellent," he said, loud enough to be heard through the closed door. "I think the cars were moving too slow for any major injuries. Pretty lucky!" He waved, and then left to help guide traffic past the bottleneck of Garrett's crumpled car in the left-hand lane.

"Lucky," Sophie mumbled quietly, sniffling. "Yeah, that's what this is."

Sirens were already starting to scream in the background, but Garrett tuned them out, squeezing her hand tenderly. "Talk to me, Sophie. What did I know that I should have said?"

With a menacing glare, Sophie let out a little laugh, and then yanked her fingers from his hand so she could tuck a stray hair behind her ear. "Oh...I don't know," she said sarcastically.

"Maybe I'm overreacting. Maybe I'm just blowing it all out of proportion, and you were right not mentioning it." Tears started falling again from the corners of her eyes, and as they cascaded down her face her emotions hit another crescendo. "Or maybe," she barked, raising her voice sharply, "you just didn't know how to say that you were completely disgusted by the fact that my family killed your father!"

Garrett's face went white and his bottom lip quivered. "How do you know that?"

"So that's it!" she shot back, angry and sad and ashamed all at once. "Well guess what! You don't even know the whole story! My parents and grandmother were just as much victims as your dad, Garrett. It was me! *I caused the accident!* So if you want someone to blame, you're looking at her!"

"What? That's not true."

"Yes." Her voice dropped to a hollow whisper as her head fell into her hands again. "Sadly, it is. No matter what anyone says, no matter how many people tell me it's not my fault or forgive me, it doesn't change the facts. I was old enough to know better. I was thinking only of what I wanted. And if I hadn't done what I did back then, my parents would still be alive. And so would your dad."

Garrett was flustered. "Sophie... how? Is that what you've thought all these years? That the accident was somehow your fault?"

"It was," she snapped defiantly.

"No," he countered. "It wasn't! And if I'd thought for a second that you felt responsible, I'd have told you about all this as soon as I figured it out. Even if you'd thought that your parents were at fault, I'd have set the record straight right away."

"There's no record to set straight, Garrett. I was there. I know what happened! And there are things that weren't in the police report that you know nothing about."

He sat quietly, fidgeting. "I could say the same thing," he said eventually.

Sophie stared at him questioningly. The first emergency responders were just pulling up to the scene, sirens blaring. They almost drowned out her words. "What are you talking about?"

Looking over his shoulder, Garrett saw that police cars were pulling up in the space between his car and Sophie's, and he knew they'd have plenty of questions. One officer was already out of her squad car, looking through the windows of his Mercedes. "I'll explain everything, just as soon as we're done dealing with... this." He motioned to the line of cars behind them. "I've got to go find my insurance papers."

WHETHER IT WAS the rain, the cold, or the miles-long traffic backing up along the highway at rush hour, everyone on the scene was doing their best to expedite the accident cleanup. Tow trucks were on the scene within ten minutes and began hauling away cars left and right. A beefy female officer spent less than two minutes talking to Garrett about how the wreck started. He'd only given a brief overview of what he'd seen before she cut him off. "Let's cut to the chase. In your opinion, was anyone being reckless?"

"Reckless? No. Overly cautious, perhaps," he said with a hesitant chuckle, thinking of Sophie clenching the steering wheel at forty-five miles per hour. "But not reckless."

As soon as the officer was through with him, a tow truck backed up and hauled his vehicle away. The officer left to talk to Sophie, who was standing beside her car under an umbrella.

Garrett followed, listening as she asked Sophie the same set of questions. He had to bite his tongue when he overheard her say, "It was all my fault, Officer. It always is."

The officer gave her a funny look. "But you were driving at a safe speed, right?"

"Yes."

"And you got hit from behind, right?"

Sophie nodded.

"Well, then according to the law, it's not your fault."

"But—"

"But," she interjected before Sophie could object, "it's too cold for debate. If you have anything of value in the car, you should get it now. Do you have someone coming to pick you up?"

Sophie started to shake her head, but Garrett heard the question too, and said, "I'll give you a lift, Soph. A rental car is on its way."

She nodded again.

The police officer moved on to the next car, and Garrett joined Sophie under the umbrella. They watched silently from the shoulder of the road as the tow truck twisted her car around in the right direction and winched it up off the ground. It was starting to pull away when Sophie realized she'd forgotten something.

"The letter!" she shouted as she handed the umbrella to Garrett and took off running after the truck. "Stop!"

The driver didn't hear her, but he saw her in his rearview mirror and stopped before he got very far. For liability reasons, he couldn't let her get into her car while it was attached to his truck, but the man saw that she was desperate, so he got out and retrieved the letter for her. She thanked him, then jogged back to Garrett.

"What was that about?" he asked.

Sophie considered trying to explain it, but she didn't want to get into another convoluted conversation before finishing the one they'd started twenty minutes earlier.

"Nothing," she said. "How long until your car shows up?"

"I don't know. Fifteen minutes. Maybe longer with all this traffic."

Pursing her lips, she said, "Great. That should be plenty of time for you to finish what you were saying before."

He grimaced. "I want to. But before I do, can I ask one more thing?"

She tilted her head. "Maybe."

"How did you find out my dad was in the crash with your family?"

For the first time since leaving her store, Sophie's mouth curled slightly at the ends in something that resembled a tiny, smug smile. "I figured it out on Sunday when I met Grandma McDonald."

Garrett's mouth dropped open. "You mean *that* was your trip? But...how did you find her?"

"It all started with our silly little want ad." She paused, trying to think how to bring up Alex without giving too much away. "One of the guys who responded was a local, and he sent me something that really...touched me, I guess you could say. And I decided I wanted to meet the person who sent it."

"So you just showed up at his house?"

"With Ellen and Evi, yeah. And it turns out we had a lot in common.

"It's a long story. The short version is that what he sent was a huge giveaway. So I went to see him."

"So that's—"

"Alex? Yes." Sophie watched his face, and was pleased to see that he seemed disappointed. "Anyway, we hit it off right away, and he sort of...motivated me, I guess, to put my past behind me once and for all. I figured the best way to do that was to go talk to the other family who lost someone that night." She stopped again, watching him watch her. "I didn't realize that your mom had raised you with her maiden name, but it became perfectly clear that your father's last name wasn't Black when Lucy told me she was your paternal grandmother."

Garrett ran his fingers through his dark hair and sighed.

"I'm such an idiot. I-if I could turn back the clock, I'd have told you this on the night I broke off our engagement. I just didn't know how to say it. And I convinced myself that you knowing the truth would have been harder to swallow than losing me." He shrugged. "Plus, I figured I was going to lose you either way, so I chose the way that saved me having to explain it, and saved you having to know the bitter truth."

"Garrett," she intoned softly, "in the words of your grandmother, what's the punch line?"

He let out a quiet hoot. "The punch line, Sophia Maria Jones, is that you didn't cause the accident that night. *I did.*"

Impulsively, Sophie slapped his arm. "That's cruel! What are you doing? Making fun of me?"

"I'm being serious, Sophie. I didn't know how to say it to you before. Knowing the effect that the accident had on your life, it made me sick to think that I'd caused you so much pain. I knew telling you would break your heart, and I knew that I couldn't go the rest of my life hiding something like that from you. So I left."

"You're beyond nuts. You weren't even there."

He sighed again. "True. But I wasn't far."

She lowered her chin and folded her arms across her torso. "Explain."

"My father always made it clear not to contact him while he was at work." Garrett kept his eyes locked on Sophie's. "However, he said if there was an emergency, I could call the UPS receptionist, and she could patch me in to his radio if it was important enough." He paused, lowering his eyes briefly. "It was never important enough when I called. On the day of the accident, I got in a fight with my mom. I said things to her that I regretted afterward, and one of those was that I wanted to move out and live with my dad. He'd never really been a part of my life, but I was getting older and I desperately wanted to feel like I had a father, so I called the receptionist and asked her to put me through. He should have been just finishing his shift when I called, but I couldn't wait until he got home. I had to talk to him right then. She put me on hold, then came back a minute later and said she couldn't reach him. So I told her it was an emergency—it seemed like one at the time. I told her to keep trying, that he had to call me back immediately." He stopped talking and looked at her expectantly.

"And?" she asked, wondering if she'd missed part of his story. "How does that tie you to the accident?"

"I thought you said you read the report?"

"I did," she shot back. "And for the record, I know you did too—just a week before you left."

"Well maybe you didn't read it as closely as I did."

"What do you mean?"

Garrett sighed, and a look of agony swept across his features. "Sophie, before I say what's in the report, there's something else you need to know."

A familiar pit formed in Sophie's stomach. "So help me, if you tell me you've also discovered that we're, like, related, or something twisted like that, I swear I'll puke all over you."

He pressed his lips into a quick smile, but it faded just as fast. "Nothing like that, but you're probably not going to like it."

"It can't get any worse than it already is," she said pragmatically. "Fire away."

With a deep breath, he began. "Even if I wasn't real close to him, losing my dad as a boy was tough. You know that better than anyone. Mom kept all of the newspaper clippings and stuff from the accident, and whenever I'd get to feeling sorry about what happened, she would say, 'Yes, you lost your father. But read this, and tell me you're not grateful for what you have.' She'd give me those newspaper clippings and point out—" He stopped, choking back tears. "—and point out a little girl, not much younger than me, who'd lost everything that night. 'Sophia Maria Jones lost her whole family,' she would say. 'So count your lucky stars, Garrett. You've still got a mom who loves you.'"

Sophie was crying now, too, but Garrett continued.

"I often thought about that little girl—what happened to her after the accident, how things turned out for her. So when my mother was transferred to Ellen's precinct two years ago and she got to know her on a personal level... well, she figured out pretty quickly that Ellen was the officer from the accident who had taken in that little girl. Of course, Ellen would have had no reason to connect my mom to my dad, since she'd taken on a new married name by then. When it came out that they both had single adult children, they decided it would be fun to set us up on a blind date."

Sophie's emotional engine fired up again. "So you knew!" she bellowed. "You knew even before we met that our parents were in the same accident!"

He tipped his head ever so slightly.

"Then why the hell did you agree to the date in the first place? Was I just some charity case to you? Make the poor girl who lost her parents feel good about herself?"

"It was nothing like that, Soph."

"Then why?" she demanded.

He shrugged. "You'd always been this person in my mind who I admired. You'd given me hope at a very difficult time in my life. Even though we'd never met, I'd always told myself, 'If that girl can make it, then so can I.' And so I guess I was just intrigued. I wanted to meet the grown-up version of the little girl I'd read about in the newspaper. But I swear, I never..." His voice tapered off into nothing.

Sophie studied Garrett's face. He looked like a wounded dog, and as mad as she was, part of her felt sorry for him—even understood him. "You never what?" she pressed.

His response was hardly audible, but Sophie could read his lips. "I never expected to fall in love." Garrett looked up when

Sophie didn't reply. He cleared his throat. "I only wanted to meet you—to see for myself what a phoenix looks like after rising from the ashes. But meeting you was...intoxicating. After we met, part of me wanted to tell you the truth, but most of me just wanted to leave the past alone. To me, the history that we shared as children was just that—*history*. And when I thought that there was a legitimate chance for us to have a future together, I didn't want anything to get in the way of that, especially a twenty-year-old car accident."

Sophie was completely still, quietly contemplating everything she'd just heard. "Then what changed?" she asked at length. "Why did you suddenly decide that the past mattered?"

"The police report," he said softly. "I wish I'd never read it. After seeing how visiting the accident site upset you, I really did want to know as much about it as I could. I figured the more I knew about what you'd been through, the more you could lean on me for support. So I went to Ellen's, and she said she had a copy of the report that I could read. And that's what screwed things up."

"I don't understand," she said. "There's nothing in the report."

"No? Did you happen to read that bit about the UPS driver holding a CB radio in his hand when they pulled him from the wreckage?"

"Yes," she said, her voice growing more concerned. "But that doesn't mean anything."

"Maybe not to you, but to the kid who'd been pestering to talk to his dad immediately, it means a lot. After reading about the CB in Ellen's file, I tracked down that old UPS receptionist. It took a private investigator nearly a week to find her, but eventually I got my hands on her phone number." He paused.

"And?"

"And she said she remembered talking to him that night on the radio. He was annoyed and wanted to know what the emergency was, and of course I hadn't told her, because I knew he wouldn't think it was important enough. But she was a mother herself, and started arguing with him. And then she said he stopped responding. She thought at the time he was ignoring her, but she found out later it was because of the crash. So just like I said before, *I* caused the accident. Not directly, maybe, but if I hadn't called... who knows? Maybe he wouldn't have been so distracted, and things would have ended up differently for your parents."

Sophie's eyes were now very wet. "I don't know what to say," she admitted. "You're... you aren't making this up, are you?"

Shaking his head slowly, Garrett exhaled through his nose. "I'm sorry, Soph. I should have told you last year, as soon as I knew myself. I just didn't know how to."

Just then a car pulled up next to them. The driver rolled down the passenger window. "Are you Garrett Black? I'm from Enterprise Car Rental."

Garrett bent down to see him better. "I sure am. Thanks for coming."

The man smiled. "You're welcome to sit in the front or back, whatever you prefer."

"We'll just get in the back. Can you drop my friend off in Gig Harbor?" The driver agreed, so Garrett opened the door and he and Sophie both climbed in.

The Enterprise driver had lots of things to say—mostly questions about the accident—but a few minutes later he quieted down enough for Sophie to whisper a question to Garrett. "Just so I'm clear, when you decided not to tell me last year, it was because you thought the news would be hard for me to hear, or hard for you to say?"

He thought about how to respond, and then said simply, "Yes."

"So breaking my heart was a better option than swallowing your pride? I meant that little to you?"

His shoulders slumped forward. "After two decades I'd just

learned that I was partially to blame, not only for the death of my father, but the loss of *your* family as well. I figured your heart would break no matter what I said. It took so long for you to trust me—I promised I'd never hurt you, and this would have devastated you."

"So you took the easy way out," she deadpanned.

"There was nothing easy about it. But like I said, if I could turn back the clock, I'd have done things much differently. Especially knowing what I know now. I was stupid."

"Yes. You were." Sophie turned away and looked out the window. Garrett kept quiet, allowing her time to think. "You didn't even give me a chance to decide how I felt about it. *You* decided alone that *we* couldn't get past it."

When they got to Sophie's house, Garrett walked her to the door. "Soph," he said before she turned the handle, "I said before that I'd turn back the clock if I could."

Sophie didn't speak, but told him with her eyes that she was listening.

"If I could undo what I did last year, I would in a heartbeat. I'll never forgive myself for not being honest about what I knew. It was selfish of me, and I'm sorry."

She shifted her weight. "I understood you the first time." She dropped her hands to her side. "We really are something, aren't we? Both of us feeling guilty for the same accident. You know what Ellen would say about that, right?"

"*Divine providence, Sweets, so help me God,*" he replied in his best imitation of Sophie's foster mom.

Smirking, Sophie said, "Exactly. But then I'd have to remind her that providence would have brought us together on a more permanent basis."

Garrett frowned. "Good point."

"Divine intervention can only get you so far, I guess." Sophie shrugged her shoulders, turned around and opened the door, then stepped inside.

Garrett waited for her to turn back around. "So…that's it then?"

"I guess so." She looked straight at him, regretting that they'd let everything between them crumble. She wished he'd come to her with the truth sooner, even though she understood why he didn't. But it was a moot point now. He'd moved on, and there was nothing she could do about it. "Good luck with…what's her name? From the phone the other night?"

Garrett's mouth tightened. "Jane."

"Jane. Well. I wish you two the best. Whatever happens, it can't turn out any worse than we did, right?"

Turning on his heels, he quietly said, "Good-bye, Sophie."

"Good-bye, Garrett," she whispered back. Sophie closed the door, locked it, and then leaned against it for support. It had been a long day, and she was ready for it to be over.

Chapter 35

What you thought was happiness wasn't. It's time to move on.

LYING ON HER BED AN HOUR LATER, SOPHIE RECOUNTED everything that had happened since leaving work. Because she blamed herself all these years for causing the accident by distracting her father, she could understand why Garrett blamed himself as well. But he hadn't trusted her enough to tell her the truth, hadn't given her the opportunity to forgive him. But if she had known it was his father who was killed, too, could she have admitted to Garrett it was her fault? And would she have expected *him* to forgive *her*, or would she have done the same thing he had?

The accident that took her parents accounted for less than a minute of her life, yet the effects of that brief moment had caused her a lifetime of pain. No matter how much she tried to move forward, it seemed that accident always dragged her back. Like Andromeda, she was forever chained to her past.

As she was replaying everything that Garrett had said

again in her head, she remembered that she still hadn't read the letter from Jacob Barnes. Reluctantly, she got up and trudged to the kitchen, found the letter in her purse, then sat down and tore open one end. Reading the date in the top corner of the letter's first page, she noted with some dismay that it had been written just a few days before Jacob passed away.

With a stomach full of butterflies about what it was going to say, she started to read. By the time she reached the end, her emotional levees were in ruins, with tears running freely down her face. For the first time since she was eight, Sophia Maria Jones felt completely unfettered by her past. And utterly sick over her future—*a future that should have included Garrett Black.*

August 17, 2009

Dear Sophia,

With any amount of luck, you don't remember me at all. But I cannot forget you. How could I? It is the agony of remembrance that now compels me to write to you. Though it pains me to do so, I could not leave this world without putting down on paper all of my thoughts and feelings concerning our brief encounter so many years ago.

My name is Jacob Barnes. Believe it or not, you and I shared a few words and a small patch of sidewalk together in the aftermath of a horrific accident on your ninth birthday. I lost four fingers that day, but I know you lost much more than that. I'm so sorry for your loss.

Please know that I've wanted to seek you out, or at least write to you, for years. I should have done so a long time ago. At first I told myself that you were too young to understand. As you got older, I convinced myself that too much time had passed to dredge up things like this. Neither excuse was really true; I was simply a coward.

I've tried over the years to keep tabs on your welfare, just to make sure you were getting along okay. Last September I saw in your local newspaper that you were about to be married to Dr. Garrett Black. Congratulations! Hopefully married life is treating you well. My heart leapt for joy when I saw the photo of you and him. The smile on your face told me that you've somehow managed to deal with the weighty burden that you were left with on the night we met. Which burden? The burden of guilt for causing the accident that claimed the lives of your family.

Sadly, that burden should have never been yours to bear. It rightfully belonged to a coward. It belonged to me.

Should you ever be so fortunate, I hope you have the chance to meet my son, Alex Barnes. If you are reading this letter, then you can be sure that he's the one who put it in the mail. He is the greatest joy I've ever known, and, regrettably, my guilt and shame are inextricably tied to him. Allow me to explain.

Alex was born just before the stroke of midnight on September 20th, 1989—less than 24 hours before our collision. His mother, Katherine, and I could hardly wait for him to join our family. We were both lawyers and had put off having children longer than most first-time parents. I was nearly forty-five, and my wife was forty-three, when she became pregnant. The entire pregnancy went off without a hitch, right up until labor began. I was notified while trying a case in court that Katherine's water had broken, so I went straight from the courthouse and met her at the hospital.

Then everything turned sour. My wife started hemorrhaging badly while she was pushing, but the baby was far enough into the canal that they had to focus on getting the baby delivered before they could do much for her. They worked as fast as they could to bring Alex into the world, and then they turned immediately to my Katherine's needs. We all breathed an enormous sigh of relief when they were able to stop the bleeding and stabilize her pulse, which had gotten very weak.

The doctors took Alex to run some tests on him, but I was too caught up in the worry over Katherine to wonder why. I assumed the tests they were performing were just standard procedure. For the next four hours I sat next to my wife in her hospital room. She had a steady stream of oxygen pouring into her through a mask, but other than that she seemed fine. However, while I was watching her, all of a sudden she looked up at me in a panic. She gasped a few times, closed her eyes, and was gone. She died, just like that. No good-byes. No I-love-yous. She never even had a chance to hold our son. I learned later that a blood clot from the earlier bleeding had gone to her brain, effectively shutting down her vital organs in one quick stroke.

Needless to say, I was in shock. I spent the better part of that day in a stupor, filling out hospital paperwork while trying to wrap my head around the fact that she was gone. It wasn't until five or six at night that I finally had a quiet moment to sit and think about our son. When I asked for him, an entire team of doctors responded to my request. The head of pediatrics explained that my new baby had some chromosomal abnormalities, and that raising him was going to present some unique challenges.

When I heard the words "Down's syndrome," I panicked. And though they tried to get me to hold him, I refused. My head was spinning. How could I hold him without my wife? How could I raise a child like that on my own? Those thoughts led to self-pity. Why me? How unfair and cruel was life that I, who just lost the love of my life, should have to endure the burden of a child with special needs?

I'm not proud of those feelings, but my regret over my thoughts at that moment pale in comparison to the shame of what I did next.

I left.

I told the doctors I couldn't do it, and I simply walked out of the hospital into the night. I was mad at everything: mad at the doctors for letting my wife die, mad at my wife for dying, mad at the world for the perceived injustice, and, sadly, mad at my new son for his genetic makeup. In a rage, I went to my car, and I drove away. I didn't have a clue where I was going; I just wanted to drive, and I wanted to drive fast.

The weather that night was ridiculous, but that didn't stop me from being careless. I should have slowed the first time my car hydroplaned, but I didn't. When I saw a UPS truck in my lane, it upset me. Why, I wondered, should I have to crawl along behind a big brown truck at a time like that? Suddenly I was mad at the truck and its driver, for no other reason than they were slowing me down. Since I couldn't get around it on the left due to oncoming traffic, I flew alongside it in the right-hand lane, then swerved in front of it as I passed. Just to show the UPS driver that I owned the road, I tapped my brakes as soon as I got in front of him. It was stupid, I know, but I didn't expect it to cause an accident. When I touched the brake pedal, my car hydroplaned again, and I slammed the brakes even harder. Worried that the UPS truck was going to rear-end me, I looked quickly in the mirror while I was sliding and I saw that instead of hitting me, he'd swerved to the left. Who knows, maybe he was hydroplaning by then as well, as a result of slamming on his brakes to avoid hitting me. Either way, he was too far left. He missed me, but hit your car head-on.

It's sickening, I know. The accident was entirely my fault. If not for me, your family would still be alive. The driver of the UPS truck, too.

After I saw—and heard—the first impact, I lost complete control of my car. It turned sideways, then caught an edge and rolled—twice, I think. Everything beyond that was a bit of a blur. It is believed that I lost my fingers on the second roll, probably being pinched between the road and the car when my arm swung out through the shattered window. Who knows. It doesn't matter anyway. Four fingers is a small price to pay for my carelessness...one finger for every person that died.

I don't remember how the other cars got involved in the mess, but I recall sitting in my car once it came to a stop, feeling utterly sick for what I'd just done. I wanted to vomit. I couldn't get out of my door, but the rear window was popped completely out, so I shimmied through it. The first place I ran was back up the road to your car. What I found was a little girl—you—in the rear seat, crying. Your door was the only one that would open. Not knowing what else to do, but believing that you needed to get away from the scene inside that Volvo, I pulled you out and carried you a safe distance away along the side of the road, setting you down next to a fire hydrant. That's when I passed out.

Sometime later—I don't know how long, exactly—I came to. I was foggy at first, and unsure what was going on. You were there, still crying, and you were saying that the accident was your fault. While I was getting my hand worked on, I learned that your name was Sophia Maria Jones. A police officer took you to an ambulance, and a few minutes later I was escorted to a nearby ambulance as well. That's when I saw you throw away your fortune. It floated right down the street near where I was sitting on the back of the ambulance. It was wet and in a tiny ball, but I picked it up and read it. I kept it as a reminder of whose life I'd ruined.

At first I resisted when the ambulance team tried to take me back to the hospital I'd just left an hour before. Looking back, I believe it was providence, drawing me back to my responsibilities as a father. When I got there, my thoughts kept turning back to you—all alone in the world. I imagined what your life was going to be like without parents, and I decided that I could not inflict that same fate upon my own son, too. I called the doctors upstairs and had them bring Alex down so I could hold him in the ER. Once I had him in my arms, I never wanted to let go.

So why am I writing this letter now? I've wanted to apologize for what I did at least a million times; not only for causing the accident, but for knowing that you believed it was your fault and not correcting that notion. I shouldn't have allowed you to carry that guilt all these years.

It was my shame that prevented me from saying anything, and even now I cannot bring myself to face you in person. In the years since the accident, I have come to love Alex like no son has ever been loved before. He is a rare gift. Instead of being a burden, he has been my greatest joy. Each time I told myself that I needed to apologize to you and tell you the truth about what happened, I found myself unable to own up to it, because doing so would have forced me to admit to two disgusting truths. First, that when he was born, I left Alex parentless—if only for an hour—because I thought he was less than perfect. How insanely wrong I was! And second? That I would have never had the joy of raising Alex at all, if not for the accident that claimed the lives of your family. I'd have just kept right on driving and never looked back. It's cruel, isn't it? Your horrible loss was my incredible gain.

I've never been a particularly religious person, but that hasn't stopped me from thanking God every day for that accident that sent me back to my son. And those same prayers have always included the one unending "wish of my heart": that someday God will make right what He allowed me to mess up in your life.

I'm so sorry for everything. I wish you and your husband every happiness in the world. Hold on to each other, and live each moment as if it were your last. Someday it will be. Later rather than sooner, I hope, but as long as you've lived well, how long you live won't really matter.

God bless,
Jacob P. Barnes

P.S.: If you're ever feeling sad or discouraged, I encourage you to meet my son, Alex. He can lift spirits like nobody else. I promise!

P.P.S: Each year on your birthday Alex and I place rocks on the graves of your parents. I hope you'll let him continue the tradition. I'd like to be able to say there is some profound meaning to it, but that's not the case. To me, it seems like too many things in life are temporary. The rocks are just reminders that not all things dissipate so quickly. Some things, in fact, last for eons...maybe even forever. My love for my wife and son, for instance, and I'm sure the love you have for your parents as well. And hopefully, too, the love you feel for your new husband. God bless, Sophia Jones.

Chapter 36

You have overcome everything in your life,
except for your own shortcomings.

SETTING JACOB'S LETTER DOWN ON HER NIGHTSTAND, Sophie wiped her tears on her sleeve, and then immediately called Ellen.

"You're not going to believe the day I've had," she said as soon as her foster mom answered.

"It's late, but try me."

For the next thirty minutes Sophie shared in great detail the ongoing saga of her and Garrett, starting with him showing up unexpectedly at Chocolat' de Soph, followed by the accident, and his admission that he knew who she was before their first date. Then she explained his claim of responsibility for the accident that killed their parents, and ended with a verbatim reading of Jacob Barnes's letter.

"Good Lord," Ellen said slowly when Sophie was done. "If you don't see something more at work here than dumb luck or happenstance, then you're as blind as a bat, and I feel sorry for you."

"Ellen—"

"Don't 'Ellen' me. I've been saying right from the beginning that something good would come out of that accident. Mr. Barnes saw the good of it in his life, and I hope you recognize it, too." She paused to let Sophie speak, but there was only silence on the phone. "You were meant to be with Garrett, Sweets," Ellen continued. "It's been twenty years in the making, but now's the time. So what I want to know is, are you going to keep sitting there moping about the past, or are you going to do something about the future? Remember—God's steering the boat to shore, you just need to paddle."

"It's not that easy, El—"

"What's not?" she shot back.

"He has a girlfriend. Jane."

Ellen laughed. "Is he married to her?"

"No."

"Are they engaged?"

"I don't think so."

Ellen's voice dropped. "Do they share a history that started two decades ago?"

"Probably not," said Sophie tenuously.

Chuckling again, Ellen said, "Then I have just one more question. *Do you still love him?* In the end, that's all that really matters."

Sophie waited before responding. "Do I have to answer that right now?"

"You don't have to answer it at all. Not to me, anyway."

Sophie exhaled loudly into the receiver. "Thanks for listening, Ellen. And for your advice. I'll think about what you said."

"So do you think you know what you're going to do?"

While Ellen was speaking, a text message popped up on Sophie's phone. It was Garrett. A gust of hope filled her lungs, and a grin spread across her face. "Ellen," she said, "I gotta go."

"Why? You got somewhere else to be at this hour?"

"No, but I'm going to try putting my paddle in the water, and see what happens."

"That's my girl! Love you, Sweets. Let me know how it goes."

"Good night, Ellen."

Sophie pressed a button to open Garrett's message. It said, *FYI: I stopped by your store on way home, let Randy know you're okay.*

Typing with both thumbs, Sophie wrote back. *Thanks. Very thoughtful.*

He said a bunch more letters arrived today. I took a peek.

And???

100 letters, all from the same sender. ☹

Shut up. Serious??

Yep. All of them are from your guy, Alex.

What??

Yep. Don't worry, I only read a handful. He's very optimistic. U R lucky.

At first Sophie wasn't sure how she should respond, mostly because she didn't want to continue letting him think that Alex was anything more than a friend. To a large degree, her failure to be completely honest with Garrett—and he with her—had been the thing that had torpedoed their relationship in the first place, and she knew that if she had even the slightest chance of ever winning him back, she had to be truthful with him. It was that line of reasoning that suddenly prompted an idea.

Can I call U? she typed.

She didn't have to. Five seconds later, her phone rang. "What's up," Garrett asked. "Thumbs out of practice?"

"No," said Sophie, more reserved than normal. "I just wanted to say this to you in person."

"Uh-oh."

"No, it's not bad."

"Then why do you sound so gloomy? What's going on?"

She took a deep breath. "Okay. Don't freak out, but...I'm getting married."

There was a prolonged silence.

"Garrett?"

"Wow...Soph. I mean...*wow*. Don't you think maybe you're rushing things?"

"Nope. Not this time."

"Well...are you sure you love him?"

"More than I ever thought I could love anyone."

"Ouch. That stings a little," Garrett mumbled. "Well, I guess you know what you're doing then. So...congratulations...or something like that."

"Thank you," she whispered. "Hey, I know I've been kind of a pain about all of the want ad responses; I want to apologize. And I know me getting married puts a bit of a damper on our deal, but I'd still like to read what all of this mail says. It's starting to pile up again. Do you think you could come by the store sometime and help me finish going through it?"

"Of course. Just tell me when."

"How about tomorrow night?"

"I think that'll work. What time?"

"Is eight thirty too late? I'm covering for Randy tomorrow, so I won't really be free until then."

"That'll be fine, Soph," Garrett said. "I'll see you tomorrow."

"Great," she replied. "Good night, Garrett."

Biting her lip nervously, Sophie hung up the phone. "Well, this should be interesting," she stated out loud to herself. "I guess I'd better get baking."

Chapter 37

Between the sun and the rain, there are rainbows.
That's where you'll find the pot of gold.

It was raining outside the next day when Sophie walked out to the bus stop, but she didn't care. In fact, unlike previous rainy days, she welcomed the moisture as a way to wash away the past and start anew. As she paced along the street without an umbrella, the water pelting her face made her feel strangely alive. She smiled and strode confidently onward.

The bus driver was surprised to see Sophie step onto the bus with dripping hair and a bright smile. "Oh, snap," the woman grumbled, eyeing Sophie from head to toe. "Hell must'a froze over when I wasn't lookin'. What's gotten into you, girl? Don't you know it's droppin' cats and dogs out there?"

Sophie smiled even bigger as she paid the fare. "Without a storm now and then, how would we ever appreciate sunny skies?" She didn't wait for an answer, but just walked to the rear of the bus and took a seat.

Chocolat' de Soph was always busy in the weeks leading up to Thanksgiving, but this day was especially hectic. In addition to a large, last-minute order of pumpkin truffles for a corporate party, Sophie was scrambling to complete something special for Garrett before he showed up later that night. To make her schedule even tighter, she lost an hour in the afternoon because she had to temporarily close the store to accommodate a trip to the auto repair shop where her car had been towed.

After the evening rush, Sophie focused every spare second on her newest creation, wanting it to be just right when Garrett arrived. It took multiple rounds of failures before she got the cookies just the way she wanted them, but she was pleased to have them done to her satisfaction by the time she turned on the Closed sign in the front window at eight o'clock.

For the next half hour Sophie cleaned furiously. She started with the display case and serving area out front, then moved quickly to the kitchen, and in the final minutes before eight thirty she wiped a few flecks of chocolate and flour from her own face, then tussled her hair lightly.

A series of loud knocks on the front door echoed through the store right at half past the hour.

Tucking a strand of hair behind her ear, Sophie glided around the wall that divided the front of the store from the kitchen and waved at the face peering back at her through the window.

"Hey, Sophie," Garrett said as she opened the door for him. A cold wind blew in from the street as he entered. Under one arm he held a small box.

"Hi."

"Did you make out all right tonight without Randy? That's a long day."

"I managed," she said.

Garrett looked at her like he wanted to say something, then

his face changed. "Well, shall we get started on the mail? I probably shouldn't stay too long...you know, Jane might start to think something's up."

"Understood," said Sophie, wanting to cringe, but maintaining her composure. "But before we start, can you spare a minute for something else? I have a new creation I'd like you to try. An unbiased opinion would be helpful before I put them out to sell."

"Sure," he told her with a dimpled half smile. "I'd love to."

Sophie led the way to the back of the store, past two large copper vats, to a small counter on the opposite side of the kitchen from the new bins of mail. Sitting on the counter was a plate with two chocolate-dipped treats that looked suspiciously like Misfortune Cookies, with the exception that instead of only having dark chocolate exteriors, they also had thick stripes of white that curved all around in an ornate zebra pattern.

Garrett frowned when he saw them. "Misfortune Cookies? Umm, no thanks. Fool me once, shame on you. But not twice. I've still got the aftertaste from the one you gave me in September."

Sophie tilted her head and grinned. "Oh ye of little faith. Trust me. I promise, these will be better than the last ones."

"They can't be worse. They are Misfortune Cookies, right?"

"Well, yeah. But the recipe is very different. Seriously, Garrett, trust me." Biting her lip, she picked up the cookie that was closest to the front of the plate. "First, try this one."

Skeptically, Garrett took the striped cookie from her hand and sniffed it. "You seem awfully eager for me to put this in my mouth, and that has me worried."

"Chicken," she said, egging him on. "Just eat it."

"Fine. But if this is a trick..." He lifted it again and hesitantly bit into the chocolate shell, allowing a chunk to sit on his tongue long enough for his taste buds to make a decision.

Then he closed his mouth and chewed. He smiled just before he swallowed. "Wow, Soph! That was... I don't even know how to describe it. Uniquely delicious. I can still taste the bitter chocolate from before, but mixed with the sweet it's a completely different experience."

She curtsied playfully. "Thank you, kind sir. I'm glad you approve."

"So why the change?"

"It just felt right," she said matter-of-factly. "I think my perspective has changed a lot in the last couple of months. Yes, life can have many bitter moments. But those are tempered here and there by sweet bursts of happiness, which make the whole experience more palatable."

"I'm impressed. Have the fortunes changed as well?"

"Sort of. They still have Misfortunes in them, but now each cookie has two slips of paper—one positive, and the other, well, the same as the one you got last time. I guess you could say you get the good with the bad. Read yours," she told him, grinning.

Garrett carefully pulled two slips of paper from the cookie, and read the top one aloud. "*You have a knack for hurting those you love. Be grateful they still love you*. Ouch. Thanks for the reminder. I take it that's the bad one?"

Sophie nodded as Garrett pulled the second paper closer to read. He noticed that the second fortune was typed, not handwritten, and was printed on paper that felt old and wrinkled. Some of the ink was even smudged. "*Happiness is a gift that shines within you. The wish of your heart will soon come true.* Sophie, is this the fortune you told me about that came with the want ad responses?"

She took a deep breath and nodded. "It's also the fortune I got the night my family died. I just thought... your dad died that night too, and you might like to share in my good fortune."

He nodded appreciatively. "Thank you."

"Now try the second cookie," she said, taking another deep breath to quell her nerves.

"Is it different?" he asked, questioningly. "I thought that one was yours."

"Umm, no. It's definitely... different."

"Ah. Is this the one that'll have me spitting in the bathroom for the next ten minutes?"

"No, nothing like that. In fact, you may not even taste a difference. But I still need to know what you think of it."

Shrugging, Garrett set down the remnants of the first cookie and picked up the other one, then he took a bite and smiled as before. "Tastes the same."

Sophie tried to force a smile, but the knots in her stomach were making it difficult. All she said was, "Hmm."

Cracking off another piece of the black-and-white cookie, Garrett lifted it closer to his face and studied it briefly. "There aren't any fortunes in this one," he said.

"Oh? That's... odd."

As he tore off another chunk, the cookie broke completely in half, and something shiny and metallic fell out onto his palm. "What in the world is this?"

Sophie held onto the counter to steady herself. Her moment had arrived. *Paddle for shore, or sink trying*, she told herself. Taking a final, extended breath, she said, "That, Garrett Black, is an O."

"I see that," he chuckled. "It looks like something from a car."

Grinning awkwardly, she said, "It is. But more specifically, it's the O from the rear logo on my Explorer. You know, the one I killed yesterday. I had the guy at the auto body shop pop it off for me today."

"But why would you do that? And why is it in this cookie?"

Paddle faster! "Because... really, it belongs to you."

"The O?"

"The *car*."

"Huh?"

Breathe. Just breathe. "Did I ever tell you how I paid for that thing?"

"Uh... no."

She forced a chuckle. "It's actually a funny story. Well, maybe not exactly funny. See, when I was absolutely sure that we were through, I took the engagement ring you gave me down to a local thrift store and turned it into cash."

Garrett swallowed. "You hawked the ring at a pawnshop to buy a car?"

"Uh-huh."

With a look of stupor, he glanced down once more at his open palm, and then back up at Sophie. "So why the O?"

Sophie willed herself to keep looking him in the eyes. "Well," she started, her hands trembling, "no matter what happens, when the insurance check comes, I want you to know that I'm handing it all over to you. It's your money."

"You don't have to do th—"

"Let me finish," she interrupted. "It's your money, and I'm giving it back, like it or not. But I chose the O..." Her voice trailed off as she reached out to take the chrome letter from his hand. "I chose the O," she said again, much quieter, "because out of that entire car—which used to be a beautiful ring—it was the only shiny part I could find that I could squeeze into a cookie and still, well..." As her voice trailed off, Sophie stuck her pinky through the center of the O, and then carefully slid it all the way to the base of her hand. "It's too small for my ring finger, but close enough."

Garrett's eyes nearly popped out of his head. "Sophie, what are you—"

"I'm not done! Hear me out, Garrett. I've lived a long time

with regrets, but I'm done with that. So even if I don't get what I want, if I don't say everything I want to say to you right now, I know I'll regret it later."

"Sophie, just let me—"

"Nope! Not done yet. The first cookie that you opened tonight had two fortunes. The first one may be a little cryptic, but what I meant for it to mean is that even though you hurt me, I understand why you did what you did, and…I still love you. And I don't care that you've met this…*Jane*. I know she can't love you as much as I love you. And the second message is really for me more than it is for you. My father promised me when I was a girl that I'd get the wish of my heart. That same night Ellen promised me the same thing." She gulped for air. "Garrett, there's no way I could have ever known that while I sat there crying along the side of the road, that the ultimate wish of my heart—*and the greatest fortune of my life*—was sitting at home wishing he could get through on a radio just thirty yards away from me. *You* are the wish of my heart, Garrett Black. My happiest moments are when I'm with you, and I'd love nothing more than to take the good with the bad, *with you*, for the rest of my life."

Garrett's eyes were still bulging. He let a moment or two pass, listening to the sound of Sophie's rapid breathing. "Are you done?" he asked finally.

She nodded reluctantly, unable to read the expression on his face.

"Good." In one swift motion he leaned into her, wrapped his arms around her back, and kissed her. It felt just like the first time they'd kissed in the very same spot.

"What about Jane?" Sophie asked, blushing, when she came up for air.

Garrett leaned back and laughed. "Jane's her middle name. Olivia Jane Black DeMattio."

Sophie gasped. "Your mother?"

He chuckled again. "All I said that night was that I was on the phone with a woman. I didn't say with whom. If you thought I meant a pretty young woman, then good! I was jealous, and I wanted you to be too." As he said that, his smile dimmed slightly, and his brow furrowed into a knot. "What about Alex and the wedding."

Standing on her tiptoes, Sophie kissed him again. "I said I was getting married. I didn't say to whom. If you thought I meant Alex, then good! That was part of my little plan." She winked. "I guess it worked."

"Wait a minute. So is there even a guy named Alex? Who sent all those letters yesterday?"

She giggled. "Yes, Alex is very real, and the fact that he sent those letters is so sweet. Alex Barnes is very special to me. And hands down the happiest guy I've ever met. He just has this innate ability to make me smile and laugh, and to remind me of all the things in life that there are to be happy about."

"But you're not in love?"

"Oh, I do love him. He's incredibly lovable. But it was never what you thought." Sophie unwrapped herself from Garrett's embrace and went to her purse on the opposite counter, then searched its contents for the letter from Jacob Barnes. "Here, you need to read this. It's from Alex's father. Not only will it tell you what makes Alex so special, but it also clears up a few of our past, umm, *misconceptions* about the accident that killed our parents."

"Huh?"

"Just read," she said as she handed it to him, and then gave him another little kiss.

Garrett grimaced. "Not yet." He reached into his back pocket and pulled out a folded piece of notebook paper. Every line was filled on both sides. "I wasn't planning on giving this to you until later. But you can read it now. It's my own list of happiness. I figured since your dreamboat, Alex, was able to come up with one hundred different things that make him happy, then I could too. You'll notice as you read that every single one of them is about you."

Small tears started to form at the corner of Sophie's eyes. "And when were you planning on giving it to me?"

Garrett winked. "Well, according to you on our first date, a truly romantic man will do whatever it takes to win a lady's heart. So I was getting all geared up to crash your wedding. It was all planned out in my head. I was going to march right up to the front like they do in the movies and read my list. Then, assuming Alex hadn't already taken a punch at me, I was going to profess my undying love."

She stretched to kiss him again. "And then we'd ride off into the sunset?"

"Yeah," he said softly, before kissing her back. "Something like that."

"I'm glad to know you're still a hopeless romantic," she joked.

"Hopeful romantic," he corrected. "There is a difference."

WITH GARRETT BY her side, Sophie read his list of happiness, and smiled.

Garrett read Jacob's letter, and cried.

Then they embraced and ate the last few pieces of the new Misfortune Cookies, grateful to share every bittersweet bite.

Acknowledgments

I'M GOING TO LEVEL WITH YOU: WRITING ACKNOWLedgments stresses me out. Even as I type this, my blood pressure is spiking. I'm pretty sure this anxiety is directly related to my certainty that whatever I say will be woefully inadequate—the words *thank you* simply don't capture the full measure of what I feel for those who have helped with this and previous books.

Since there's no way I could possibly say everything I want to every person who deserves a nod for their contributions, I've chosen instead to try something, er, a little different. Haiku! (No, not a sneeze. It's poetry.) I'm certainly no poet (as you'll soon see), but putting my thoughts and feelings into this format was way more fun, and considerably less stressful, than crafting boring old sentences. So without further adieu, I'd like to thank the following individuals and groups for everything they've done to help me as a writer…

Acknowledgments

Haiku! (Gesundheit)

Rebecca my wife—
True sounding board and Muse of
Infinite love, Life.

C. Boys, Editor—
Why so insightful and nice
With words and advice?

Joyce Hart—Joys and Heart.
You, gentle agent of mine,
We've signed on the line.

A publishing Zen—
Rolf Zettersten, leader, friend.
Thank you once again.

The great Hachette team,
Sales, edits, art, marketing—
Talents, some unseen.

Sharp eyes reading quick:
Gram, Mom, Kacie, Becca, Jen—
Family with red pens.

For guidance often
Jason Wright delivers well.
Oh, and writes too well.

My children, all five—
Lots of noise in little home,
I'll miss you when grown.

For everyone else
Who reads my books (and enjoys):
Friends, thanks as always!

Wanted: Happiness

Lasting happiness only, please. Nothing that fleets. Please send suggestions to happiness@kevinamilne.com

As one might expect, after receiving so many responses to the newspaper ad, Sophie Jones eventually had to change her PO box number. However, those closest to her know that she is still keenly interested in learning what other people view as true, lasting happiness. To that end, Kevin Milne is collecting suggestions on her behalf. If you would like to share what happiness is to you, send an email to happiness@kevinamilne.com. Kevin will periodically post his favorite responses to his blog (http://kevinamilne.blogspot.com).

First Verse:

Solo, allegretto scherzando

Chapter 1

"LET'S START AT THE VERY BEGINNING; A VERY GOOD place to start." Julie Andrews sang those words while methodically strumming her guitar in *The Sound of Music*, just before she and the kids broke into their famous do-re-mi's. Then together they danced, climbed, sang, spun, and peddled their way, up and down, through the rolling hills of the Austrian countryside. When concerned friends (and a few nosey acquaintances) have asked how my life got to the point it's at now, I've been reluctant to share the excruciating details. Instead, I tell them simply that, like Captain von Trapp and his musical wife, it all began quite wonderfully in Austria with a song and a guitar, but somehow it ended up in San Francisco... with nothing.

Okay, *nothing* is a bit of a stretch, but that's how it feels sometimes when your entire world is crumbling before your eyes.

A lot has transpired since Austria—most of my life's biggest disappointments, for instance. But if we're to follow my grandfather's (and Frauline Maria's) admonition, then the snow-capped Alps of Europe's cultural heart is a very good place to start, because that's where everything fell into place. That was *the beginning*, the place where I received my very first note.

I'd just graduated from the University of Rochester's Eastman School of Music and was on my way overseas for graduate studies at the University of Music and Performing Arts in Vienna, Austria, when Grandpa Bright announced he was loaning me Karl.

As odd as that may sound, it really wasn't. Karl was the name of Grandpa's guitar, though why he'd given it a name was anyone's guess. More importantly, Karl was the instrument I'd been openly coveting since I first heard Grandpa play it when I was a kid. Not only did Karl sound great, but it carried a certain reverence and mystique among the Bright family, mostly because Grandpa was so tight-lipped about how he'd acquired it and why he'd named it Karl. All he would say was that he owed his very life to that old guitar, and that he'd cherish it until "the great conductor of the universe calls me home to play in his symphonies on high."

Taking all that into account, I was more than a little surprised when he lent it to me. I was also deeply honored. But it was nonetheless fitting that Grandpa's beloved six-string should accompany me on my journey to Austria, if only for nostalgic reasons. We all knew he'd gotten it there while serving in the war. We just didn't know *how*.

I'd chosen Vienna over other possible graduate programs for the express reason that I wanted to see and experience all of the places Grandpa must have traveled with that guitar as a soldier. Nobody had a greater impact on my life than Grandpa, and Karl was part of that legacy, so going back to Austria, where both of them had such strong roots, was like a dream come true.

After arriving on European soil and settling into my two-year music program in Austria's capital city, I began soaking up as much as I could of the sights, sounds, and culture of my new surroundings. During my first semester abroad nearly all of my spare time was spent playing tourist. If there was something to see in or around Vienna, I saw it. There were frequent visits to the opera houses, countless hours staring at the intricate details of St. Stephen's Cathedral and Karlskirche, and more than a few excursions to the Imperial Palace—the monstrous home of the Habsburgs, rulers of the Austrian Empire for more than six hundred years. I saw the Lipizzaner horses, the Vienna Boy's Choir, a Sigmund Freud museum, and enough first-century castle ruins to last a lifetime. Before the weather turned cold I took a paddleboat ride along the Danube River, and during a long holiday weekend I hopped on a southbound train through the Alps to the city of Graz, just so I could see the home where Arnold Schwarzenegger grew up.

Like I said, if it could be seen, I saw it.

Unfortunately, all such tourist activities cost money, which was something I didn't have a lot of. And so, on the day before Christmas, after paying an exorbitant price to see Diana Ross perform live with the Vienna Symphony Orchestra and two of the Three Tenors, I realized that I was flat broke. I'd secured loans to cover the big-ticket items, such as tuition and housing, so that wasn't a worry. But money to get around town? Cash to buy groceries? Funds to simply exist? Those coffers were empty.

Other students might have called their parents for financial assistance, but that wasn't an option for me. My mom couldn't help because she was "gone." That's how dad explained it to me when I was five and she didn't come home from the hospital. Not passed away. Not dead. Just *gone*...and not coming back. And my dad? Well, after mom left, he just sort of died, too. Not physically, but in every other way—stopped going to work, lost his job, slept most of the time, started drinking heavily. After three months of depression he decided raising a child by himself was more than he could handle, so he handed me over to my grandparents.

Dad pulled out of his tailspin a few years later. He never asked to take me back, though. In fact I rarely saw him. He became the Bright family ghost, appearing unexpectedly to say "hi," and then disappearing again for a couple of years at a time.

Following where my mother had gone, Grandma Bright "left" just before I turned seven, so Grandpa and I had to learn to look out for each other. Grandpa was a psychologist by trade, but his passion in life was music, and he shared everything he knew about it with me as often as he could. When he wasn't psychoanalyzing patients and I wasn't busy with schoolwork, we'd immerse ourselves in all kinds of music. Sometimes we'd listen to the radio and he'd have me write down the lyrics that spoke to me the loudest. Other times we'd learn about the classical masters and their contributions to musical history. But more often than not, we'd sit and play the guitar.

Grandpa began teaching me how to play as soon as I moved in with him and Grandma. By the time I was ten I was pretty good, and by the time I was thirteen the student had become the teacher. Eventually I got my own guitar, though not as nice as Karl, and together we would write songs and play music until the wee hours of the night. Those were the experiences that helped mold and shape my dreams. It wasn't until college that I set my sights on a particular career goal, but it was those late nights playing music with Grandpa that convinced me my future was tied to the musical arts.

Although my childhood wasn't perfect, it could have been worse. I survived, which is the important thing, but only thanks to Grandpa. So naturally, Grandpa is the one who got the call when I spent myself into the poor house in Austria.

"You spent *how much*?" he asked after I explained my predicament.

I was on a pay phone, spending my last pocket change at a rate of two dollars per minute, so I had to speak quickly. "All of it," I repeated. "I'm really sorry. Can you just wire enough money to tide me over so I don't starve? By then maybe I can figure something out."

I knew I was in trouble when Grandpa suddenly switched to his thoughtful psychologist voice. "I would, but I think this will be a good growing opportunity for you. Here's my advice. *Use Karl*. It won't let you down."

The automated female voice of the payphone chimed in. *"Noch eine Minute."* One minute left.

"What is that supposed to mean?"

"Why don't you play the guitar for money? I'm sure tourists will appreciate music from a skilled street musician. At least they did last time your grandmother and I visited."

I'd seen grungy looking musicians playing at various tourist locations all the time, sometimes to good-sized crowds, but I'd always assumed those were just deadbeats trying to siphon liquor-change from other people's pockets. And the thought of doing that myself? Well, it hadn't yet occurred to me that I was a deadbeat. "Really?"

"Ethan, why do people visit Austria? Why did *you* go there? For music! It's the heart of classical music in all the world. They want to hear music everywhere. I'm willing to wager if they hear you play, they'll pay. I would."

"Dreissig Sekunden." Thirty seconds.

"Seriously? Even in this cold weather, you think people will stop and throw money in the hat?"

"Isn't it worth trying?"

"Yeah, but... what if you're wrong."

"What if I'm right?"

"This doesn't sound like a very good plan. Wouldn't it be easier if you just sent me a little cash to get me through New Year's?"

"That *would* be easier. But the easy way isn't always the best way. You got yourself into this mess, and I think it'll do you some good to get yourself out. If you want to stay in Austria bad enough, you'll find a way to make it happen. If you don't, call me back and I'll arrange a flight back to the States—which you can pay me back for."

The phone beeped three times in my ear. I had just enough time to say, "Good-bye Grandpa," and then it clicked off.

The next day, following an afternoon practicum with a small ensemble at the university, I hauled Karl down to Stephanplatz, an upscale pedestrian area surrounding St. Stephan's Cathedral in the center of the city. I'd seen musicians there before, when it was warm outside, and figured it was as good a place as any for a solo performance.

I laid a small piece of cardboard on the ground at the base of a building to protect my backside from the elements, and then sat down. Ignoring the butterflies in my stomach, I checked to make sure Karl was still properly tuned, then I propped the hard-shell case open in front of me. It wasn't a hat, but there was ample room in there for donations. Finally, with a few curious onlookers already gathering, I closed my eyes and started to play.

I loved playing that guitar. I always had. Given its age, Karl wasn't the most stunning instrument to look at. Its wood was heavily worn, with nicks here and there from decades of use. But what really mattered was the sound, and in that it was a masterpiece.

Whenever I held a guitar—plucking strings, pressing frets, making music—I entered my own little world, like a private sanctuary in my head. There, in the middle of Vienna, with strangers gawking and making breath-clouds in the chilled December air, it was no different.

Grandpa's old guitar sounded as good as it ever had. Its nylon strings were perfectly suited to the classical selections I'd chosen to play. I began with "Clair de Lune," a piece by Claude Debussy that I'd learned when I was sixteen. I knew it backwards and forwards. When I was done, I lifted my eyes to see the crowd's reaction. Only...there wasn't a crowd.

No money in the guitar case either.

The only person remaining was a man in his early twenties. His hands were shoved as deep as they would go in his pockets, and he wore a thick, hand-woven scarf around his neck. "Dat was wery güt," he said with a heavy Austrian accent. "You are Americaner, ya?"

"How could you tell?"

He shrugged. "You look it. May I offer adwice?"

"Okay."

"Do you know songs dat are more...eh...*femiliaré*?"

"Familiar?"

"Ya. Und faster. Wit more *zing*."

"Zing?"

"Zing."

"Um...sure." Mentally, I raced through the list of songs I'd prepared, but they were all as lethargic as the one I'd already played. They were plenty difficult, but they lacked speed and intrigue, which probably meant "*no zing*." Then my mind landed on one of the earliest neo-classical pieces I'd ever learned. "I got it," I said. "'Bohemian Rhapsody,' by Queen."

He smiled with a nod. "Dat should do it."

I blew into my hands to warm them up, and then started into the song. It was slow at first, but clean and crisp, with enough notes to make it interesting. I kept my eyes up this time to better assess the response from pedestrians. Sure enough, when they heard the familiar tune, people stopped to listen. And as the melody kicked in and the tempo flared, with notes flying off my fingers like fiery darts, the crowd of onlookers grew.

And grew.

Some of them closed their eyes to focus on the sound. Others keyed in on my hands, obviously impressed with the speed of my fingers along the neck of the guitar. A few mouthed the words. The man who'd offered his "adwice" was bobbing his head in time with the music; he took several steps back to make sure he wasn't distracting from the show. Before the song ended at least five people stepped forward and dropped money into the case. When the last note sounded, another three lined up to reward my efforts. I thanked them all with a courteous nod or smile.

"Vell," said the man as the happy crowd moved on, "I tink you found your money maker."

"*I tink* you may be right," I replied. "Thank you."

I didn't count it right then, but I could see at quick glance that there was at least two hundred fifty schillings in the case, a mixture of coin and cash. *Twenty five dollars! From one song!*

From that moment on, finances were no longer a problem. I certainly wasn't swimming in dough, but neither was I destitute. At least I had enough to buy food on a regular basis and pay for transportation around town, and I even had a little extra for an occasional show.

Several days a week I would lug Karl onto the subway and ride around to various tourist sights in the city; mostly the same places I'd frequented before going broke. I didn't always have as much success as my first time on Stephansplatz. Sometimes the crowds were thin and the cash even thinner. But then there were days that money flowed from pockets like air from a flute, which more than compensated for the down times.

I soon discovered that three or four compelling songs were plenty for one "show." Most people wouldn't stay and listen for more than ten or fifteen minutes anyway, so periodically I would just start my set all over again. To make sure I maintained sufficient zing, I always ended with "Bohemian Rhapsody." Even if the other songs produced nothing more than a few interested onlookers, that one always seemed to draw out loose change.

Thank heavens for Freddie Mercury.

I continued playing and studying throughout the remainder of that semester, and right on into spring. During the summer session my class load was light, allowing me more time to make money as a street musician. As expected, the warm months brought a marked increase in foreign tourists, and it showed in the amount of cash I was taking in. By the start of my second, and final, school year in September, I had enough saved in my bank account that I could cut back to playing once a week without any fear of straining my budget.

By my second Christmas in Austria I was in the thick of my masters project, which kept me busy all the way through the end of the semester in April. That left me with just one capstone course and a summer practicum before graduation ceremonies were to be held in August. I'd been in college for six straight years—four in Rochester and two in Vienna—so it was hard to believe the end was so near. Time had flown by, and I wondered if it would ever slow down.

Then in the middle of June, as my schooling was winding down, the passage of time suddenly shifted. In fact, for a couple weeks it seemed to stop altogether, as though God's metronome was somehow broken. But what I perceived as a slowing of time was actually just a side-effect of a strange illness I'd contracted. This particular infirmity hit me like a drummer on steroids. Physical symptoms included high blood pressure, shortness of breath, fever, and occasional chills. Heart palpitations came and went, too.

I knew what I had was rare—love-sickness of such severity only comes around once in a lifetime.

I also knew that the *cause* and the *cure* were one and the same: *Annaliese Burke*.